David Shepherd was born in Bolton-le-Sands, near Lancaster, in 1942. He was educated at Abbotsholme School in Derbyshire and at St John's College in Durham. After University, he was a probation officer in Linlithgow, West Lothian, and a student at the Episcopal Theological College in Edinburgh. From 1968-1979, he was Chaplain of St Paul's Cathedral, Dundee and Anglican Chaplain in the University of Dundee from 1973-1979. Since 1979, he has been Rector of St Mary Magdalene's Church, Dundee.

Six detective novels have now been published:

Who Killed Sophie Jack?
Murder Within Tent
Slaughter at the Polls
A Christmas Cracker
A Mishap in Majorca
A Prospect of Rye

Copies are available from:

Meadowside Publications
14 Albany Terrace
Dundee DD3 6HR

Telephone 01382 223510

Further details can be obtained from our website:
http://www.crime-fiction.com

A PROSPECT OF RYE

A DETECTIVE NOVEL

BY

DAVID SHEPHERD

MEADOWSIDE PUBLICATIONS

DUNDEE

2002

Meadowside Publications
14 Albany Terrace, Dundee DD3 6HR

© *Meadowside Publications, 2002*

Printed by
BHF2001
Dundee, Scotland

ISBN 0 9520632 55

Meadowside Crime
is a © imprint of
Meadowside Publications,
Dundee.

CONTENTS

The story is set in Rye
and in Grasshallows
in March – April 1989.

1: *The Morning Letter*

Raynes waited till he had reached his second cup of sweet, black coffee before he opened his mail. Much of it could instantly be torn up and cast into the bin – particularly the latest copy of the *Police Gazette* and a final reminder from the Gas Board.

But one envelope caught his eye. It was one of those cheap and nasty-looking envelopes, overprinted in lurid green ink, which proclaim that they have been rescued from the Corporation rubbish tip, pulped down and recycled – thereby preserving the rain forests of darkest Saskatchewan and depriving the humble lumberjack of honest toil. The handwriting was black and fanciful. Raynes had the feeling he had seen it somewhere before. Using his bread knife, he sliced open the flap.

"Dear Dick," (said the letter),

"Your picture is now ready for collection. I had a bit of trouble with the right knee but I think you will agree with me that I have out Goya'd Goya and put poor Boucher out to grass.

"You know how prone I am to understatement (especially where my own work is concerned!) but I think I can truthfully say that the end result is positively delicious. Mouth-watering, even. Let me know when you will be coming down to collect it . . ."

Raynes was instantly reminded of a visit he and Debbie had paid to Rye the previous summer when his painter-friend had offered to immortalize Mrs May in oil.

The first sketches had been created during an afternoon of wild celebration when a vast amount of champagne had flowed and everyone had been laughing so much that many of the initial daubs had had to be scraped off and applied again. It was amazing to think that anyone could create anything worthwhile out of such chaos. But as he had always said, Simon was a painter of great talent.

The prospect of owning an artistic masterpiece enlightened an otherwise dismal March day. The wind was blowing violently round the house; the garden was almost a swamp. Raynes walked through the hallway and into the sitting room, trying to imagine how the picture would look.

"*. . . The canvas is about 60" by 40" and I have found you a nice frame in the local antique shop which suits it rather well . . ."*

Raynes measured the wall above the mantelpiece. Good heavens! It was huge. The whole room was going to be dominated by the picture. He might even have to buy a larger house.

Though it was still early in the morning, Raynes picked up the phone and dialled Mrs May.

"Guess what!" he said. "Simon's finished your picture. Yes . . . At last . . . He wants us to go down to Rye to collect it. We could go down for a long weekend . . . Would Friday be all right?"

He scowled at the telephone. "But we all need a holiday! You can't work all the time . . . Well, Saturday, if you insist. We can stay in that nice hotel again . . . The one where you nearly gave the waiter a heart attack by bending too far over the sweet trolley! Saturday, then? Bye."

He put the phone down and smiled.

Despite the awfulness of the day, there was something bright and cheerful to look forward to. He returned to his cup of coffee and the second page of Simon's letter.

"*. . . You will be interested to hear that even our own peaceful community is not entirely devoid of crime. A local huntress – Lady Mallowan – died in suspicious circumstances whilst she was being painted by a friend of mine. You remember Brackles? He was the one who got us the brandy. Well, now he's been arrested! Lots of excitement! Of course, Brackles wouldn't hurt a fly, but he's being grilled by your lot who obviously think he's another Dr Crippen. You probably read about it in the papers.*

Anyway, I'll tell you more when you come down.

See you soon,

Simon.

PS. Bring your own champagne. The boys in blue have nicked all the brandy! Why can't the bastards buy their own booze? Why pick on innocent folk like us?"

Raynes smiled.

No one seemed to like the police. Come to think of it, he didn't like them very much himself! Some of the crooks, on the other hand, were really charming people – imaginative, entrepreneurial – though perhaps a shade careless with other people's property.

Which reminded him . . . before he left the house, to switch on his security alarm. Not that there was much worth stealing! But once that picture arrived, things would be different.

He rubbed his hands together with enthusiasm. It promised to be a memorable weekend. Art, crime – and passion! Who could ask for more?

2: *Sweet Champagne*

Four days later, Raynes was sitting on an uncomfortable wooden chair in a rather untidy kitchen, watching his artist friend pouring champagne into three non-matching mugs.

"If I'd known you were so hard up for glassware, I'd have brought you glasses as well as the champagne!"

"They keep getting broken," said Simon apologetically. "I had four beer mugs only last month – all pinched, of course – but the last of them died yesterday."

"So unromantic," said Debbie, shaking her head. "One does expect a professional man to keep up appearances."

"It's what's inside that matters! Not the outward trappings." He looked at Debbie who was turned out as immaculately as ever, in a white silk blouse and plain grey trouser suit with brass buttons. "Though I dare say you score on both counts!"

"I score to order!" said Debbie with a sweet smile. She picked up her mug. "Cheers!" she said.

"Cheers," said Raynes, who was glad the journey was over and he could relax for the next forty-eight hours.

He looked at the pink plastic clock on the kitchen dresser.

"When are we going to see the picture?" asked Debbie.

She asked the question in a light-hearted fashion even though she was still feeling rather nervous about seeing the finished product. Would he have done it properly or would he have turned her into some cubist monstrosity with only one eye? One never knew with artists.

"I thought we might have an official unveiling at cocktail time. Brackles is coming round with some brandy at about 7.00pm and I thought we'd do the honours then."

"I thought he was still in custody?"

"No. He was released on Monday night. They've grilled him on and off for a whole fortnight – but eventually they had to let him go. Lack of evidence."

"I thought you said the police had pinched all his brandy?" said Raynes suspiciously.

"He had a couple of bottles stashed away in a boathouse they didn't know anything about. Doesn't keep all his eggs in one basket, does Brackles." Simon topped up Debbie's mug.

"No. He kept his iron reserves safely tucked away, thank God! But he's been watching me doing the picture and he felt we should mark the occasion in some suitable manner. So now we can celebrate his release as well."

"The police must have been very sure of his guilt if they kept him in custody that long?"

"Well, it wasn't so much the body in the studio which caused all the trouble. It was the brandy in the cellar. Two hundred cases of it!"

Raynes raised his eyebrows.

"Good job they didn't come the week before! Then there were two thousand cases of the stuff. Brackles stores it, you see – for a friend. Well, when the police found that lot, it became really serious. At least, it gave them something genuine to pin on him. The Excise people have charged him with smuggling. That was to be expected. Just like the olden days down here: 'Brandy for the parson, baccy for the clerk; five and twenty ponies trotting through the dark – watch the wall, my darling, while the Gentlemen go by.' Kipling, I believe."

"Do you think he was framed?"

Simon shrugged his shoulders.

"Who knows? Someone had it in for him. It couldn't have been an accident."

There was a thoughtful silence whilst Simon topped up Raynes' mug and emptied the rest of the bottle into his own.

Debbie broke the silence.

"Who was she?"

"Lady Mallowan? Wife of Sir George Mallowan. Local big-wigs. They live in a large house about five miles away. He's quite a nice bloke but she was as brazen as hell. The sort of woman who could wrap men round her little finger. Once she'd got her claws into him, Brackles hadn't a chance. Seduced at the first fence! Hardly had time to get his brush out and she was on to him. The affair's been going on since Christmas."

"Did he paint her in the nude?"

"Good heavens, no! This one was for the drawing room. Lady Mallowan's a keen member of the local hunting fraternity. She wanted to be remembered in her full glory. Black coat, white breeches, a firm grip on her black leather crop. You can see it later. Brackles has almost finished it. It's a very good likeness – though I think he gave her buttocks the benefit of the doubt. In real life, she was a bit chunky, you know; but Brackles has given her the most mouth-watering curves. Supremely rapeworthy!"

Debbie looked at Simon coldly.

"If you'd met some of the men I've known, you wouldn't joke about rape. It may be sheer fantasy to you, but for us women, it's a constant nightmare . . ."

Simon apologized.

Raynes quickly brought the conversation back to the murder victim.

"Had Lady Mallowan been . . . interfered with?"

"No. She was fully clothed."

"Still in her full riding gear?"

Simon nodded.

"So how did she die?"

11

"Some sort of poison."

Raynes looked surprised.

"Not in the brandy?"

"How did you guess?"

Raynes smiled.

"What else do you people drink down here? You have a cellar packed with French brandy. Brackles hands out bottles of the stuff at every opportunity. What else would Lady Mallowan drink when she visited the studio? If she was to be poisoned, it would have to be the brandy."

"Well, you're quite right. She poured herself a brandy. Slung it straight down the hatch – and that finished her off. Only one set of fingerprints on the bottle – her own."

Raynes pursed his lips.

"That makes it highly suspicious."

"You mean someone doctored the bottle?"

"Obviously. They knew she would be at the studio. They knew she would have a drink. They knew it would kill her. Perhaps him as well? He didn't drink any, did he?"

"He wasn't there. She turned up at 2.00pm – but Brackles was out shopping. He wasn't expecting her that afternoon. She just appeared. Helped herself to the brandy – and collapsed in a heap – right in front of her picture."

"Who found her?"

Simon drained the last of his champagne. "That was the nasty bit. A woman and her daughter. They were due at 4.00pm. Came early. Just walked in. People do that round here. Brackles was painting the child's portrait – a birthday present for her father. Just a bread and butter piece. Nothing spectacular. But they came in and found Lady Mallowan on the floor. I'm not sure they realized she was dead. At least, not at first.

"You find a lot of strange things in an artist's studio – plastic models without heads, torsos made of pink plaster, heaps of theatrical clothes . . . They probably thought it was a bit of still life! Eventually it dawned on them that it was a dead body. They came running downstairs and into here. I went next door to see if they were having me on. It gave me one hell of a shock, I can tell you. There was no sign of Brackles – so I phoned the police."

"So you were the architect of his downfall?"

"I'm afraid I was. But I knew he was out. He was at the supermarket, getting stuff for both of us. I didn't know Lady Mallowan was there. So I thought Brackles was completely in the clear. As I'm sure he is. As I said to you in my letter, Brackles wouldn't hurt a fly. If he was really angry, he might break up a canvas or stick a knife through it. But I can't see him murdering anyone. Least of all Angela . . ."

"Angela?"

"That was her Christian name." Simon re-assembled the empty mugs on the kitchen table. "I suppose some people disliked her. She was brash. She was rude. She was dominating. She was immoral – flagrantly immoral. But I can't see why anyone would want to kill her. She was so full of life."

Raynes observed that his friend was close to tears.

Clearly, he too had been fond of . . . Angela. Debbie had also noticed the change in his tone of voice.

"Did you have her too?"

Simon nodded sadly.

"Just once or twice. She was irresistible."

3: *Dressed to kill*

There was silence for several minutes. Simon washed up the mugs and put on the kettle to make some coffee. Debbie looked at Richard with a look that said: "Why on earth do people muck about with such bungling amateurs? It only ends in tragedy."

Raynes completely mistook her look. He thought it was an expression of disgust at the state of Simon's kitchen. He was glad they would be staying at the hotel.

Still, the coffee was good.

He waited till his friend had sat down again.

"How old was her ladyship?"

"About 42 or 43. But she looked younger."

"Did she get on well with her husband? Despite all the affairs . . .?"

"Seemed to. George is a very easy-going bloke. Salt of the earth. Of course, he's much older than she was. He must be over sixty."

"A second marriage?"

"Second or third."

"So there may be other Lady Mallowans going about?"

Simon shrugged his shoulders.

"Could be. Who knows?"

"Did she have any children?"

"Not that I know of. George has a married daughter. In her thirties, I would say. I don't think she really approved of Angela. Felt she was making a fool of her dad. Which, of course, she was."

"Did he resent it?"

"Didn't seem to. She brought a lot of colour into his life. Had lots of friends. Lots of parties. He enjoyed being the host. She deferred to him in public; but in private, she went very much her own way."

Raynes looked at Debbie.

She smiled.

"I defer to no one."

Simon laughed.

"With a figure like yours, you don't need to!"

Raynes asked: "How did Sir George react to Brackles painting her?"

"He didn't seem to mind. He came over once or twice to see how it was going. I think he was quite impressed. Brackles has done a pretty good likeness. He was hoping to get a few more commissions from Angela's friends . . . but this murder business will put the cap on that."

"Is Sir George blaming him?"

"No. He's been very decent about the whole thing. Even sent him a cheque for £500 whilst he was in custody."

"I find that surprising."

"So did Brackles. Mark you, old George might benefit from all this."

"In what way?"

"Well, I shouldn't say this . . . I didn't tell the police . . . but George has got a lady-friend of his own. A Mrs Travers. Quite a little eyeful. Red hair and a temper to match. She's not all that tall but she's got a perfect figure. She really has. It wouldn't surprise me if she became the next Lady Mallowan."

Raynes smiled to himself.

"So Brackles isn't the only suspect?"

"Good heavens, no!" Simon looked amazed at such a blinkered suggestion. "There's Sir George, his daughter, her husband. There's Mrs Travers. Perhaps even a Mr Travers? The groom at the stables . . . I believe she was having it off with him. And then there's that young firebrand who works at the pub in Winchelsea – Philip something . . . Philip Royle . . . he was gunning for her."

"Another old flame?"

"No. Not at all. He's one of the anti-blood-sports brigade. He tried to break up the local hunt at their last meet. Boxing Day, it was. He organized a demonstration just as they were about to set off. Threw a couple of fireworks at the horses. Dowsed the dogs in pepper. Almost caused a riot. Angela slashed him across the cheek with her whip and then kicked him in the face. I think she broke a couple of his teeth. There's a court case pending. He's been saying that he intended to get even with her . . . I should think he'd be one of the most likely suspects."

"Have the police spoken to him yet?"

Simon shook his head.

"I don't know. They've asked Brackles to tell them everything he knows about Angela, so I expect he told them about Philip. Everyone knows about the incident. He really hated her."

Raynes listened with quiet detachment.

It was nice to think that this was not his problem. He was sure the local police would tease out all the details and make a swift arrest. It was a well-known fact that most murders were committed by someone close to the victim – a husband, a friend, a lover or neighbour. The Inspector realized that, living next door and having been one of Angela's lovers, Simon himself would also be a leading suspect. He thought it was significant that his painter friend should be able to vouch for there being only one set of fingerprints on the bottle. Who had told him that? Surely not the police?

Did Simon have an alibi?

That was another question deserving an answer.

For the moment, part of Raynes' inner nature rejoiced that, for once, he was a mere spectator. A bystander observing how others tackled a delicate problem. But the other part of his nature (and – if he were to be honest – the greater part) was absolutely longing to plunge into such a juicy, fascinating case. He had an unhappy feeling that, as in so many other spheres of his life, he might be quite unable to resist temptation.

Debbie was looking at him.

"I know what you're thinking," she said.

"I wish you didn't."

"You're going to get involved!"

"No, I'm not."

Simon laughed.

"Well, it would be nice to think that we had one policeman on our side. They've been poking round here for the last three weeks. I don't know what they're looking for. They won't say. But they ask all sorts of personal questions." He turned to Debbie. "They even asked who you were."

"Me?"

"They were looking at your picture. Mark you, they could hardly miss it. Especially in that huge frame. They wanted to know if you were my mistress."

"And what did you say?"

Simon managed to look a trifle embarrassed.

"I said I was working on it!"

"You should have told them she was too expensive for you!" Raynes touched upon his friend's weakest point.

But Debbie was determined not to let that statement pass unchallenged. "We do give discounts for beginners!" she said.

"He's not a beginner!" said Raynes indignantly. "If I told

you how many women had passed through his hands – at University alone – you'd be amazed!"

Simon cradled his coffee mug in both hands.

"Part of the creative urge."

"Any excuse!" said Raynes.

"It spares one all the complications . . . An artist's life is not exactly a free meal ticket. You grab what you can when you can."

"Are you going with anyone at the moment?" asked Debbie.

Simon thought for a moment.

"No. Not really."

"That means 'yes'," said Raynes.

"It means I'm hopeful."

"So you can live without my picture?"

Simon smiled – a sly smile. Perhaps a jealous smile.

"Dick," he said, "you should have learnt one lesson long before now. There are some things that money just cannot buy!"

4: *Olympia*

Brackles arrived at about a quarter to seven.

He was a small, middle-aged man with a slightly balding head and protuberant, olive-coloured eyes. He was wearing a brown corduroy jacket and a dark red silk cravat.

He bustled in carrying a couple of bottles of three star Napoleon brandy which he put down on the kitchen table.

"Splendid to see you again, Inspector."

He shook hands with Raynes and gave Debbie a warm hug.

"Lovely to see you in the flesh, my dear! I'd come to think Simon was exaggerating your charms – but now I see he wasn't . . . You look positively radiant."

He rubbed his hands together.

"Has Simon jumped the gun? Has he shown you the masterpiece?"

"No. We were waiting for you."

"Splendid! Haven't known such self-control . . ."

17

". . . not since your first night at the police station?"

Simon had touched a raw nerve.

"Don't mention it. Dreadful people – the police! Such suspicious minds. Determined to pin one on you if they can. Got me so confused, I almost began to believe I'd done it! Angela, I mean. Might have been better if I had. I think you get longer for smuggling than you do for murder . . ." He smiled apologetically. "Not that I've ever done any smuggling. Stored it, yes. Abetted a felony, yes. Accessory after the fact, perhaps. But I hardly knew what was going on downstairs. A knock on the door some dark night. A couple of bottles to keep me sweet. A lot of heavy breathing up and down the cellar steps. And away they go. I told them it was nothing to do with me."

"But of course they didn't believe you?"

Brackles shook his head.

"Not a word."

Debbie looked at the bottles.

"I think we're wasting valuable time," she said.

"Of course we are, my dear! Prolonging the glorious moment as long as we can." He looked at Simon. "Glasses?"

"Sorry, they're all broken. We're down to mugs."

Brackles looked horrified.

"You can't serve brandy in mugs! Hold on!"

He rushed out of the house and came back with a box of engraved goblets.

"Present from her ladyship," he said. "Note the family crest. *Semper fructus* – always fruitful. We called it something else!"

He poured out the golden liquid and sipped it critically.

"Perfect!" he said. "Lovely stuff."

Simon sniffed at his glass before drinking.

"I love that beautiful flame feeling, don't you?" He looked at Debbie. "You've drunk half of yours already!"

Debbie twinkled her eyes at the painter.

"Trying to build up some Dutch courage."

"You don't have to worry," said Brackles. "He's done you proud. What he'll charge the Inspector, I hate to think. But

18

you'll love it."

"We'd better go and do the honours," said Simon. "A fill-up before we go?"

"Thanks," said Debbie. "Right up to the brim."

Simon led the way out of the kitchen and up the rickety wooden stairs to the studio. On the opposite wall, a dark blue curtain covered a large, unseen object. Simon turned on all the lights in the studio.

"Are you ready?" he asked.

"As ready as I'll ever be," said Debbie.

Raynes stood in the background, saying as little as possible. This was the moment of truth.

Simon handed Debbie a piece of blue ribbon.

"I just pull it?"

The painter nodded.

"It won't fall down?"

"No."

There was a deep silence in the room. Debbie could feel butterflies battering away in her stomach. Perhaps it was the brandy? She tugged at the ribbon. The blue curtain fell to the floor. There was another long silence while everyone took the measure of the painting.

Debbie was for once completely speechless.

It was beautiful. There was no doubt about it. The colours were rich and warm. Her body looked just the way she wanted it to look. But it was her face – the look on her face – which especially excited her. Did she really look like that?

She was so used to the face she saw each morning in the mirror. The smudged make-up. The tousled hair. The slightly bleary eyes. The dark lines. The creases and wrinkles which heralded the onset of middle age. The despair with which she reached for the cleansing cream to repair the damage. But Simon had waved his magic wand and blotted out all that.

He had painted her lying back on a large, dark red, Louis XIV settee with a gold-painted wooden frame. When you looked at it closely, you could see that it had maroon and grey stripes. One of her legs was slightly raised on the settee – the other hung loosely, just touching the floor. Her stomach was slightly in shadow but her breasts had been lovingly sculpted and rendered, each touched with a warm, golden glow.

But as one looked up the length of her body, one came back every time to the face. It was not looking out of the picture shamelessly or wantonly, but was turned to one side as if someone had opened a door and a light had shone in. The eyes were alive and sparkling as if she had just seen her ideal man coming in through the door. Her hair was soft and wild – a little more hair than she normally had – but you could almost touch it. It was a sort of halo to her face. It was – beautiful.

She tried not to – but she couldn't help it. She burst into tears.

It was the first time Raynes had ever seen her cry. For once, the tough, hard-baked exterior had been cracked open – and the real person inside exposed. Richard instinctively moved forward and put his arm round her.

Debbie reached for her handbag but then remembered she had left it downstairs. Richard gave her his handkerchief. Brackles understood precisely what she was feeling.

"It's the face, isn't it?"

Debbie nodded.

"Do I really look like that?"

Simon said: "That's the look I saw on your face when you were last here. Dick said something to you and as you turned to speak to him, that's what you looked like. I spent an age trying to recapture that look. I can't tell you how many times I had to scrape off the paint and start again. The rest of you was quite easy."

"So they say!" said Debbie, cheering up.

"But do you like it?"

"It's wonderful. A great boost to any woman's morale. She's the sort of person I've always wanted to be . . . What do you think, Richard?"

Raynes was slow to give his considered opinion. He too could understand what Debbie was feeling – and a good deal more deeply than Simon or Brackles. When you thought of yourself as a cheap tart, selling your body to one customer after another every night of the week, trying to build up your bank balance before your assets finally wore out . . . it must come as quite a shock to see yourself portrayed as a beautiful work of art. To rediscover a person you thought you had said goodbye to a long time ago.

Of course, Mrs May was not a cheap tart. She was quite an expensive woman – certainly for Grasshallows and especially when one visited her as often as the Inspector did. Nor could one say that she was indiscriminate in her choice of customers. She was very "picky and choosy". If she didn't care for a client, she would readily say "no", no matter how much money was waved under her nose.

But that was not the point.

It was how she saw herself deep down which mattered. The painting had turned that image upside down. She had spent so long building up the appearance of the hard-bitten professional. The woman who had no real feelings. The woman who thought only about money. The woman who had endured two beastly husbands and would never stoop to matrimony again. The woman who accepted the demands of her job without a scintilla of guilt. That woman had suddenly been blown to pieces.

She had expected to be shocked by the picture. She had been secretly afraid it might be some garish, modernist extravaganza – shapeless, ugly, depicted in lurid colours. She had assumed it would be a nude. That was what Richard had wanted for his sitting room; something crude to ponder over in his leisure hours. What she had not bargained for was a vision of loveliness that transformed her from an object of lust into a figure of innocent joy.

She looked nervously at Richard.

How would he react?

Raynes was perfectly honest.

"It's not what I was expecting," he said, "but I think it's superb. I shall be absolutely delighted to have that in my sitting room."

An unworthy suspicion suddenly entered Debbie's mind.

"Once you've got her," she said, "you won't want me!"

"That's a thought," said Simon.

"Could lose you quite a bit of trade!" said Brackles.

Raynes smiled.

"Don't give me ideas!"

But Debbie's astute mind had already conjured up the ideal solution.

"I'll buy the picture!" she said. "Then he'll have to come and see me before he can see *her*!"

"That's most unfair!" said Raynes.

Debbie looked at Simon.

"He hasn't paid for it yet, has he?"

"Not a penny."

"So it could be bought by anyone?"

"Dick commissioned it. It was his idea."

"But if I offered you a higher price, you'd sell it to me?"

Simon did not know whether she was being serious.

Raynes assumed that she was.

"Look at it this way," he said. "If you like the painting that much, you could always come and see me." He smiled more confidently. "Besides," he said, "a picture like that could really upset your customers. They might think they were ravishing the Archangel Gabrielle. Might spoil their fun!"

Debbie could see that Richard had a point, but she wasn't giving up without a fight.

"I could always buy another flat!"

Raynes shook his head.

"You're being very selfish. Typically selfish, if I may say so. I wanted a picture of you . . . " He chose his words carefully. " . . . because I'm very fond of you. We both do fairly sordid jobs, but when I come home, it will be a pleasure to relax and look at something really beautiful. And," he added, "if you were there too, it would be even better."

"Crawler!" said Simon.

"We'll discuss the matter later," said Debbie.

Brackles lifted his glass.

"And may the best man win!" He laughed. "Now what about some more brandy?"

Everyone replenished their glasses and the atmosphere became more relaxed. Simon explained the finer points of his painting; the trouble he had had with the right knee; the way he had caught the look in her eyes; the reason he had made her hair that bit longer; and why neither of them should touch the picture for a couple of days because, like most artists, he couldn't leave his creation alone. Only that morning, he'd been touching up one or two pieces.

Brackles waited patiently till the masterpiece had been thoroughly explored and passions seemed to have been stilled.

"Now," he said, "would you like to come and see the other lady? She's waiting for you next door."

5: *The Painter's studio*

Brackles flung open the door.

"Welcome to the site of the murder!"

He walked into the centre of the room and with an expansive gesture, demonstrated the exact spot where the body had been found.

"She was lying just here. Her head was face-downward – as if she was trying to burrow into the carpet. Her arms were stretched out but her legs were fairly close together." He smiled broadly. "Quite out of character! But she was in her boots and things. The little table was sitting here with the brandy bottle open. She had the glass in her hand when she fell. It didn't break. But some of the stuff in it spilled out across the carpet. That's why the police took it away." He looked around apologetically. "I'm sorry it looks so bare."

Raynes took in the studio with a single glance.

It was very similar to Simon's studio next door. A big room – about twenty-five feet square – with high walls and large glass window panels built into the roof to give the painter plenty of extra light.

To the right of the door, there was a large bookcase, full of art books with titles like: "The Dutch School", "Samuel Palmer. The Complete Works" and "Seurat and the later

23

Impressionists". In any other home, they might have been the sort of books to grace a coffee table but, to Brackles, they were very much the tools of his trade.

Beyond the bookcase was a deep Belfast sink, a table with an electric kettle, a jar of coffee and a couple of mugs. Beside the table there was a heap of canvases and frames and, above them, orderly shelves with tubes and tins of paint, all neatly arranged. In the far corner, there was a large, grey chesterfield half-covered with a sheepskin rug. It looked as if it had been well-used.

To his immediate left, there was a semi-circular dais, flanked by two large, grey plaster pillars with a backdrop of red velvet curtains. A couple of spotlights in the ceiling focussed on an ornate Jacobean chair with a high back and twisted legs. Beside it was a small brown leather footstool.

It was all very much as Raynes had expected.

However, just as Simon's studio had been dominated by Debbie's portrait, so Brackles' studio was overwhelmed by the full-length canvas of Lady Angela which occupied the wall between the dais and the chesterfield. The canvas was not in any frame or stretchers. It hung against the wall, about eight feet by four.

Raynes considered the picture carefully. It was extraordinarily life-like. Lady Angela was in her full riding gear, with one hand on the saddle and the other holding a leather crop. The painting had caught her a second before she lifted her foot to the stirrup, pausing as if she had been asked a question.

Her eyes had a warmth, a sparkle, a touch of naughtiness. Her mouth was just open as if she were about to reply. The only things that seemed unfinished were her riding boots and the horse's neck. The rest of the painting exhibited Brackles' fanatical attention to detail. You could almost feel the texture of the hair on the chestnut gelding.

"Another remarkable picture," said Raynes admiringly.

Brackles looked pleased.

"The background still requires some attention – the trees and the stones in the road. I hadn't really bothered about her feet – but I'll have to get them right. Then it'll have to be stretched and framed. That'll take another month."

"I should think her husband must be delighted with it," said Debbie. "She looks so real. So alive . . ."

Brackles said nothing.

A tear ran down his cheek.

He wiped it angrily away.

Simon intervened.

"Where's he going to put it?"

"In the hallway. He was going to put it in the main drawing-room over the Chippendale cabinet – but now he thinks it'll cut him up if he has to keep looking at it." He sniffed. "Besides, the next Lady Mallowan might not like it . . ."

Simon looked surprised.

"Surely Lesley's not staking her claim quite so soon? That would be the height of indecency."

Brackles nodded.

"She's already set the wheels of divorce in motion."

"That's dreadful!"

"Can't do anything about it. George is a bit embarrassed – as you might expect. But you don't pass up a chance to join the aristocracy. To a social climber like Lesley, a title would mean a great deal."

Simon looked at Raynes.

"Lesley Travers – the lady I was telling you about."

"She's no lady!" said Brackles bitterly. "Just a money-grubbing bitch. She latched on to Sir George and now he can't get rid of her. I expect he made some sort of promise – and she's holding him to it. They've been carrying on for quite some time. Angela told me what was going on; but there was nothing she could do about it."

There was a long silence.

Raynes was looking at the floor, trying to imagine the actual scene which had greeted Simon when he found the body. Debbie had moved round the studio and was now looking at a smaller painting, sitting on an easel. The painting was of a small girl in a straw hat and a pink dress.

"Is this the birthday girl?" she asked.

Brackles was glad of the change of subject. He had been

feeling increasingly distressed about Angela's death ever since he had been released by the police. The more he spoke about her, the more uncomfortable he felt. It was becoming clear to him that she had meant far more to him than he had realized at the time. He wondered if she had felt the same about him.

"Yes," he said, "that's Cherry. Her mother wanted it painted for her dad's birthday. It's supposed to be a surprise for him – but I think he knows. Cherry's not very good at keeping secrets. Pretty little thing . . ."

Raynes was speaking to Simon.

"Did you see her face?"

Simon nodded.

"Horrible sight."

"Purple?"

"Blue – and twisted. Her eyes – just staring."

"Smell of almonds?"

"Yes! That must have been it. It was a smell I recognized but I couldn't place it. Cyanide, was it?"

Raynes nodded. "There's only two things that kill people that quick. Potassium cyanide and sodium azide. With other poisons, you've got time to get to a sink, drink some water, try to vomit it up. If you've got any sense, you'll phone a doctor or an ambulance right away. The hospitals know what to do. You may still die, but it takes time. With these two, you've no time to do anything. You're pole-axed on the spot."

"She wouldn't have had any pain?" asked Brackles.

"Nothing to speak of. She'd have been suddenly choked. Her blood supply to the brain would have been cut off. She'd have had a violent spasm. After that, the brain wouldn't have registered anything. Within three minutes, she'd have been dead."

Raynes looked at Brackles.

"You didn't see the body?"

"I wasn't allowed to. They wouldn't let me in. They were too busy taking photographs. Measuring things. Searching my cellar. They stopped me at the front door. So I went into Simon's – and he told me what he had seen."

"Did Cherry's mother speak to the police?"

"No," said Simon. "I sent them home. I thought that if they had to hang round waiting for the police, it might upset the child. I thought the sooner she got home, the quicker she might forget. But I'm sure they'll have been round to see her by now. I told the police who they were."

"Cherry . . .?"

"Baxter."

"And they live where?"

"In Rye. On the outskirts – just beyond the arch."

Raynes found himself sinking ever deeper into the case.

"And the bottle – the brandy – was it one of Brackles' current stock?"

"It looked like it."

"So whoever doctored it must have access to this house?"

"No problem there!" said Brackles. "People just walk in and out round here. Borrow things . . . return things. We trust people. The only place I keep locked is the cellar. But I always have a bottle or two sitting around. Anyone could slip in and pinch one."

The next question was painfully obvious but Raynes felt obliged to ask it: "Have you been conscious – at any time in the last few weeks – of losing a bottle?"

Brackles laughed.

Raynes hoped he was going to say yes – a bottle had been stolen. But all Brackles said was:

"You policemen all think the same! That was one of the first questions they asked me down at the Gestapo headquarters."

"And did you lose one?" Raynes asked patiently.

Brackles shook his head.

"I don't think so. But everyone knows what I drink. It wouldn't take more than a few minutes to go down to the local supermarket and get one. Anyone could have done it."

"It was a good job Angela turned up," said Raynes coldly. "If she hadn't, you might have drunk it yourself."

Brackles nodded.

"I've been thinking about that. It could have been meant for me. The police asked me if I had any enemies. I haven't, have I?" He looked at Simon.

"Not that I know of."

"I thought Sir George might have had it in for me. He might have guessed we were having it off. But then he sent me £500 whilst I was in custody. Now he wouldn't do that, would he, if he hated me? He wouldn't waste his money on his wife's lover?"

Debbie chipped in.

"He could've had a guilty conscience."

Brackles shrugged his shoulders.

"I suppose so – but George is not like that. He's a quiet, easy-going fellow. He doesn't go out causing trouble . . ."

Raynes looked sharply at the artist.

"He's not involved in your brandy-smuggling operation, is he?"

"Good heavens, no! What gave you that idea?"

"Just wondered."

Brackles shook his head.

"If you met George, you'd realize what sort of person he is."

Raynes abandoned all his good resolutions.

"I'd very much like to meet him."

Brackles smiled.

"Well, that's no problem! No problem whatsoever. He's invited me over for Sunday lunch – tomorrow, 12.30pm – to celebrate my liberation. If you and Debbie wish to join me, I'm sure you'll be most welcome. George runs an open house. Trouble is, you'll probably bump into that wretched Travers woman. She's bound to be there."

Raynes tried to look disappointed but, inwardly, he was delighted. What a splendid way to interview two more suspects.

"Are you sure he won't mind? Another policeman?"

Brackles laughed.

"One more won't make any difference. He's got his story and he's sticking to it."

"How interesting!" said Raynes.

6: *The Van Dyck room*

"Good to see you, Inspector!"

Raynes' first impression was that his host looked very like the American comedian, George Burns, except, of course, that he was very much younger. In his mid-sixties, he reckoned. Sir George had a well-lined face, a pair of rather comical horn-rimmed spectacles, a rich, fruity voice and a cheerful smile. He also had a strong, confident handshake. Raynes was surprised to find that he took an immediate liking to Angela's husband.

"It's very kind of you to invite us."

"Couple more won't make any difference." He turned to Debbie. "And this is your lady-friend? Lovely to see you, my dear. You're not frightened of giving an old man a kiss?" He gave her a friendly kiss on both cheeks. "What a lovely girl, Inspector! You people certainly know where to find them!"

His eyes twinkled.

Raynes wondered what exactly Brackles had told him.

But Sir George did not give him time to ask. The three guests were bustled through the imposing hallway and into a sumptuous green and gold drawing room where the drinks cabinet was already wide open.

"Now, my dear," he addressed Debbie, "what's it to be? Brandy, whisky or gin?" He smiled. "If you're associating with this rogue" (he indicated Brackles) "I bet you've already drunk a bucketload of brandy! You'll be ready for something else. What's it to be?"

"A large gin and tonic would be nice."

"Everything's larger than life round here, my love!" Sir George laughed. "I wouldn't dream of giving people half measures. People come here to try and drink me out of house and home; but they go away disappointed." He looked at the Inspector.

"Another gin and tonic, please."

"And I don't need to ask you!"

"The usual."

As Sir George opened the bottles and poured out the drinks, the Inspector wondered where all the money had come from. Was it earned or inherited? The man certainly seemed to have plenty of it.

As he took his large, bubbling tumbler, he asked:

"Were you in business, Sir George?"

Their host grinned happily.

"In business? Of course I was in business! Earth-moving, boring, trucking – you name it, I did it. South Africa. Great country. You make plenty of bucks out there."

He poured himself a large whisky.

"Well," he said, "to whom shall we drink our toast? To my dear wife? Why not?" He lifted his glass. "To Angela. May she rest in peace!" He drank a very large mouthful of the golden liquid – and then looked at Brackles.

"Stop bubbling, man! She meant more to me than she ever did to you. Damn it! We've been through everything together. She was more than a wife to me. She was a true partner. Everything I am today is thanks to her." He took another hefty swig.

Raynes reckoned that he must have an iron constitution. It looked like neat whisky – with no water.

Sir George looked at Raynes – this time in a less than friendly fashion.

"Well, Inspector," he said, "have you solved the mystery yet? Do you know who killed my dear Angela? I must say the local police have done fuck-all to find out. All they do is to come round here and ask me the same stupid questions. As if I should know!"

Raynes was at his most diplomatic.

"We only got here last night. Brackles has shown us where her ladyship died – and his friend has filled us in on some of the details; but I'm supposed to be off-duty this weekend. Professionally, I'm not allowed to poke my nose into other people's cases."

Sir George grinned.

"Bet you will though! Can't stop a bloodhound sniffing at

the trail! Bet you're dying to get your teeth into it!"

Raynes admitted that it appeared to be a fascinating case but all he and Debbie had come down to Rye for was the picture.

"Ah, the picture!" said Sir George.

"You've seen it?"

"Given a private viewing two or three weeks ago. Gorgeous colours!" He looked at Debbie. "It's even better to see the real person – in the flesh." He smiled broadly. "You know what I mean!"

From the look in his eyes, it was perfectly obvious what Sir George meant. He was a deeply lecherous old man.

"Brackles has also done a splendid picture of your wife."

"I know. I know. And that's the pity of it . . ." Sir George shook his head sadly. "Those blind bastards should have known that an artist would never lay a hand on her till the picture was finished. Till he'd got his money. I should have thought it was obvious to any fool – but what did they do? They arrested him! I ask you!"

"I think it was mostly because of the brandy," said Brackles modestly. "And I didn't have an alibi."

"Neither did I," said Sir George expansively. "Neither did I; but they didn't arrest me. But I took her across to the studio in the car. Hers was at the garage. I delivered her to her assassin at 2.00pm. And she told me to come back for her at five." He smiled at Brackles. "I know what you artists get up to with your models! Come back at five and look at the fresh paint on the horse's tail! My fanny! You expect me to swallow that?" He put his arm round Brackles' shoulders. "Never mind. I forgive you – because you loved her. I knew you wouldn't hurt her."

"But somebody did," said Raynes quietly. "There must have been someone very jealous – or very angry. Someone who hated her with a very deep passion. The murder was carefully prepared."

"So it was," said Sir George. "And Angela had enemies. There's no denying it. That young thug who busts up the hunt . . ."

"Mr Royle?"

31

"Yes, him. He's been threatening her for months. Sending her death threats. Pestering her over the phone. I expect he's got his new set of teeth by now." He looked at the Inspector. "Angela kicked him in the face when he tried to cut off her stirrups."

"So I heard."

"I blame him. Him and his crowd. They have no principles. Trying to destroy one of the most precious traditions in English country life." He waved his empty glass in Raynes' direction. "You people should be more active in protecting folk like us. We're not doing anything illegal. We're maintaining a great British tradition. Nothing finer than to see a pack of hounds chasing across the fields, followed by all the riders on their splendid horses. Wonderful sight! But these young thugs who've only been in the district five minutes, they think they've got a divine right to tell us what to do! Think they can get away with murder. I'd put them behind bars – for a long time."

Brackles was swift to back up Sir George.

"After all, Philip Royle works in a pub. No problem for him getting his hands on a bottle or two . . ."

"None whatsoever."

There seemed to be no doubt where Sir George's suspicions lay. Raynes wondered whether he might concede that there were others – nearer home – who might have wanted to get rid of Lady Angela.

"They do say that poison is normally a woman's weapon . . . Is there any lady who might have had a grievance against her?"

Sir George looked anxiously at his empty glass – as if he would rather not answer the question.

"Well," he said, "most people know my daughter – my daughter from my first marriage – young Katie; they know she never liked Angela. Fought like cat and dog they did – for years. Whenever they met, fur used to fly."

"Does she live round here?"

"About five miles away."

"And she works in a laboratory," added Brackles.

"For God's sake, don't give the Inspector ideas! It's bad

enough as it is. The local police immediately latched on to the connection. Could hardly miss it, could they? They've been through the poisons book with a fine toothcomb. Really put her through it. Of course she had access to the stuff. Of course she was used to using it in her work. But she's hardly likely to have waited this long to murder her stepmother. Why do it now? Why not do it ten years ago? That's what I said to the local police. Not that they paid any attention to me . . ."

Raynes looked sympathetic.

"Did she have an alibi of any sort?"

Sir George shook his head.

"She was off with a migraine. She says she was at home – in bed – till 6.00pm. But there's no way of proving it." He shook a weary head. "I know young Katie wouldn't do it. She knows how much Angela meant to me. She wouldn't do anything to hurt me."

Sir George looked at the grandfather clock which stood near the door. "I'm sorry to be keeping you waiting for lunch – but I'm expecting two other guests, Inspector. Two old friends. A Mrs Lesley Travers and her friend, Janet. They've both been a great help to me since Angela died. I'm afraid they're a bit late, but they said they'd be here before 1.00pm. Let's have another drink while we're waiting."

Sir George returned to the cocktail cabinet.

"Same again?"

The glasses were duly replenished.

Raynes looked closely at Sir George as he asked his next question. "Has Mrs Travers been seen by the police?"

Sir George turned round and glared at his guest.

"I consider that a very offensive remark, Inspector. Especially when you don't even know the lady involved."

Raynes was unmoved.

"My friend, Simon, the other painter, told me that you and Mrs Travers were very close. And Brackles told us last night that she was intending to get a divorce from her husband. I just wondered if there was any connection in all this?"

"You shouldn't believe every bit of tittle-tattle you pick up!" said Sir George angrily.

"Oh, come on," said Brackles. "Everyone knows you and Lesley have been having it off for months. You've been boasting about her charms every time I've met you. And Angela knew all about her too! There's no secret about you and Mrs T."

Sir George had the good grace to look embarrassed.

"I'm sorry. Inspector. Didn't mean to be rude. But it's a delicate matter. Lesley and I have been having a little on the side. Nothing serious – just a romp. At my age, it's nice to have a young thing egging you on." He looked at Debbie. "Angela had all her men-friends. I called them the 'Fly-by-Night Division'. So when Lesley came on the scene, I didn't resist. She's quite a little spitfire when she gets going. Red hair and all that! I was intending to ask Brackles here to paint her – when he'd finished with her ladyship. Not that I'd have left her on her own with him! No way!"

"Lesley would have been quite safe with me," said Brackles coldly. Clearly he did not care for the woman at all.

"Well, you may not like her," continued Sir George, "but I find her a real cracker! Such a change after going to that massage parlour in Brighton! Those girls – no souls! No finesse! But Lesley's been kindness itself. As I say, she's been a real brick since Angela died. She's been down here every weekend. Stopped me moping. Taken charge of all the things Angela used to do about the house . . ."

"And now she's getting a divorce!" said Brackles.

"I think it must be Tom's idea. They've been living apart for almost two years."

Brackles shook his head.

"It won't look good, Sir George. If she moves in here so soon after Angela's death, people will talk. It could be very embarrassing."

Raynes intervened.

"Did you know she was getting a divorce?"

"Not till last Tuesday."

"And does she want you to marry her?"

There was a silence in the green and gold drawing room. Outside, there was a sudden crunching of gravel as a red

BMW swung round the drive and pulled up beside the front door.

Sir George's face lit up.

"At last! Thought something might have happened to them." He looked at the Inspector. "If you want to know the answer to your question, the best thing is to ask Lesley herself!"

7: *La Ghirlandata*

Debbie took an instant dislike to Mrs Travers. Her feeling was not motivated by any sense of jealousy or rivalry. It was a gut feeling. For although Lesley Travers was a strikingly attractive woman, Debbie sensed immediately that she was greedy, selfish and false.

None of this was apparent to the three men in the room. What they saw was a slim, girl-like figure, sheathed in a wispy, pale green dress, with an expensive gold chain about her waist. Her thick red hair was cut 1920s style in a page boy bob. Her skin was fresh and clear; her eyes sparkled green; and her lips were full and passionate. Her legs were bare and her small feet were encased in tiny gold sandals.

Her entrance into the drawing room was as commanding as that of any actress.

"George, darling! I'm sorry we're so late. We got stuck in the most frightful traffic jam outside Gatwick. Terrible accident! Bodies everywhere. We just couldn't move till they cut them out. Could we, Janet?"

Her companion confirmed the truth of her statement.

She was a plump, dark-haired woman with a sad face. Raynes reckoned she was in her early forties. She was wearing a two-piece pink suit with blue edgings.

Janet knew full well the reason why she and her friend were late. It was because Lesley had stopped off at a charming little pub just outside Rye for a cocktail. There, she had been flirting with a young farmer who had come down to his local for a Sunday pint. Lesley had been determined not to leave until she had given him her phone number and made him promise to call her.

"But I'm a happily married man!" said the young farmer.

Lesley looked at him with mock sorrow and ran her long fingers all the way up his corduroy thigh. "Don't be so square and old-fashioned," she said. "Everyone needs a bit on the side! You just phone me up and I'll be down here, leaping into your haystack, doing things to you your wife'd never dream of."

The young farmer had looked faintly dazed but had written down her number on the back of a beer mat. As they left the pub, Lesley said to Janet: "I do like them rough. It makes it so much more exciting."

If Debbie had known all this, it would have confirmed her deepest suspicions. But to the outward eye, Sir George was the single object of Lesley's passion.

She flung herself into George's arms and gave him a long, body-tingling hug – her feet way off the floor.

"We're not late, are we?"

"No," said George. "We've been waiting for you."

Lesley disentangled herself from his embrace, straightened her dress and looked at the other guests.

"I didn't know we were having company."

"Well, Brackles has just escaped from the police . . ."

"A great mistake!" said Lesley coolly. "They should have kept you in."

"Thank you," said Brackles.

"And this is Detective-Inspector Raynes – a visiting policeman, and his lady-friend, Debbie . . . she's been having her picture painted . . ."

"I've heard about it."

The two women looked at each other. Debbie said nothing but Lesley could sense the younger woman's hostility.

"And this is Lesley's friend, Janet."

Sir George smiled happily.

"We've met," said Brackles briefly.

"Have you?" said Sir George. "And where was that?"

"At Art College," said Janet.

"She was one of my models."

"Well, you don't say!" Sir George was delighted to see old friends – perhaps old lovers – reunited. "I suppose you painted her in the nude?" He smiled salaciously at Janet.

"I was much slimmer in those days."

"Bet you were a cracker!" said Sir George.

Raynes noticed that Brackles was twisting his empty glass in a nervous manner. Obviously, this was an embarrassing encounter for both of them.

"Were you lovers?"

"He promised to marry me!" said Janet accusingly. "And then he ditched me."

"We'd grown apart," said Brackles. "You knew that."

"A promise is a promise," said Janet. "You were a rat. I don't suppose you've changed. You're probably still leading gullible women up the garden path."

Raynes reckoned that it had the makings of a very unpleasant lunch party.

Lesley was anxious to spike her rival's guns.

"And what do you do for a living?" she asked Debbie.

It was the sort of question Richard dreaded – especially in a tense atmosphere like this.

"I work in a dress shop," said Debbie modestly.

"That's not what I heard."

Her green eyes tore into Debbie.

But Mrs May was not to be intimidated.

"It takes one to know one!"

Sir George seemed quite unaware of the bitter tides swirling around him.

"Now, now, girls!" he said. "Stop bitching and scratching each other. We're all here to enjoy a splendid lunch. Mrs Beaton has been slaving in the kitchen all morning, preparing a delicious meal. We must go through and enjoy it."

They passed through the hallway and into another elegant room overlooking a broad terrace at the back of the house. The large table was set for six. There were silver candelabra and silver napkin rings, heavy crystal glasses and two large decanters of wine, Raynes was glad that a decent lunch was in prospect – even if the company was likely to be poisonous.

Sir George placed Janet and Debbie on either side of him. Mrs Travers occupied the other end of the table with Brackles and the Inspector beside her.

Mrs Beaton bustled in with a large silver salver and served smoked salmon salad with seafood *en croute*. Sir George poured out a very dry Chablis.

Raynes decided that perhaps the safest subject of conversation was Lesley's relationship with Sir George. She could hardly say unpleasant things about that. He ate two forkfuls of smoked salmon and then turned to Mrs Travers.

"Is your divorce being contested?"

Lesley looked at the Inspector suspiciously.

Why was he asking her that question?

"No," she said. "Tom hasn't got a leg to stand on. He's a crook and a cheat. I should have divorced him long ago."

"How long have you been married?"

"Ten years. But it's never been much of a marriage. He wanted me as a respectable face for his business. To entertain his cronies. To soft-soap the unwary . . ."

She paused.

Perhaps she had said too much?

"And what is your husband's business?"

Lesley looked at Raynes with contempt.

"You don't expect me to tell you that! You'd probably arrest him!"

"He runs a casino," said Sir George. "A very popular place. Goes like a bomb!"

"And sells plenty of brandy?"

Raynes looked at Brackles.

"I wouldn't know."

Lesley turned her fire on the middle-aged artist.

"Of course you know! Don't pretend you don't. Every time you come up to London, you go there. Never forget, when you were down on your luck, Tom got you those two good commissions. That Arab guy and that company director. They must have paid you a packet!"

"Small world!" said Raynes mischievously.

He wondered why Brackles had disclaimed all knowledge

38

of Lesley's husband. Perhaps it was too close to the bottle?

"And has your husband got someone else?" he asked innocently.

Lesley was chill itself.

"Has he ever not had someone else?"

Sir George explained:

"Lesley worked for Tom as a croupier, Inspector. Then she became his personal secretary. It might have been better if she'd stayed that way. Marriage has brought her nothing but unhappiness. Isn't that so?"

It wasn't so. Lesley knew very well that she had been more than eager to marry Tom. To share his wealth and his bed. He had been a good catch and she had well and truly sucked the orange dry. But now she was beginning to see that Tom was on the downward track. He was drinking heavily and making mistakes that would soon bring him into trouble with the law. His reputation was no longer what it had been and others were waiting in the wings to ease him out. She could read the writing on the wall. It was time to go. His having an affair with the latest young croupier was nothing new.

"Will you be keeping the BMW?" asked Brackles maliciously.

"She's keeping everything she can get her hands on," said Sir George. "Sensible lass!"

Lesley dug unenthusiastically into her seafood *en croute*. She didn't like being reminded that she was greedy and selfish.

"And when are you two getting married?" asked Raynes.

"As soon as the divorce comes through," said Sir George. "I don't think there's any doubt about that."

Lesley could think of one or two reasons why their marriage should be delayed as long as possible — and even why it should not take place at all. But this was not the time or the place to express doubts. She looked down the table with clear, radiant, hopeful eyes.

"As soon as we can."

It made Debbie feel quite sick.

"So you will become the next Lady Mallowan?" said Janet.

Lesley smiled.

39

"That's the least of it. This beautiful house. The estate. The horses . . ."

"Do you ride?" asked Debbie.

Lesley looked at her coldly.

Why did that little scrubber ask that? Was she being sarcastic?

"Not yet," she replied. "But I hope to learn. How many horses have we got at present?"

"Six," said Sir George. "Not a large number but they're splendid beasts. Angela loved horses . . ."

A tear rolled down his cheek. He wiped it away with his napkin.

"She also loved the groom!"

Brackles looked at Lesley.

"Better not make the same mistake!" he said.

Lesley stared at the artist as if he were some mongrel which had disgraced itself in a public place.

"Brackles," she said, "I thought you were a friend. My friend. Sir George's friend. Why are you being so nasty to me this afternoon?"

Raynes watched the two of them with interest.

Brackles did not flinch.

"I think," he said, "I'm still feeling very upset at Angela's death. I loved her . . . not as much as Sir George did . . . or his groom . . . but I loved her. She was so full of life." He paused. "I'm still painting her picture. A little bit, every day. To me, she's still very much alive. I just think it's . . ." He was going to say "indecent" but he changed his mind at the last minute. " . . . I think it's very sad that she's hardly been dead three weeks and you're talking about marriage. Stepping into her shoes. It seems . . . too soon."

Mrs Travers looked down the table.

"Don't blame Lesley," said Sir George. "It's not her fault. She's not been pushing me to get married. She's just tried to comfort me at a very difficult time. A very difficult time for her as well as for me. We're like two people clinging together after a shipwreck. Marriage gives us both something to look forward to. But it won't be happening in the immediate future. You know what lawyers are like. They make mountains out of molehills. String the whole thing out as long as they can. Charge you the earth. By the time we get round to tying the knot, the period of official mourning'll be long since over. I don't think anyone'll have cause to complain."

He looked at Brackles.

"You're just upset because you've got no one to console you."

Brackles shook his head.

"No," he said. "It's not that. I'm just frightened what people will say. You know what they're like round here. Even if there's no truth in it, tongues will wag. People will point the finger. You're a very popular figure, Sir George. I wouldn't like you to lose that respect."

"Respect?" said Sir George. "It's not respect. It's money! Because I give people work . . . because I buy stuff in local shops . . . because I give donations to good causes – people grovel. Whatever they may think of me, they'll say nothing so long as they're being paid." He looked at Brackles sharply. "Just like you! You won't say a harsh word against me till you've been paid for that bloody picture. Yes! And now you're no longer committing adultery with my wife, perhaps you'll get it finished. Pronto . . . Double quick?"

Lesley's eyes lit up with pleasure as Sir George laid into Brackles. That was the way to treat him. When she thought of all the times Tom had tried to rescue him from the gutter, when he was down on his luck . . . "Poor Brackles," he used to say, "we must do something for him. We can't leave him like that." My God! What a viper he had nursed to his bosom.

Mrs Travers ignored the fact that she had done her best to prevent her husband helping the artist. She had always said that if he couldn't get himself out of the gutter, he should be left there. She had said this more than once – even when Brackles was present. He had not forgotten.

Raynes watched this exchange of blows with considerable detachment. After all, it was Simon who was his friend. Brackles' invitation to lunch with Sir George was just a convenient way of meeting the other characters involved. And what characters! It would be splendid to discover that Mrs Travers was the murderess – and unmask her. To silence that vicious tongue.

However, Mrs Beaton brought an end to any further comment. She bustled in with yet another silver dish containing a magnificent roast and a steaming tray full of Yorkshire pudding. She collected the plates and looked distressed that Mrs Travers had eaten so little of her seafood *en croute*. Everyone else had eaten theirs.

Sir George carved the joint, distributing generous portions to each plate. Mrs Beaton handed them round and then fussed over the vegetables.

"More brussels sprouts, Inspector? Some mangetout?"

Sir George was soon at his elbow.

"Claret, Inspector?"

"Thank you."

Debbie decided that she should make an effort to re-direct the conversation into more peaceful paths.

She looked across the table at Janet.

"And what do you do?"

"I work in a jewellery shop."

"In London?"

Janet nodded.

"Do you enjoy it?"

"Not very much."

"She used to have her own business . . ." Sir George explained.

"It was my parents' business."

" . . . but it went bust."

Janet nodded.

"Various people tried to help. Lent her money – but it didn't do any good. Never had enough stock. Couldn't keep up with the latest fashions. Customers went elsewhere. Expensive business – jewellery."

"So now you work for someone else?"

"She helps Tom," said Sir George, again butting in. "When people can't afford to pay their gambling debts, Tom often takes in a bit of jewellery and sells it off. Janet re-cycles it

42

through the shop. Her boss doesn't mind. Quite a useful little sideline. Doesn't appear in the books."

Raynes looked at Lesley's face.

It was tense and angry.

Sir George looked at the Inspector. "I shouldn't be telling you all this. But," he shrugged his shoulders, "it's life." He looked at Raynes' glass. "Help yourself to some more claret."

Debbie continued her efforts to draw Janet out.

"Are you married? Have you any children?"

It was a desperate mistake.

Janet burst into tears.

Lesley looked at Brackles.

"It was your fault. You persuaded her to have an abortion. That finished her. She never had any more after that."

Brackles said nothing, but Raynes could see that his knuckles were clenched white around his glass. Would he hit Mrs Travers? Would he get up and walk out? And what should he and Debbie do if he did?

Sir George was comforting Janet.

"Don't cry, my dear. It's a long time ago. You've come through it. There's more to life than husbands and children."

He put his arm around her and gave her a warm hug.

Lesley poured herself another glass of wine and looked down the table at Debbie.

"This scumbag," she said, indicating Brackles, "met Janet at college. She was just a model. Six shillings an hour. Young, impressionable, naive. He seduced her. Promised to marry her. Put her in the family way. And then ditched her."

"There was more to it than that," said Brackles.

"Not much more," said Lesley. "Think of all the damage you've done. She's taken seven overdoses. Been in a psychiatric hospital. Had ECT. Been drugged up to the eyeballs. It's a miracle she's managed to hold down any job. Small thanks to you! You were the only person she ever loved."

"That's not true."

"It is true." Janet suddenly re-entered the conversation.

Brackles said nothing.

"You're a coward!" said Lesley firmly. "You were

responsible for all this."

"No, I wasn't," said Brackles. "Whether you like it or not, she was unstable before I met her. I discovered my mistake – just in time."

"*Your* mistake?" said Mrs Travers.

Brackles looked at her with undisguised hatred.

"I didn't know she was a lesbian!" he said.

He turned to Sir George.

"If you will excuse me . . . I have a painting I have to finish." He folded his napkin. Stood up. He looked at Raynes and Debbie. "I'm sorry for spoiling your lunch. I shall walk home."

He pushed in his chair and walked calmly towards the door. As he reached it, Janet hurled one of Sir George's heavy crystal glasses at him. It missed – but shattered against the wall.

Following his departure, there was complete silence for several minutes. Raynes continued to sip his wine, wondering what he should say – or do.

Sir George finally came to the rescue.

"I'm sorry about that, Inspector. Lot of old wounds re-opened. Very painful." He turned to Janet. "Are you all right? Feeling a little better? Wish you'd thrown one of my plates. A bit cheaper." He laughed. "Can't help admiring him though. Took a lot of provocation. You were a bit hard on him, my love . . ."

Lesley shook her head.

"Yes, you were. He's a great artist. A very great artist." He turned again to Janet. "I think even you would agree with that?"

Janet nodded glumly.

"Yes – and artists are highly-strung people – more highly-strung than the rest of us. Live very unbalanced lives. Nothing matters to them but their painting. They've no understanding of other people's feelings. Too full of themselves. They just use people. As he used you. As he used my dear Angela . . ."

As an apology for Brackles' life. Sir George's words did

not cut much ice with the assembled company – but Raynes thought Sir George was not far out in his assessment of Brackles' character. He had noticed the same traits in his friend, Simon. He too had got a girl into trouble at the university. He had deserted her. Since then, he seemed to have moved restlessly from one affair to another, never finding a suitable partner. It was remarkable how similar the two men were.

Raynes looked at Sir George.

"I think you're right. I've noticed precisely the same characteristics in other artistic people."

Janet had now recovered.

"We were both young and stupid at the time. Very foolish and immature." She looked at Lesley. "You know it wasn't Brackles' fault I ended up in hospital. It was my parents' death." She looked at Debbie. "They died in a car crash. Hit a tree on a stormy night. It was all very sudden. But I had to blame someone. I always blamed Brackles. Took a long time to get over it."

Sir George patted her arm.

"Well, you did get over it – and that's what matters." He pushed an empty glass in her direction. "Have another drop of claret. It'll help. Yes, it will." He filled the glass up to the brim. "Drink it up – and be brave." He smiled. "And I know you're not a lesbian – and so does Lesley."

Mrs Travers frowned.

Sir George looked at Raynes' empty plate.

"A little more beef, Inspector?"

"Thank you," said Raynes. "It was delicious. And perhaps a couple more roast potatoes?"

Sir George filled up Raynes' plate.

He looked over to Janet.

"D'you think you could clear up all that glass? Mrs Beaton'll be wondering what we've been up to."

Raynes thought Sir George had handled the whole incident with great diplomacy. The glass was swept away. The conversation resumed; and everything returned to normal by the time Mrs Beaton made her final appearance with a rich, fruity, summer pudding served with farm-fresh cream.

"Oh," she said. "Has someone gone?"

"Mr Brackles had to go and finish a picture."

"What a shame! And only had half his lunch."

She cleared away the plates and served the dessert.

"Now," she said, "will that be all? The cheeseboard's on the side, if anyone wants it. The coffee's in the lounge. And . . ." as if she had almost forgotten ". . . your daughter phoned. She'll be around in about half an hour. She wants to speak to you . . ." She looked at Mrs Travers with a face devoid of all expression " . . . privately."

Sir George was pleased.

"You must meet my daughter, Katie, Inspector. She's the intelligent member of the family. I told you, she works in a laboratory. Graduate in chemistry. Loves horses. Only thing she and Angela had in common. They both loved riding. You must stay on and meet her."

Debbie felt the visit had already lasted quite long enough. Inwardly, she groaned. She hated wasting her time with such worthless people. She would willingly have left at the same time as Brackles. She hated scenes. She wished that she and Richard were back at the hotel, having coffee and liqueurs in their room, snuggled together in the four-poster, warm, cosy, naked together. Stroking, caressing – even sleeping their way through the afternoon. Anything would be better than enduring these pathetic people.

But Richard was keeping his end up. Asking intelligent questions; and being careful to avoid offending Mrs Travers. He seemed to be genuinely interested in her divorce case. He talked to Janet about electroplating as if it was a subject he had been wanting to talk about all his life. And then Sir George had taken him out of the dining room. He had said he had something to show him. And she was left with Janet and Lesley.

As he left the dining room, Sir George mopped his brow.

"Glad we got out of that," he said. "Quite exhausting. Need a breath of fresh air."

Raynes assumed that they would be going outside but Sir

George took him into his study and showed him the Mallowan family tree.

It was encased in a handsome black and gold frame with lots of crests and shields in bright colours with the broad lines of descent and lineage clearly marked out. It was an impressive document and Sir George was obviously proud of his heritage.

He poured out a wealth of detail about his family history. His eyes twinkled.

"And, of course, Inspector, there may be more to come."

"A son and heir?"

"Why not? Things have taken an unexpected turn. Perhaps in some ways for the better. There's all to play for." He pointed to the family motto: "*Semper fructus*, Inspector. Always fruitful. As I told you, there's life in the old dog yet."

Raynes smiled.

"Don't waste it all in Brighton!"

Back in the dining room Lesley Travers looked at Debbie.

"I'm sorry I was a bitch."

"That's all right."

"No. I'm sorry I was so nasty. It was just – seeing Brackles here. He always brings out the worst in me. I want to hit him."

"Perhaps you should."

Mrs Travers looked at Debbie thoughtfully.

"I can't help thinking that all this murder business is his fault. It was his studio. His booze. And he was having an affair with her."

"But did he benefit in any way from her death?"

Mrs Travers bit her lip delicately.

"No," she said. "I'm the person who's going to benefit."

"So?"

The green eyes narrowed imperceptibly.

"Yes. I know it looks bad. But," she smiled. "I'll pull through. I always do." She looked at Debbie critically.

"Are you good at your job?"

"Very good."

Lesley nodded. "So am I."

8: *A Bay Hunter*

After the unpleasant ordeal in the dining room, Katie was a breath of fresh air. She was plain – not pretty – a solid, sensible, practical person, wearing a grey jumper and blue jeans.

Sir George introduced her to Debbie and Richard and asked her to show them round the stables. He would be busy for the next hour or so.

Once her father had left them, Katie asked:

"What's happening?"

"Your father's entertaining two ladies – Mrs Travers and her friend."

"Not them again?"

"Have they been round a lot lately?"

"Every weekend since the funeral – and sometimes during the week as well. Dad's a fool where women are concerned. He gets himself into one mess after another."

"Was it any better when Angela was alive?"

Katie shook her head.

"No. Just the same. He went his way; she went hers. One scandal after another. Sometimes both at the same time. I learnt – long ago – never to get involved. They'd sort it out somehow."

"Your mother was Sir George's first wife?"

"He wasn't Sir George then."

"No. But what happened to her?"

"She died. Septicaemia, I believe. I was too young to know much about it. I was shipped off to my grandmother. She brought me up."

"But you came back to your father?"

"Not till I was grown up."

"Once he inherited his fortune?"

"Yes. About then."

"Was he married to Angela at that time?"

"Just back from his honeymoon. Dad'd been away in South Africa. I hadn't seen him for several years. Once they were married, they settled here – and I came to stay with them."

"But you didn't like Angela?"

"Who told you that?"

"Your father. He said you fought like cat and dog."

"Well, she was very difficult to live with. So dominating. So fickle. So obsessed with money – and clothes. She was very vulgar. Didn't make any effort to hide her affairs. I was very sorry for Dad – but he didn't seem to mind."

"Your father said that Angela made him what he is."

Katie scowled.

"Well, I suppose she did. She organised everything. The house, the stables, their social life. The sort of things they both liked. But I think I preferred Dad as he used to be."

"You think money has changed him?"

"Completely. And mixing with all those county types. They're all so false."

Katie went silent.

"Mrs Travers doesn't seem a county type," Raynes observed.

'No, she's a leech. A professional leech. She'd latch on to anyone with money and suck them dry."

"D'you think that's what she intends to do to your father?"

"Probably."

"Will he be able to resist her?"

"It's up to him."

"D'you think she'll become the next Lady Mallowan?"

Katie shrugged her shoulders.

"I hope not." She thought for a moment. "I can't really see it happening. She's not a country person. She's more of a night-club hostess. That's where she excels. Down here, she'd be like a fish out of water."

"She doesn't ride . . ." said Debbie.

Raynes raised his eyebrows.

" . . . horses," she added quickly.

"Might sell off the stables," said Raynes.

"She'd better not!" A flash of real anger came over Katie's face. "That's the one good thing about Dad's inheritance. The only benefit as far as I'm concerned. Would you like to come and see them?"

Katie led them down to a small courtyard of new buildings where six horses were stabled. One of them was out in the open being saddled by a groom.

"That's Pat," said Katie.

"Was that the one your mother was having an affair with?"

Katie stopped.

"First of all, she was not my mother – and secondly, she wasn't having an affair with him. She wanted to – but he refused. She made his life hell – almost broke up his marriage – but she didn't get her way. I think it says a lot for him that he refused." She waved to the groom. "Hi, Pat! Be with you in a minute. These are some friends of Dad's – just showing them round."

She went over to the first stable door.

"This is Angela's horse – Natal. All their names have South African connections. He's a beautiful horse. Come over, boy. They won't hurt you."

The large chestnut hunter refused to come forward. He stayed deep in his loose-box and pawed the ground restlessly.

Katie looked at him sadly.

"He knows she's dead," she said. "Been like this ever since she died. Restless. Vicious, even. Never used to be like that. Angela used to ride him every day. Beautiful jumper. Cost Dad a fortune – but it was worth it."

She tried to entice the horse closer – but without success.

She moved on to the next green door.

"And this is Durban. Dad likes him. Very comfortable and reliable. Lovely nature. Not too fast. But steady. Doesn't try to fight you. You're a sweetie, aren't you?"

She stroked Durban's nose and talked to him.

She pointed to the horse out in the yard which was now saddled up but was impatiently throwing his head up and down.

"That's my horse. Jo'burg. Smashing nature. I've had him for three years. Goes like a rocket. A bit wild sometimes. But we understand each other, don't we?"

The horse clopped over to her and nuzzled her.

"Waiting for his afternoon run. I shall have to go in a minute." She took hold of the reins. "The other three are younger horses we bought last autumn. Pat's just breaking them in. Kruger, Zulu and Elizabeth. Zulu's going to be a great horse. A real winner."

She turned back to Jo'burg.

"Don't be so impatient!"

She returned to Debbie and Richard.

"D'you want to join me?"

"I'm sorry," said Raynes, "I've never ridden a horse."

"I couldn't control a thing that size!" said Debbie.

Katie laughed.

"It's quite easy when you know how."

She swung easily up into the saddle.

Jo'burg straightened up immediately – his ears pricked – snorting vigorously.

"Longing to go," she said. "I'll have to leave you. Have a word with Pat. I'll be back in about twenty minutes."

9: *Whistlejacket*

Raynes and Mrs May watched her go.

Pat, the groom, was standing nearby, holding a bucket of feed.

"Loves her horses," he said.

"So did her ladyship."

"Yes. It was thanks to her we got these stables built. Money no object. Still, it was her money."

"Are you the only person who works here?"

"The only full-time. We have a few people who come in part-time to help."

"Are you from Ireland, Pat?"

"No. From Norfolk originally. Been all over the place."

He sounded a well-spoken sort of man with no accent.

"And you love horses?"

"Easier to cope with than human beings – that's for sure."

"Katie was saying that you found her ladyship rather trying."

Pat put down his bucket and folded his arms.

"Trying isn't the word!" He shook his head sadly. "I know one shouldn't speak ill of the dead, but there's no other word for it – she was a right bitch. Had to have everything her own way. She was nice enough to my wife and myself when we first arrived. Made us welcome. Made sure we were settled comfortably. Gave me a good wage. Good holidays. But she didn't just want your labour, she wanted your body and soul as well."

Raynes laughed.

"But mostly your body?"

Pat remained serious.

"It was no laughing matter. She didn't say: 'Please can I have you . . .' She cornered you in the shed and grabbed you. 'Come on,' she said. 'I need it.' Well, I didn't need it. My wife and I were perfectly happy and I wasn't going to deceive her. But she came on so strong. And perverted: 'You can whip me if you like,' she says. 'I'd enjoy that.' She took down her trousers and flaunted herself. She'd come up behind you and grope you. She was insatiable.

"I said to her: 'Look, I'm a happily married man. I couldn't go back and face my wife if I'd being doing things with you.' 'She'd never know,' she said. 'What damage would ten minutes in a loose-box do? All I'm asking for is a bit of a cuddle.' But the look in her eyes showed she wanted more than that.

"She was so used to getting her own way. She didn't like people who said: 'No'. She felt she could buy you. And the more I refused, the more . . . what shall I say? . . . rampant she got."

"And when you refused?"

"She turned really nasty. Very sarcastic and rude. Put on all her airs and graces. Sometimes, she just cut me dead. Later, she tried to give me the sack, but I spoke to young Katie and she had a word with her dad."

"Did that help?"

"Well, I kept my job. But she went round telling everyone that she'd had me and what a good lover I was. She boasted about it. Well, that was worse! Everyone looked at me. People talked about it in the town. My wife believed her. She was livid. With *me*! I told her there was no truth in it. I told her what she'd tried to do – and how I'd rejected her. But she said: 'There's no smoke without fire. Angela wouldn't go round lying about something like that.' But I said: 'That's just what she did'."

"Did you convince her?"

Pat sighed deeply.

"No. She left me. She went away for two weeks to stay with a friend. Her and the kid. I was bloody angry. I mean, if I'd done something wrong . . . fair enough. But I hadn't. It was bloody unfair. I told Katie what had happened and she went round to see her – and explain. I don't know what she said, but she came back. Not very friendly – but at least she came back. Then she insisted I went along to the hospital for tests – to make sure I hadn't caught anything! It was a nightmare, I can tell you."

"Did things improve after that?"

Pat nodded.

"She accepted my story. Eventually."

"And her ladyship?"

"Still a bit chilly – but gradually she came round. Got involved with someone else. An artist chap. Got her claws into him. Perhaps one or two others. Anyway, it took the heat off me. She's been fine since Christmas. Then, of course, she got bumped off . . ."

"By whom?"

Pat shook his head.

"No one knows. I think it was probably one of those nasty people who come down from London."

"Mrs Travers?"

"I don't know what her name is. But they're always down here rooting about. A red-haired, cheeky little piece. And her husband, who's a slimy crook."

"They're at the house – at this moment. The redhead and a

female friend."

"Are they friends of yours?"

"Certainly not!" said Raynes.

"We've had the most awful lunch," said Debbie. "Hysterics and weeping . . . people throwing glasses . . ."

"That's not the half of it," said Pat. "Three in a bed's what I hear."

"Really?" said Raynes.

Pat nodded.

"That's what the cleaning lady told me. Walked into the bedroom and there they were – at it – all three of them. Sir George in the middle. They're a dirty lot. Just like animals." He looked towards Zulu, who was straining to get out of his loose-box. "No," he said, "not like animals. They're decent – compared with humans."

Richard looked at Debbie.

She pulled a face at him.

"What about Mr Travers?" asked Raynes. "The one you said was a slimy crook. Was it just his manner?"

Pat gave the bucket of feed to Zulu who chewed noisily.

"No," he said. "Just hearsay. People are very close down here. Don't say much. Speak out of the corner of their mouths when they think no one is looking. They tell me he's been seen loading up his van with booze in the middle of the night. Boxloads of it. He takes it up to London; gets rid of it there. One of the boatmen told me what he was up to. I'm surprised the police haven't caught him yet."

"Perhaps they're waiting for him to lead them to bigger fish?"

"Perhaps."

Raynes wondered how much he should say.

"Still," he said, "they did arrest that artist chap. I'm told he'd been storing the stuff. They got him for that – even if they didn't get him for the murder."

"Yes," said Pat, "but he's just a pawn in this whole business. And it is a business. They're making thousands out of it. He daren't squeal. If he did, they'd bump him off too."

"You think they killed her ladyship?"

54

Pat nodded.

"Why?"

"To get their claws into Sir George. He's got a lot of money. A lot of ready cash. That red-haired piece and her chum are going to screw it out of him bit by bit. You'll see. If her ladyship had been here, they wouldn't have got a penny. She was very careful about money. But with her gone, Sir George is a sitting duck. They'll get him all excited about their business ventures. He'll sink money into it. But he'll never see it again. The whole estate'll go down the plughole."

"And the horses?"

"The whole caboodle."

Pat looked quite depressed.

"And what about you?"

"I'll just move on. Find work somewhere else. It's no skin off my nose."

"But very sad?"

"If it comes to that, young Katie might put her foot down. She's quite a girl. Been a good friend to me."

Raynes looked around the immaculate stableyard with its freshly-painted green doors and white walls. When he had first seen it, he had thought what a splendid little empire Lady Angela had built up with Sir George. Now he saw it – poised on the edge of an abyss.

"The impermanence of money," he said. "Like shifting sand."

"Root of all evil!" said Pat and spat on the ground.

A sound of thudding hooves reminded them that young Katie was about to return from her afternoon ride. Jo'burg clattered into the yard, snorting heavily and steaming with sweat.

"Was he all right?" asked Pat, grabbing the reins.

"Terrific," said Katie. "Couldn't be better."

She took both feet out of the stirrups and swung her leg over the saddle and dropped lightly to the ground. Her face was red and her eyes were shining.

She turned to Pat.

"Have you had a good chat with the Inspector?"

Pat looked horrified.

"Inspector? You didn't tell me he was a policeman. And all the things I've been saying. If I'd known, I should never have said a word."

"It's all right," said Raynes. "I'm not a policeman down here. We've just come down for the weekend – to visit friends."

But Pat shook his head.

"I'm sorry, Inspector. I don't believe you. You policemen are all the same. You scratch my back. I'll scratch yours. Just remember! I said nothing to you. Nothing!"

Raynes smiled.

"I'll remember that: 'Pat said nothing'."

He took the groom's hand and gave it a firm squeeze.

10: *Molly Longlegs*

Katie walked back with Debbie and Richard.

"What was Pat telling you?"

"About Mrs Travers and her friends. He thinks they're going to take your dad for a ride."

Katie stopped.

"They may think it," she said, "but they won't succeed. Angela made quite sure the family fortune was tied up in a trust fund. Only so much can be spent in a year. You can borrow against future income, but you can't touch the capital."

"And the capital comes to you?"

She shook her head.

"Only the income."

"Do you have any children?"

"Two boys. Five and three."

"But they won't inherit the title?"

"No," said Katie, "the line stops with Dad – and that suits me. I'm not interested in all these titles."

"Your dad was showing me the family tree . . ."

Katie laughed.

"It's a load of rubbish! Those people who make them, I

think they must dream it all up. Apparently, we're all related to Charles II through one of his mistresses – and because he had so many, we've all got royal blood. It's quite ridiculous."

Raynes said: "Don't you think there's any truth in it?"

"Well, obviously some of it is true. But the further back you go, the more bizarre it is."

"Is there anything in it you know to be true?"

Katie looked thoughtful.

"Well, I know Sir Ian Mallowan . . ."

" . . . the fourth baronet . . ."

" . . . he died in 1977 when Dad got his title."

"I noticed that."

"Well, he lived in Grasshallows."

"Did he?"

Raynes was quite surprised.

"Yes. Dad told me. He said how strange it was that I should be going back to the old family home . . ."

Raynes looked blank.

Katie noticed the look.

"That's where I went to university. That's where I got my degree."

"What a small world!" said Raynes.

"That's where we come from," said Debbie.

"Really?" said Katie. "It's a lovely place. The river. And the Meadows . . . I had some wonderful nights down there. What a coincidence!"

Debbie did not admit to any knowledge of the Meadows, although she had spent many profitable hours there.

Raynes smiled indulgently.

But he was busy thinking. Could this be the vital opening he was looking for?

He turned back to Katie.

"You got a degree in chemistry, I believe?"

"Oh, don't start on that! I've had it up to here with the police. They think that because I have access to chemicals, I must have been the person who provided the fatal dose – even if I didn't administer it myself."

"You have cyanide in the laboratory?"

57

"Plenty of it. Enough to poison half the population. But it's not something I ever use. I work on tranquillizers. That's my line of country."

"Did the police say it was cyanide?"

"That's the only thing they talked about, so I suppose it must have been. Someone put a sizeable dose into the brandy and left it for Angela. She was so greedy, she just picked up the bottle and swigged it down. Killed her stone dead. If she had to go, it was probably the best way. The quickest, anyway. But she looked pretty awful – afterwards."

"You saw her?"

"I went with Dad to identify the body."

"You had recovered from your migraine by then?"

Katie was reminded that she had beside her a very astute police inspector. Who had told him about the migraine?

"Not really," she said. "But when something like that happens, you tend to forget yourself. It's so awful. I'd never seen a dead person before. Lots of dead animals in experiments – but never a real person."

"And do you have theories as to who did it?"

"Well, it wasn't me."

"And it wasn't your dad?"

"I shouldn't think so. But then – you never know. They both had sharp claws. They'd been going for each other ever since Christmas. He didn't like her spending so much time with Brackles. She didn't like him having it off with Lesley . . ."

" . . . and Janet?"

Katie looked annoyed.

"Pat must have told you that. He told me. It's disgusting. Especially at his age. If Lesley had been the one to die, I would have pointed the finger immediately at Angela. She'd been so worked up about it. Said that Lesley had wormed her way right into Dad. Like dry rot! And she was right."

"But would your dad have ganged up with Lesley to kill Angela? Do you think they were that desperate to get married? I imagine Angela would never have agreed to a divorce?"

"Never. She'd got her title and she was sticking to it. It was very important to her."

"So murder might have been the only way?"

Katie shook her head.

"It seems far-fetched – but you can never tell with Dad. On the surface, he seems a cheerful Charlie, but underneath, he's as hard as nails. He had to work his way up – from the bottom. Didn't expect any favours. He had to struggle for most of his life. It's only in the last twelve years that he's been in the lap of luxury."

"So you think it was someone else?"

Katie nodded.

"The anti-blood-sports brigade?"

"They've been threatening her. Especially since Christmas when she kicked one of them in the teeth. They reported her to the police. She's been charged – but her lawyer told her to plead not guilty. He said that they would have great difficulty bringing a case against her. The hunt people wouldn't say anything. And there was such a commotion going on at the time, no one would have noticed what she did . . . It could have been an accident."

"I believe she also hit someone across the face with a riding crop . . .?"

"Well, he was throwing fireworks at the horses. They were panicking. Jumping in the air. It was terrible. And then he tried to pull her off her horse."

"You were there?"

Katie nodded.

"It was a dreadful business. Jo'burg got singed. Just under his neck. I had to bring him home and get the vet."

"And Angela's been receiving threatening letters?"

"And phone calls. It was beginning to get her down. She used to carry a hand gun in her car." She caught the Inspector's eye. "It's all right. She had a licence. Don't worry about it."

"And you think Philip Royle may have taken the law into his own hands – since the case wasn't going his way?"

"He certainly had access to the brandy."

"But not to the cyanide?"

Katie tossed her head.

"You can get cyanide from all sorts of places. It's used for a wide range of industrial purposes. Electroplating, jewellery."

Raynes said quietly: "Janet works in a jewellery shop."

"Does she? I didn't know that."

"She gets jewellery from Mr Travers at the casino and then re-cycles it illegally. If she's capable of doing that, she would be quite capable of pinching a gram or two of cyanide."

Katie looked worried.

"I don't trust her. I think she's unstable."

"She certainly is," said Debbie. "She threw one of your father's best crystal glasses against the door and smashed it."

"Sounds like her," said Katie bitterly. "Lesley seems to be her only friend. She'll do anything she tells her to do."

"An unholy alliance," said Raynes.

Katie agreed.

"Did your father know about the threatening letters and phone calls?"

"He may have done. But I think Angela tried to keep it from him. He might have gone out and dealt with Philip Royle himself. Then we'd have had another murder."

They reached the steps of the house.

Sir George appeared at the front door.

"Hello, my dear! Did you have a good ride? Did you get the Inspector and his good lady up on a horse? You didn't? What a pity! Still, you must all come in and have another drink. Our guests have departed. They said they had to be back in London by six. So – in you come."

Sir George seemed full of gaiety and good humour. Raynes wondered whether he had had a good ride.

11: *Taxi*

Raynes was glad to see Debbie safely back inside his car. He felt a certain sense of relief as the door closed with a satisfying clunk and she strapped herself into her front seat. There was a feeling of escape. Sir George had been so unrestrained in his descriptions of his sexual experiences that there seemed to be little doubt that he was thirsting for more.

He had obviously seen Debbie's picture at the studio; and as he said – more than once – he was delighted to see her "in the flesh". During the afternoon, his eyes had never ceased to range over her body. Raynes reckoned that it was highly unlikely that Debbie would give him any encouragement, but one could not rule out the possibility that George himself might make some desperate lunge whilst the Inspector's back was turned. Then there would have been an embarrassing scene, which might have prevented him coming back and asking any more questions.

And further questions would certainly have to be asked.

Having listened to Simon's description of Sir George, Raynes had been led to expect some amiable old buffer who would hardly say boo to a goose. But the reality had proved very different. George was an energetic, forceful personality with a suspicious mind, a short temper and prone to sudden outbursts of anger.

His relationship with Lesley Travers was dynamite. She was the sort of female the Inspector would have expected to meet in a night-club, standing over the body of an ex-lover, brandishing a pistol or a knife. A raw, brittle personality with little but her sexuality to commend her. Lesley was as hard as nails – but so was Sir George. They were both people who had worked their way up from the bottom. Both were ruthless and greedy. What was she after? Money? Position? A title? Perhaps all three? And why had she brought along that stooge – Janet – who was little more than a psychiatric case? One would have imagined that the two of them would have been enough to satisfy George, but clearly he was gagging for more.

He seemed disappointed to see them go. He stood on the front steps and waved goodbye. Debbie and Richard smiled and waved back. Neither said a word until they had passed through the ornamental gateway and were out on the main road.

Debbie was the first to speak.

"Thank God that's over!"

"You didn't enjoy it?"

"Did I hell! It was one of the most unpleasant afternoons I've ever endured. Like sitting on the edge of a volcano."

"I know what you mean."

"He's a vicious, dirty old man."

"I think he was hankering for a bit more."

"I'm sure he was. I was all ready to hit him with my handbag. Straight in the pusser!" She smiled. "I would have done too. I wouldn't let a man like that touch me."

"D'you think he was capable of bumping off his wife?"

"Quite easily. With *her* egging him on. She's a devious little bitch."

"It takes one to know one!"

"Don't you start!"

"I'm just quoting you."

"I know. I saw through her right away. She didn't like me being there. She knew I could read her like a book. All that stuff about an accident at Gatwick. It was all lies."

"I can easily check."

"Do. You'll find I'm right."

"What d'you think she's after?"

"Money. What else? When I went to the toilet after lunch, I saw her in one of the bedrooms, moving the pictures, looking inside the cupboards . . ."

"Looking for his safe. Probably trying to get hold of Angela's jewellery so that Janet could make a bit on the side."

"I felt sorry for her. I should never have asked her whether she was married or had any children. It just made things worse."

"And deprived Brackles of an excellent meal."

"I think he was lucky to get out in one piece. Lesley had it in for him. I think it might have been better if we'd got up and left at the same time."

"Probably. But then we'd have missed the horses. They were nice. And Katie was all right."

"All you're thinking about is the case. It was all right for you. The more people shouted and screamed, the more information you got. But what did I get out of it? Nothing!"

"You got an excellent lunch."

"I'd rather have done without it. A sandwich and a glass of champagne would have been quite enough for me." She paused. "Well, two glasses . . ."

Raynes was thinking about Simon's friend.

"Perhaps we should invite Brackles to dinner tonight at the hotel?"

"It's the least you can do."

"It might have been much worse for him if we'd not been there."

Debbie disagreed.

"No. She only attacked him because we were there. If they'd been on their own, she'd have said nothing. She wanted to humiliate him in front of his friends. And in front of Sir George. I think Brackles handled it with great dignity. And I'll tell you another thing. I bet she won't have that picture in the hallway. It'll be consigned to the back bedroom – or to the stables."

"I don't think Pat would appreciate that."

"Poor man!" said Debbie. "Fancy putting up with Angela!"

"Fancy not giving way! Most men would. He must have incredible moral strength. Or else he loves his wife very much."

Debbie again disagreed.

"I think it's probably because he just didn't like her. He found her repulsive. Like I found Sir George. I'm sure they were very similar sort of people. Grab what you can from other people. When you think about it . . . they did it rather well."

"So it's out of the fat and into the fire for Sir George?"

"Very much so. Lesley'll certainly grab everything she can. George'll hit back. There'll probably be another murder, I shouldn't wonder."

* * * *

63

Their journey was a short one.

They left the car in the station car park, there being no room for parking in the narrow streets. They walked hand-in-hand up the hill and past the church.

"We need some exercise," said Richard, "especially after all that food."

"That's precisely what I was thinking!" said Debbie.

Raynes squeezed her hand.

"Do I detect a little lateral thinking?"

Debbie smiled.

"Horizontal, Inspector! Always horizontal!"

12: *The Potato Eaters*

"I thought you ought to have at least one decent meal. Especially considering the excellent lunch you passed up."

"That was a very kind thought, Inspector."

Brackles had joined Debbie, Simon and Richard for dinner at the *Mermaid*.

Outside, the rain was lashing against the leaded windows and cascading down the narrow cobbled streets. But inside the ancient hostelry, with its heavy wooden beams, its deep, comfortable chairs, its warm, peaceful atmosphere, it was quite easy to forget the miserable world outside.

They were sitting in the cocktail bar, studying the menu.

"I fancy the lobster," said Debbie.

"It's off," said Simon. "I heard the waiter telling someone."

"Roast beef'll do me," said Brackles.

"I couldn't eat it twice in one day," said Raynes. "I think I'll go for the duck – *canard à l'orange*. Always sounds better in French."

"I don't know what to have," said Debbie.

"The lamb's very good," said Simon. "Locally grown. The lambs are reared on Romney Marsh, just beneath the town. I don't know what they eat down there, but it gives their meat a certain tenderness."

"Are you recommending it?"

"I'm not only recommending it; I shall be eating it myself."

"That solves the main course," said Raynes. "What about the starters?"

Another five minutes passed before they had made up their minds.

Raynes had quickly settled on the deep-fried scallops with a cream and garlic sauce. It was not the sort of starter Debbie would have approved of in normal circumstances – but tonight there was a feeling of celebration in the air. A time for self-indulgence.

Simon had declared that Richard's painting was well and truly finished. There was nothing more he could add. Richard could now sign his cheque and take the thing back to Grasshallows and sort out with his lady-friend where it was going to be hung.

Brackles too had good news to report.

"I've also finished my picture. After what Sir George said at lunch, I thought: 'Why the hell should I waste any more time on it?' So I filled in the final details – not as carefully as I would have done for Angela – but George'll never notice. He can have it as soon as he likes! Peasant! He can stuff it in his hallway, if that's all he cares! Or the lavatory if it suits him better! I'm never going to set foot in that blasted house again!"

"Not even to collect the cheque?"

Brackles laughed.

"Well, I suppose we all have to sink our principles some time."

"You've been sinking them for years!" said Simon. "And look where it's got you."

"I'm still painting – which is the only thing that matters. And I'm still being invited out to dine. Twice in one day. I consider that my life has been extremely fortunate."

So there was further cause for celebration.

Raynes, of course, was savouring the pleasures of an

unsolved murder – his favourite occupation. He had already picked up a few leads and was running his mind over each of the suspects – Brackles and Simon included – to see how they fitted into the picture.

He caught Debbie's eye – and smiled at her.

She was probably the chief source of his happiness at that moment. But for her, there would have been no painting – and no prospect of Rye.

She was wearing little more than a black velvet dress, supported by a couple of thin straps over her soft, brown shoulders. (That at least was how they looked in the gentle, pink light.) He took pleasure in running his eyes up her shapely legs and relished the thought of all that lay beneath the black velvet. She probably knew what he was thinking . . .

"I'm having snails," she said.

* * * *

For a short while, the conversation revolved around food, but soon it came back to the events of the afternoon.

"What sort of person is Katie Middleton?" Raynes asked.

"I don't really know her," said Brackles. "I've only met her once or twice. Angela used to say that she was devious, two-faced – but the two of them didn't really get on. Strong clash of personalities."

"I thought she seemed very natural and straightforward," said Debbie.

Brackles was also sympathetic.

"It's always difficult having a stepmother."

"Especially when you've got one like Angela," said Simon. "What does she do for a living?"

Raynes laughed.

"A research chemist! Unlimited access to the poison in one form or another."

"But nothing to gain from the murder," said Brackles. "If you think Katie'll fare any better with Lesley as a stepmother . . .! Like me, she'll never set foot in Blake House again."

Simon remembered some chance remark.

"Angela didn't like her husband either, did she?"

"No. She despised Max. He's an academic – a lecturer at the College in Hastings. Angela said he was gay – but whether that's true or not, I don't know."

"Well, she's always got the horses."

"That was the only bond between them."

"They were lovely creatures," said Debbie. "Almost human. They seemed to understand what she was saying."

"I hope Lesley won't persuade George to sell them. That'd provoke another murder!"

"I don't think he would be so stupid. He seemed very fond of Katie."

"But it's amazing that he doesn't see through Lesley."

"I disliked her immediately."

"And she hated you. That was obvious."

"She struck me as utterly false, selfish and greedy."

"She's always been like that," said Brackles. "I've known her and her husband for the past eight years. She's cold and heartless. Only interested in money. And she'd do anything to get it. She spends most of her life fleecing the punters at the club. I think she gets a percentage. All those old codgers get excited having a pretty woman sitting beside them and showing a friendly interest in their game. The higher the stake, the more the interest. I've seen her at work. They might think they're in with a chance; but, slowly, the pile of chips goes down and the siren slips away. Fun whilst it lasts, I suppose. But totally mercenary; devoid of all feeling."

Raynes avoided any eye contact with Debbie. It was one of his most frequent criticisms – that she was money-mad.

"So her interest in George must be financial?"

"I can't think of anything else."

"Sex?"

"I'm sure George is getting a bit past it."

"He can't be too bad if he can cope with two women at once."

"Probably induce an early heart attack!"

"Hence the rapid recourse to marriage," said Simon. "The new Lady Mallowan wants to cash her chips at the earliest opportunity."

"But would she have been able to obtain the poison?"

Raynes nodded.

"Janet and her jewellery shop."

Debbie intervened.

"I didn't understand what you were talking about . . . What's the connection?"

"It's quite simple," said Raynes. "Cyanide is used for various industrial purposes. For coating base medals; for electroplating. Anyone who has a bona fide reason for using it can buy cyanide balls which are then melted down. A jeweller might be just the sort of person to have such stuff. Janet is in the jewellery trade. She will do anything for Lesley or her husband. If they needed the poison – no problem."

Brackles nodded glumly.

"She's quite unstable, you know. I wasn't making it up. She had a complete nervous breakdown. Someone told me that she poisoned her parents. That's why she was sent to a psychiatric hospital. That was why she had to give up the family business."

"She said they died in a car crash."

Brackles shook his head.

"I don't think so. I think it was Tom who told me. And he should know. The two of them are hand in glove. More so than him and Lesley. He uses Janet to keep an eye on her."

"A dangerous combination?" said Raynes.

"Very much so," said Simon.

He threw back the final dregs of his rum and green ginger.

"I probably shouldn't say this – not with Dick listening all ears." He laughed. "But someone told me that Tom was down here on the day of the murder . . ."

Brackles seemed annoyed.

"You shouldn't believe everything you're told."

" . . . talking to one of the fishermen."

Brackles was silent.

Debbie had begun to wonder whether the chef had had to go out on to Romney Marsh to shoot the lamb – or whether the snails had escaped back to France. But just at that moment, when Raynes was longing to ask more questions, the waiter arrived to announce that their table was ready – and the moment was lost.

They were escorted to a table in a quiet corner of the dining room. As they unfolded their satisfyingly large napkins, the waiter opened a bottle of champagne.

The sight reminded Simon of his domestic needs.

"Glasses!" he said. "I need them."

"Well, you're not pinching them from the hotel!" said Raynes.

"You should be able to afford them tomorrow," said Brackles, "once the Inspector pays his dues!" He laughed. "Shall I get some for you? I think the local supermarket is doing a special offer."

Simon looked at Richard.

"He always goes shopping on Monday afternoons."

"Creature of habit!" said Brackles.

"Is that what you were doing on the day of the murder?" Raynes asked politely. "Or were you having a quiet *tête-à-tête* with Mr Travers?"

Brackles did not smile.

"I think the less said about Mr Travers the better."

13: *Nighthawks*

Tom Travers stubbed out his cigarette.

"Did you find the safe?"

Lesley eyed her husband coldly.

"No, we didn't."

Tom's dark-ringed eyes flashed with annoyance. "What the hell have you been playing at? You've been down there seven times in the past five weeks. You should have found it by now."

Lesley Travers looked sullen and resentful.

"I've done eight of the main rooms – the kitchen, the dining room, the drawing room, the study and four of the bedrooms. I've still not been in the attics or the gun room. There's two more bedrooms to do – not to mention the scullery and cellars. It's a big place."

She reached over for Tom's packet of cigarettes and lit one.

"It's not as easy as you think. George follows you everywhere. If you're out of his sight for a couple of minutes, he wonders what you're up to. He's got a bloody suspicious mind. About the only place he doesn't follow you is the loo!"

She looked at her husband. "And it's not there either. I've checked all the bathrooms and toilets. Pulled up the carpets – even looked inside the cisterns. It's just not there."

"It must be somewhere."

Lesley shrugged her shoulders.

"Why don't you go and look yourself?"

Tom ignored her suggestion.

"What about Janet? Couldn't she distract him?"

Lesley looked contemptuously at her husband.

"You obviously have no idea what George is like! He's woman-mad. You put two women in front of him, he wants both of them – at the same time! Janet may not be everyone's idea of a tasty piece of crumpet, but she certainly appeals to George." She looked at her husband, calculating to a nicety how much her report would irritate him. "He's very athletic for a man of his age. Very imaginative. He knows how to satisfy a woman . . . "

"All right! All right! I get the point. You spent the entire afternoon eating, drinking and screwing . . . "

"Basically, yes."

"And there wasn't even five minutes when you could have been looking for it?"

"Not today, there wasn't. George had a police inspector to lunch."

"A police inspector?"

Lesley nodded.

"And his mistress! Some cheap little hooker from up north."

"What was he doing there?"

"She's been having her picture painted. Brackles brought them over to meet George."

"Brackles?"

70

"Yes. Brackles. You'll be lucky if he keeps his mouth shut. He's probably told the Inspector all about the booze."

"He'd better not! He told the Big Man he'd been very discreet with the local police. Denied all knowledge. Said he was merely storing it for a friend."

"I wouldn't trust him an inch."

"You don't trust anyone."

"Not even you, sweetie!"

Lesley was feeling heartless and cruel. She was annoyed about being used by Tom to find an invisible safe. She was even more annoyed because he wouldn't tell her what was in the safe – what he expected to find. It must be something important because every time she reported failure, he looked even more haggard and desperate.

She was also annoyed with him employing Janet to spy on her. There was no other reason for Janet being sent with her. Later in the evening, he would be pumping her for information – not that she would have much to say. For Janet, the afternoon had been one of hurt and humiliation, which not even Sir George's rumbustious lovemaking had been able to dispel. Tom would bully her in vain. There would be bucketloads of tears and lots of wet tissues. Serve him right!

Tom was biting his thumbnail, staring into middle distance.

"Well, when the cops arrive, you'll discover I was right. I hope you've got your story well-prepared. You could go down for quite a long time." She quietly smiled to herself as she lashed him with words. "You might have been better giving *him* that bottle of brandy! Might have silenced him once and for all. It was wasted on Angela!"

Tom said nothing.

"It's people like Brackles who let other people down. Failures. No-hopers. Bloody creeps. You help them when they're down and in return they shop you to the police. If you're hoping to pull off some scam, you should at least give the job to someone efficient."

"Someone like you, I suppose?" He was being sarcastic. "Someone who can't find a safe in a sodding haystack!"

"Well, I've certainly looked hard enough for it. If it's there, I'll find it. Not that I'm expecting to get anything out of it."

"There's nothing in it for you."

Lesley raised a delicately plucked eyebrow.

"Really? I thought the deal was that if I found you this safe, you'd give me a 'quickie' divorce? Don't tell me you're changing your mind?"

"Of course I'm not. I'll be glad to see the back of you. I'm just saying that there's nothing in that safe that'll benefit you." Tom waved his hand dismissively. "Anyway, you haven't found it. At this rate, you'll never find it. So you'll be stuck with me for ever! That should encourage you."

"There are times when I feel like turning you in myself."

"Oh, stop rabbitting on! Go and do something useful." He looked at his watch. "It's after ten. The place'll be filling up. Go and seduce a few Americans! Relieve the punters of their chips! Don't waste your time bitching at me."

Lesley sneered at her husband.

"And what'll you be doing? Chatting up Janet? Listening to all her little stories? See if she'll tell you anything! She's another busted flush!"

Tom Travers wilted under his wife's attack. Her viper-like tongue and her blazing eyes left him speechless. She made it so obvious that she despised him.

As the door slammed behind her, Tom put his head in his hands and groaned with frustration. If she didn't find that safe, what on earth could he do?

* * * *

"Tom seems to be losing his marbles."

"I'm afraid so."

It was after 2.00am and Lesley was speaking to Bernard, trying not to yawn. It had been a long day.

Bernard was the power behind the Club – the financial power. Not for nothing was he called "The Big Man". He was over six feet in height, with a well-polished bald head, a large brown spade of a beard and watchful brown eyes. In his evening dress, he resembled King Edward VII – and was always pleased when people commented on the likeness.

"He seems obsessed about this safe!"

"I think Angela may have had some hold over him. He's terrified others might find it before him."

"His past's catching up on him."

"Very much so."

"But you can't find it?"

"I've used every spare moment – even though he doesn't think I have. But, believe me, it's not in any obvious part of the house. I've pulled back carpets, shifted furniture, looked behind pictures, pulled out whole shelf-fuls of books, tapped wooden panels – I just can't find it."

"But you know the combination?"

"Know it by heart – 718364. It was in her address book. Clearly marked. But it's no use knowing the number when you can't find the bloody safe."

"I was beginning to wonder whether it really existed."

"There's no doubt about that. But I can hardly ask George. He might get ideas . . . "

"Dangerous."

Bernard stroked his beard thoughtfully before he spoke again: "I don't like to see Tom going to pieces."

Lesley was silent. She didn't really mind what happened to Tom. As far as she was concerned, she was already in one of the lifeboats, leaving the sinking ship.

"He's not doing his job properly. He's neglecting the punters. Being rude to them. Not keeping the staff up to scratch. You can see his mind's on other things. Who's he sleeping with?"

"Tracy."

"And Janet?"

"Now and again – but he's just using her. She does those little jobs for him but I don't think there's much feeling on either side. Janet needs a lot of TLC."

"She enjoyed her day out then?"

"She enjoyed the romp in bed – but she didn't enjoy

meeting Brackles! He raked up her past. Even accused her of being a lesbian. She threw a valuable crystal glass at him."

Bernard smiled grimly.

"Brackles is another of our problems."

"Always has been. You'd be better giving him a pair of concrete boots and dumping him in the river."

"You mean – before he squeals?"

"You may be too late."

Bernard was silent.

"I wouldn't leave it if I were you. I'd twist the knife a bit further. Let him know he's going to walk the plank like her ladyship did. That'll keep his trap shut. He's a coward. I know he is."

"He's lost us a valuable link."

"You've got enough stock in hand, though?"

"Several months at least. But starting up a new link is always dangerous. It could take months to get it going. There's no telling what the pigs have found. I'm sure they've only let Brackles out to see where he leads them. Tom will have to make sure he lies low."

Lesley showed her contempt.

"They're both broken reeds. You'd be better getting rid of both of them. There's no place for sentimentality in this business."

Bernard looked at Lesley. The firm line of her lips; her cold green eyes. Sometimes, she frightened him. She was capable of any wickedness. Being married to Tom had deprived her of any ounce of human feeling.

"You're a ruthless woman," he said. "But it's easier to say these things than to do them. Tom has his uses."

"But if he muffs it, it comes back on you."

Bernard stroked his beard thoughtfully.

"I'll think about it."

"Well, don't think about it for too long. There's another sleuth on his trail. Richard somebody from up north. Another police inspector. He was at lunch with George, asking all sorts of questions. He's trying to second guess the local police on Angela's death. I didn't like the look of him – nor the cheap hooker he brought with him. I'd put him on your black list if I were you."

Bernard looked anxious.

"Not Richard Raynes?"

"That sounds like him."

"That's very bad news."

"You know him?"

"Know of him. He has quite a reputation."

"Well, you've been warned. If you leave Brackles loose, he'll blab. Then you go down the plughole – and so does the Club. Strike first. Fix another bottle of brandy – and make sure! Don't leave anything to chance."

Bernard quietly surveyed the low-pitched hum of the gaming room. It was an atmosphere he loved. Where he felt completely at home. He loved the smooth efficiency with which the croupiers handled their cards. The rise and fall of the coloured chips. The quiet way the waiters glided between the tables. The gradual crescendo of excitement as a fortune was either made or lost. The elegant grace with which rich people were parted from their money night after night. The begging; the tears; the imaginative offers made to settle debts which often brought a grateful woman into his bed.

He didn't like the harsh world which existed outside the Club. The dirty work which had to be done by others – normally Tom – chasing up debts; putting the screws on defaulting punters; blackmail; the strong arm tactics that caused people to get hurt; smuggling in duty-free goods to boost profits. But if one did not control that other world, it would only be a matter of time before that other world would destroy his. It was a balance of fear. Of knowing when to strike – and when to hold his hand.

Bernard was certainly no shrinking violet but he felt that Lesley was pushing him too quickly into action which he might regret. It was all right for her. She was carefully preparing her bolthole down in Rye; feathering her nest with Sir George; abandoning Tom who was obviously on the downhill track, but not entirely finished. He felt her advice needed to be taken with a pinch of salt.

"I think," he said, "for the moment, one murder is quite enough."

14: *The Windmill*

The pub had only been open for ten minutes and Philip Royle was not expecting any customers – at least not for another half hour. He picked up the local newspaper which had just been delivered. He leafed through the pages and noted that there was nothing more about the murder. Everything seemed to have gone very quiet on that front. He had heard that the artist, in whose studio Lady Mallowan had been killed, had been released. However, he had then been charged with storing smuggled goods – so, with a bit of luck, he might still be going to jail. Serve him right!

No friend of Lady Angela's was any friend of his. He reached up and delicately touched his front teeth – a poignant reminder of that bitter moment when she had slashed her riding crop across his face and kicked him violently in the mouth. It had taken two months of skilled dental work before he had looked decent. It had also cost him quite a bit of money.

He noticed that the newspaper was advertizing the next meet of the local hunt on Easter Monday. He wondered whether it was really worthwhile mounting another protest. This time, they would probably make sure the police were there to quell the opposition. They would be fighting on two fronts. The police might take a dim view of the spikes and fireworks they had used so effectively on Boxing Day. Then, they had scented victory. Well, it had been a victory of sorts. Several horses had been injured and taken home. One or two of the riders had been thrown off their mounts. The dogs had been drenched in pepper and only a few of them had been capable of following the fox. Happily, that wily creature had escaped. The national news had carried a report on the protest and many local people had begun to question the morality of fox-hunting. So it had been a success! Perhaps even the threat of a repeat performance would be enough to discourage the faint-hearted? However, if there were to be a repeat performance, Philip Royle was determined that he for one would take a back seat. He had no wish to lose any more teeth!

His meditations were interrupted by the arrival of a man and woman. She was quite striking – soft golden hair, big brown eyes, a warm smile and very nice teeth. (He tended to notice these things now.) He also took in the diamond rings on her right hand and the gold bracelet on her left wrist. They both said "money". The man looked quieter and more reserved.

Philip Royle put away his paper and tried to look pleasant.

"Good morning. Welcome to the *Windmill* ."

(They were obviously visitors.)

They seated themselves on stools close to the bar.

"A Dubonnet with ice," said the young woman.

She was wearing a very strong perfume.

"Make it two," said the man.

Philip Royle busied himself with their order.

"Do you know anything about imported brandy?" asked the man. "Do you buy it in on the side?"

"Of course not," said Philip indignantly.

(He would have to be careful. They might be snoopers from the Customs and Excise.)

"All our supplies come from London."

"Who's the owner?"

"Mr Campbell."

"Not Mr Travers?"

"Never heard of him."

He put the glasses down in front of the couple.

"Three eighty."

The man gave him a five pound note.

"There have been some reports of smuggling down here."

Philip nodded.

"In Rye. Not here."

"Chap called . . . Brackles . . . Was that his name?"

"I believe so. He was also questioned about a murder."

The man raised his eyebrows.

"Has there been a murder?"

He was obviously not a local.

"Yes. A woman died in his studio."

The woman's eyes never left him. He felt he was being slowly undressed. He felt that she could see right through him. It was not a pleasant experience. But there was nothing he could say.

"Was her death connected with the smuggling?"

"I don't think so. More like a crime of passion."

"Passion!" said the woman.

She had a soft, enticing voice.

"Who killed her?"

"Nobody really knows. She belonged to the county set. You know, horses and things. People think one of them might have been involved."

"Any motive?"

"Jealousy . . . hatred . . . revenge. It could have been something like that."

"It wouldn't have been the anti-blood-sports brigade that bumped her off? I hear they're pretty active down here?"

Philip Royle blushed.

He had been caught out by the sudden change of direction in the conversation.

"No," he said, "they wouldn't do a thing like that."

"I hear," said the man, "that before her death, Lady Mallowan had been receiving threatening letters. Abusive telephone calls. Would you know anything about that?"

Philip Royle kept his mouth firmly shut.

It would be dangerous to say any more.

The woman smiled ever so sweetly at him.

"How are your teeth?" she asked.

"Much better," said Philip nervously. "They're still a bit sore – but not as much as they were."

"Glad to hear you can still speak," said the man. "You must have suffered quite a lot from that kick."

"It wasn't very nice."

"I'm not here to judge the merits of fox-hunting," said the

78

man. "But putting two and two together, it seems to me that you had every reason to hate Lady Mallowan."

"I didn't kill her, if that's what you mean?"

"No," said the man. "I'm not accusing you of murder. I'm more interested in the threats which were made against her whilst she was still alive. You were responsible, weren't you?"

The woman smiled.

"We know you were."

How did she know?

Philip Royle nervously polished the bar with a damp cloth.

"Do you know it's an offence to send abusive letters through the post?" asked the man.

"I didn't send any letters through the post."

"I've seen them," said the man. "And they were definitely sent by someone closely connected with the anti-blood-sports campaign. Someone with great personal knowledge of the lady involved. Someone who knew where she lived. Someone who knew her love for horses – and her fear of having them injured. Someone who had every reason to hate her – because she had hurt him so much. Destroyed his good looks . . . Someone who had sought redress through the courts but who had not been very successful. Someone who had decided to take the law into his own hands. Who sent the letters whilst he was off work, getting his teeth put straight. Someone, who by the beginning of February, was able to speak properly again – and spat out his venom and his threats down the telephone. Day after day, night after night."

The woman smiled again.

"It was you, Philip, wasn't it?"

It was difficult to give her an honest answer.

"Are you a policeman?" he asked defensively.

"As a matter of fact, I am."

He reached into his pocket and produced his identity card. Not long enough for him to catch the name – but long enough to recognize the constabulary badge and the official photograph.

At last he knew where he was.

"I've already given a statement to the police."

"But not a very full one."

"You could have told the truth," said the young woman. "You seem such an honest person. It must have been difficult for you telling all those lies."

Philip tried hard to think what exactly he had said in his statement. Certainly he had not said all that much! He had said that he had been the victim of a serious assault by Lady Mallowan. That he had not seen her since Boxing Day. That he obviously bore a deep resentment towards her. But he had not been in Rye for any other purpose than to visit the dentist. His last visit had been in early February.

Yes. That had been a lie . . .

The woman seemed to guess his innermost thoughts.

"Who did you go to, to get your teeth put right?"

"Mr Wainwright."

"And he has a surgery in Rye?"

Philip nodded.

"And were you in Rye the day Lady Mallowan was murdered?"

Philip said nothing.

The questions were too close to the bone.

"And did you keep that appointment with Mr Wainwright?"

Philip could hardly bring himself to speak.

"Yes," he said, "I did."

"So," said the Inspector, "you were only a few hundred yards away from the studio where her ladyship was killed?"

Philip was shocked by the accusation.

"I never touched her!" he said angrily.

"Of course you didn't," said the policeman reassuringly. "No one touched her. Someone just left a poisoned bottle of brandy in the studio – ready for her to drink."

He looked round the well-stocked bar.

"Plenty of brandy here. Mr Campbell would hardly miss the odd bottle."

Philip Royle loudly proclaimed his innocence.

"I had nothing to do with it. I've told you."

"But," said the Inspector, "you are the person who sent the threatening letters to Lady Mallowan. You were in the habit of writing to her. No one else was. Who better to send her a charming little note, saying: 'Do come and visit me in my studio on Monday afternoon at 2.00pm.' She came. She drank. She died."

Philip Royle shook his head.

"You can't prove anything."

The Inspector looked at him critically.

"You had the motive. You had the opportunity. You had the means . . . "

The woman looked at him with appealing eyes.

"You know you did, Philip."

He wanted to hit her. But if he hit her, he might be arrested. Perhaps they were wanting him to do something violent – so that he could be arrested? He must control his feelings.

"No one hated her as much as you," said the Inspector. "She had a lot of lovers – but she was generous with her body. They bore her no ill will. Nobody would have killed her out of jealousy – or because they had been rejected."

He paused to let his points sink in.

"Her money was in a long-established trust – so she couldn't have been killed for her money. Her husband seems perfectly happy with her. Paying thousands to have her picture painted. No one I have met has said a harsh word against her . . . "

"That's a complete lie," thought Debbie.

But Philip Royle was not to know.

" . . . the only person who could possibly have wished to hurt her was you; because of what she did to you on Boxing Day. Everyone I've spoken to says it was you. So why don't you admit that it was you who put the poisoned brandy in the studio?"

"Because I didn't."

Raynes listened carefully – hoping to detect a lie.

Debbie continued to look at Philip with warm, appealing eyes, which he found totally irresistible.

"But you did write those letters – those nasty letters which hurt her so much?"

Philip nodded.

"Yes, I wrote them. I'm very sorry I did it – especially now she's dead. But people like her have to be stopped. All these people with their barbaric ways. Allowing a wild animal to be torn apart. Smearing their faces with blood. Taking pleasure in killing. Making a ritual out of it. It's repulsive!"

The Inspector looked at him.

"But it's not illegal – not yet."

"No," said Philip, "but it's deeply offensive to civilized people."

The Inspector raised his eyebrows.

"Civilized people don't send threatening letters to innocent people."

"She wasn't innocent," said Philip, recovering his nerve. "She was as guilty as hell!"

Raynes looked at the barman.

"Before you attack other people, I think you should consider your own behaviour, which most people would find equally offensive." He turned to Debbie. "You can switch off the tape-recorder now." He smiled at Philip. "Thank you for the drink. I look forward to seeing you again – very soon. And when you are asked to rewrite your statement, perhaps you would be kind enough to tell us the truth."

"The whole truth," said Debbie, "and nothing but the truth."

She winked. "Just for me!"

15: *Cherry Ripe*

All good things come to an end – and Raynes decided that after their thought-provoking visit to the pub in Winchelsea, it was time to make their way back to Grasshallows. But first, they had to pack and collect their picture.

For, after a lot of argument, it had been decided that the painting should be owned 50:50. As intended, it would be hung in the front sitting room of Richard's new home – but with Debbie being given permanent rights of access to view it. Should the Inspector ever wish to dispose of it, the full rights of ownership would pass to Mrs May. Naturally, the total cost of both painting and frame would be borne by Richard since he had commissioned the work. It seemed a fair agreement to both parties and the deal was sealed with a kiss and a bottle of Moet et Chandon. All that remained was to hand over a cheque for £1500. The Inspector felt that it was worth every penny.

So, after settling their bill at the hotel, they went down to Simon's studio to collect the picture. It was not perhaps the best moment to arrive. A blonde-haired woman, wearing a tight-fitting white sweater and beige-coloured jodhpurs, was sitting close to Simon beside the wood-burning stove. The woman looked embarrassed at their intrusion.

"Sorry!" said Raynes. "Didn't know you were entertaining."

Simon did not seem too bothered.

"This is Liz," he said. "Cherry's mum. The one who's having her picture done by Brackles. She felt bored so she came next door for a little TLC."

Raynes looked at the woman closely to see if there was any sign of guilt in her eyes. But no, it seemed that it was a friendly visit with no amorous intent.

Simon completed the introductions.

"And this is Inspector Raynes and his friend, Debbie."

"I've heard a lot about you."

"News travels fast down here."

"You've probably seen the picture," said Debbie.

"I think everyone's seen it," said Liz. "It's quite striking. The Inspector must be very proud of it."

"We've come to pay our dues," said Raynes.

"Anyone bringing money is always welcome to this house."

Richard sat down and opened his cheque book.

"£1500 we said?"

"That'll be fine."

"No problems with the taxman?"

"Who cares? I've nothing worth pinching."

Raynes handed over the cheque.

"Thanks!" said Simon, noting that his friend had added an extra £500 for good measure. "That's splendid!"

"Now you can afford some proper glasses!" said Debbie.

She looked at the woman cradling a cracked pink mug. Certainly no one could accuse the artist of high living.

"And when will your picture be finished?"

"Another couple of sessions, I'm told."

"When's her father's birthday?"

"The end of April. April 28th."

"Should be ready by then," said Simon.

"Are you pleased with it?"

"Brackles has done a beautiful job. So realistic."

"You think her father'll enjoy it?"

"He should be very proud."

"Has the secret been kept?" asked Richard. "Or does he know about it?"

The woman shook her head.

"He could hardly fail to find out about it. The police were round like a shot when Lady Mallowan died. He couldn't think why I was involved – so I had to tell him about the picture. But, for Cherry's sake, we're still pretending."

"He still doesn't know what it looks like?"

"No."

Raynes noted the slight hesitation.

"It must have given you a terrible shock finding her in the studio?"

"To start with, I thought she was asleep. Then I thought she was drunk. Just keeled over. She had quite a reputation locally . . . "

"You can say that again!" said Simon.

" . . . but when I looked at her face, I knew something had happened. It was a horrible colour of blue. I can tell you, I didn't linger up there. Cherry and I came down to Simon and he phoned the police."

"Did you know Lady Angela?"

84

"As much as I ever wanted to."

"You didn't like her?"

"She was a vicious dangerous woman."

"Did she ever do anything personally to you?"

Liz laughed bitterly.

"Not to me – but to my family, yes. She just about wrecked it. There was no love lost between us. I'm sorry she was murdered – and in Brackles' studio – and that we had to find her that afternoon; but I feel the world's a cleaner, better place without her." She looked at Simon. "I know you men drooled over her. Couldn't keep your hands off her. But a woman sees things differently. The falsehood. The deceit. The greed. It's not much fun watching a bitch leading your husband up the garden path!"

Any further comments about Lady Mallowan's character defects were halted by the arrival of Liz's daughter, closely followed by Brackles, wiping his hands on a blue cloth.

"Hello, you two! About to go?"

His eyes had taken in the cheque, lying on the kitchen table. "Paid your dues as well? Great! Simon'll be able to restock his larder."

He looked at Liz.

"Just one more session, I think – and then we shall be finished. She's an excellent sitter. Telling me all about her favourite pets."

Liz shook her head.

"Cherry never stops talking. She'd talk the hind legs off a donkey, wouldn't you, love?" She gave her a big hug and kiss. "Time for tea. And remember! Mum's the word. Not a word to Dad."

"I'm good at keeping secrets," said Cherry.

"Unusual in a woman," said Simon.

"You're a chauvinist pig!" said Debbie.

"And yet I paint beautiful pictures – of beautiful women."

Debbie smiled at the painter indulgently. After all he had done for her, she couldn't really be angry.

Brackles gave Cherry a small box of chocolates.

"We both paint pictures of beautiful young ladies!"

Liz and her daughter departed.

Raynes was curious.

"She didn't seem to like Angela very much. What did she do to her? Pinch her husband?"

"Tried to."

"Of course she did!" said Brackles. "No man could resist Angela. Liz was so angry she left him! It was Katie who patched things up. The painting's a sort of peace-offering. Kiss and make up."

The scales suddenly fell from the Inspector's eyes.

"Liz is Pat's wife? The groom at the stables?"

Simon nodded.

"Didn't you know?"

Raynes shook his head.

"No. I thought she was someone completely uninvolved with this whole business. That makes an enormous difference!"

"Another suspect?" said Brackles.

"Very much so. I must quiz her properly."

"Come again," said Simon. "Soon."

Raynes smiled.

"I shall take you up on your offer. Definitely."

"I hope the invitation includes me?" said Debbie.

"Of course," said Simon gallantly. "Chauvinist pig I may be; but I would rather see you than Richard any day! And I'll tell you another thing. I shall miss your picture. It cheered me up all winter."

Brackles chuckled mischievously.

"Perhaps he'll do a similar one for Liz?"

Debbie noticed that Simon did not laugh.

16: *Blue Territory*

"Did you have a nice weekend?"

Carlisle was being no more than civil; but the Inspector was not very forthcoming.

"Very cultural. Lot of pictures . . . " He smiled. "I even

bought one for my new house."

"Pricey?"

"£1500."

Raynes noted the painful impression such largesse caused his colleague. Fifteen hundred pounds would have kept his baby in milk, rusks and disposable nappies for the next eighteen months.

"I believe it would have been worth more on the open market," he said, "but the painter was a friend of mine."

Raynes felt further comment was inadvisable. He pulled the in-tray towards him and drew out two thin brown official files. "Anything interesting happened whilst I've been away?"

Carlisle shook his head.

"Student caught trying to sell a medieval manuscript up in London. Dealer had the honesty to phone up the University Librarian to ask if he was a party to selling off such a valuable piece of work. Caught in the act."

Raynes sighed.

"He'd probably have done better if he'd taken it across to Amsterdam or Brussels. They'd have had fewer scruples over there." He smiled. "Is that all?"

"Major road accident at Slipper's Hill . . . Two dead."

"Outside the golf club?"

"Yes. They never learn." Carlisle looked back at his notes. "But apart from that, a quiet weekend. Have you got anything?"

"I don't know," said Raynes slowly. "A family tree. A poisoned bottle of brandy. A member of the lesser nobility – stone dead. Seven or eight suspects. With a bit of smuggling thrown in for good measure."

Carlisle's face lit up.

"Sounds exciting!"

"Unfortunately it's not in our patch. The Sussex police are dealing with it." He paused. "Not very well, though. They've had a fortnight on the case and got nowhere."

" . . . and you're longing to take over?"

Raynes smiled.

"I did try to resist temptation," he said apologetically.

"But not for very long?"

"No. I thought it was just up our street. As perhaps it is."

He gave Carlisle a detailed picture of the background to the case. Angela's sudden death. The passions she had raised. He described her husband and the other characters he had met. Gradually, he tailed off.

"It was the family tree that gave me an opening," he said thoughtfully. "Most impressive. Four knights of the realm. Numerous lords and ladies. Sir George seems to be the last of the line. Very much so. He only has a daughter. He himself was a distant nephew of the last baronet. He was in South Africa at the time. Said the inheritance came to him as a complete surprise. I can't really believe that. But his benefactor – his uncle – Sir Ian Mallowan, lived in Grasshallows . . ."

"Really?"

"Retired here from London. Distinguished jurist. The fifth baronet is a complete peasant. Heavy drinker. Compulsive fornicator. Very little self-control. Wallowing in all his wealth. His wife was – well, I've told you about her. Funny how one generation can be so different from the next . . . "

"Like the Malboroughs?"

Raynes was surprised by such erudition on the part of his colleague.

"Yes," he said. "Just like the Malboroughs."

He pushed away the two slim brown files and put his feet up on his desk.

"I think I would like to find out a little bit more about Sir Ian. "

"Do you suspect foul play?"

Raynes stared fixedly at a distant point on the ceiling. There was a long silence.

"I don't know," he said at last. "There's so much one would like to know . . . I just need some excuse to get in on the act. We can't call up stuff on the computer. The Sussex police would immediately ask what we were doing. But we can nose around here – and see where it leads us. If it takes us back to Rye, we get a share of the action. If it doesn't . . . " He looked at the two brown files. "Well, there's nothing else to do, is there?" The Inspector sighed sadly. "I much prefer murders. It's the only bit of my work that I really enjoy. And if we can't provide our own, there's nothing better than muscling in on someone else's." He looked critically at his younger colleague. "Where shall we start?"

Carlisle looked rather hesitant.

"Mr Derek Coates-Smythe?"

He was hesitant because he knew how fervently the Inspector disliked the lawyer. But Raynes did not react quite as violently as he had expected.

He grimaced – certainly. And he also uttered one or two uncomplimentary remarks which reflected badly on Mr Coates-Smythe's mother. But after mature consideration, he nodded his head.

"It would be very nice if he could help us for a change. Might do some good. He was bound to know Sir Ian. All these lawyers swill together. Perhaps he might even have drawn up his will."

* * * *

Carlisle's suggestion proved exceedingly helpful.

After a brief phone call and the invariable cup of sweet black coffee, the Inspector and his assistant descended on the office of the senior partner of Logan, Smythe & Smythe.

Derek Coates-Smythe did not exactly relish the prospect of another bruising encounter with Detective-Inspector Raynes. He had already ample cause to dread the scourge of Raynes' tongue. But he was glad to hear that this time his tormentor sought a favour. And not just a favour. He wanted to know more about one of Mr Coates-Smythe's personal heroes.

"Sir Ian? Of course I remember him well. A great man. Very dry sense of humour. An outstanding jurist. I only knew him towards the end of his life. He used to lecture here at the University after he retired. A great benefit to several generations of students. He was an excellent speaker. What Sir Ian didn't know about case law was scarcely worth knowing. What exactly is it you want to know about him?"

"Were you responsible for drawing up his will?"

Mr Coates-Smythe shook his head.

"We didn't have that privilege. I would imagine that he had it done for him by a colleague down in London . . . "

"By a proper legal firm?"

Raynes could not resist twisting the lawyer's tail.

Mr Derek Coates-Smythe winced perceptibly.

"In the eyes of most people, Inspector, we are a very proper legal firm."

Raynes did not apologize.

"Was he married?" he asked.

"He may have been. When he lived in Grasshallows, he was looked after by his housekeeper. Is it important whether he was married?"

"Did he have any children?"

Mr Coates-Smythe paused – and cast his mind back.

"I really couldn't say." He smiled. "There's only one way to find out." He pressed a button on his desk and immediately a tall dark-haired girl in a smart black dress appeared in the office. Raynes was pleased to note that the lawyer was still being well served. "The *Who's Who* for 1970, please."

The lawyer looked cautiously at the two policemen.

"Surely he must be dead by now? He couldn't be doing anything that would interest you gentlemen?"

"He died in 1977," said Raynes. "That's what it said on his family tree."

"But he didn't die in Grasshallows."

"No?"

"No. He died – in Bournemouth, I think. Somewhere like that. I remember reading it in the *Law Journal*. He was pretty frail by that time. 85, 86 . . . I think he went south to eke out his final days."

The personal secretary returned with a large red book.

"Thank you. Now we shall know where we are. Mallowan Sir Ian. Fourth holder of the title. Born 1889. Older than I thought. Elder son of Sir Henry Mallowan – landowner. Educated: Oxford. First class honours . . . Married Margaret

Elizabeth Erskine, who died 1916. No issue . . ."

"So," said Raynes, "if he was the elder brother, any existing relations must have descended from his younger brother?"

Mr Coates-Smythe nodded.

"Very logical, Inspector!"

"Now if his younger brother was married about the age of twenty-one and his son – presumably his only son – also married about the same age, the grandson would now be in his early fifties. Is that right?"

He looked at Detective-Constable Carlisle, who did a quick calculation on his shorthand pad.

"Yes."

"And both the younger brother and his son must now be long since dead?"

Mr Coates-Smythe ploughed back into the depths of his memory.

"I think he once mentioned that he had had some relation who died in the war. He was rather bitter about it."

Raynes looked back at the *Who's Who*.

"Does it say where he lived when he was in Grasshallows?"

Mr Coates-Smythe smiled broadly and then consulted the text to see if his memory was accurate.

"64 Ranelagh Gardens. A familiar address, I think, Inspector? Two doors away from Commander Kenworth."

Raynes managed a smile in return.

"Has he married Rosalind yet?"

"Still thinking about it, I believe. He has money, you know. Doesn't want to cast his pearls before swine!"

Raynes laughed.

"I wouldn't let Rosalind hear you say that!"

"I'm trusting to your discretion, Inspector."

Raynes raised his eyebrows.

How very unwise!

"Sir Ian was also a very rich man, wasn't he?"

"I imagine so. But he didn't let it show. Always wore the same dark suit. An elegant bow tie. A silver-topped cane. A very reserved manner. He didn't speak much about himself but he was very good in company. Loved telling you stories about the olden days. All the crooks he had known. The great trials he had witnessed. Once he had had a couple of glasses of port, he was away. He loved port. In fact, I remember him saying that when he died, he would like to be pickled in the stuff and buried in Oporto."

There was a silence.

"But he died in Bournemouth?"

"Yes," said Mr Coates-Smythe. "A bit of a come-down that! I don't think Bournemouth was exactly his sort of place. He must have been losing his marbles by then. But at eighty-eight . . . "

He spread out his broad hands in a gesture of despair.

What follies might any of us commit at eighty-eight?

Raynes smiled.

"Do you have a copy of the *Law Journal* in which his obituary appeared?"

"Of course, of course. I should have thought of that right away." He pressed the button on his desk again. "The *Law Journal* for 1977 and early 1978, please."

"Could I borrow the copy?" asked Raynes.

"With pleasure, Inspector, as long as it is returned in its original immaculate condition. We do pride ourselves on our legal library." He looked reprovingly at Raynes. "Even if we are not quite so prestigious as some legal firms in London."

Raynes assured him that he would treat the book as if it was a copy of Holy Writ; but when he returned to his car and tossed the heavy volume casually into the back seat, it did not seem that the Inspector was truly a man of his word.

* * * *

"Where next?" asked Carlisle.

"No. 66 Ranelagh Gardens."

"I thought he said No. 64?"

"It's his neighbours we're after," said Raynes. "Home-helps, doctors, vicars, lecturers in the University – anyone who might still remember him."

It was to prove a very long and frustrating search.

Over the next two days, Raynes and Carlisle visited a number of people in Ranelagh Gardens but none of them had ever heard of Sir Ian. Only one senior professor of Law could remember his lectures to the students – so rapid had been the turnover in the department. He thought it must have been fifteen years and more since Sir Ian had last figured in University circles. He remembered him as a quiet, reserved, dignified old man.

They visited a Baptist minister who had once had one of Sir Ian's housekeepers as a member of his congregation. He suggested – rather unhelpfully – that the Inspector should approach some of the cleaning ladies who might have worked in Ranelagh Gardens. However, one of them was in a nursing home with senile dementia; the others appeared to be dead. The only helpful lead came from a Mrs Ellen Reid, the daughter of a cleaning lady who had once "done" for the fourth baronet. But even she was somewhat vague.

When Sir Ian had first come to Grasshallows, he had lived with his sister – but she had died soon after the move. Raynes pointed out – ever so politely – that Sir Ian was one of two brothers and did not have a sister. Mrs Reid conceded that perhaps it might have been his sister-in-law.

Anyway, once the old lady had died. Sir Ian had advertized for a housekeeper. Not in the local press – but in *The Lady*. He felt he would get a better class of woman that way. He was not a snob – but he was very particular. He interviewed all the ladies himself – but did not pay them very well.

Yes, she knew he was a rich man – but rich men were like that – very mean. Consequently, over the years, he had had quite a number of housekeepers. At home, Sir Ian spent most of the day in his study, reading, writing, keeping himself very much to himself. It was a lonely life for a housekeeper. Just preparing meals, shopping, doing the laundry, fetching and carrying whatever Sir Ian required – and, of course, answering bells. She was not surprised he had had difficulty keeping them.

In the mid-seventies, she remembered, Sir Ian had had a stroke which had made him even more difficult to deal with. His mind and speech remained clear, but his right leg troubled him. Eventually, he had been reduced to going about in a wheelchair. But the houses in Ranelagh Gardens all had steep flights of steps leading up to their front doors. It was probably this which had persuaded Sir Ian to move house.

She remembered when he had moved to Bournemouth because her poodle had died the same week. It was in March 1976. She remembered her mother telling her that Sir Ian had said one more winter in Grasshallows would kill him. Obviously, Bournemouth had been chosen because of its better climate.

Beyond that, Mrs Reid had nothing more to add.

Raynes thanked her for her help.

17: *Seascape, Bournemouth*

On the Friday morning, having nothing better to do, the Inspector and Detective-Constable Carlisle drove down to Bournemouth. The inquest following the fatal accident at Slipper's Hill had taken place on Thursday afternoon – and been adjourned. The University student had also appeared in court, pled guilty and been sentenced to one hundred and twenty hours of community service.

"They should have made him dust down all their medieval manuscripts," said Raynes. "One hundred and twenty hours of sneezing would have been punishment enough." But the University decided to rusticate the student for a full academic year.

Carlisle drove the Inspector's own car because it was less conspicuous than the police Granada in which they normally travelled. Carlisle quite enjoyed the change but Raynes had to remind him to keep on the right side of seventy – in case they were stopped and awkward questions asked. Raynes himself pretended to be thinking through the case, but since there was very little to meditate upon, he soon turned to the *Daily*

Telegraph crossword which occupied him for nearly half an hour.

Shortly after noon, they reached their destination and had lunch in the best restaurant Egon Ronay could recommend. The Inspector confined himself to half a bottle of good claret – to make sure his mind was completely clear. For at two o'clock, they had an appointment with Mr Charles Eastwood, a senior partner in Miller & Duckworth, the lawyers who handled all Sir Ian's legal affairs.

Mr Eastwood was in his late fifties – small, precise and bird-like. He had no difficulty remembering his client.

"Poor man!" he said. "He was so crippled after his stroke. Had to travel everywhere in a wheelchair. I usually visited him at his home. He had a bungalow – a beautiful bungalow – in one of the loveliest parts of the city. The tragedy was that he was too ill to enjoy it."

He had been called upon – soon after Sir Ian moved to Bournemouth – to handle all his legal business. It had been a pleasure to work with him. A man who understood every legal point; who was scrupulous over detail; who made sure that each last letter had its "i" dotted and its "t" properly crossed. He wished every client could be as particular as Sir Ian had been.

Some days, he had suffered great pain and had terminated the visit after just twenty minutes, inviting him to call again the following day. For eighteen months, he had visited him regularly. But, finally, he had died in October 1977. The second of the month, he thought it was.

Raynes congratulated the lawyer on having such an excellent memory and asked him whether Sir Ian had died at home or in hospital.

"Oh, at home," said Mr Eastwood. "He had a most dedicated housekeeper. A lovely woman. She couldn't do enough for him. She didn't want him to go into hospital. As he got weaker, she arranged for a series of nurses to come in round the clock – to look after him. She couldn't have done more."

Mr Eastwood paused.

"And after his death, she was a great help to me, tidying up his estate. She had all his business files in perfect order. All his bank statements and dividend slips neatly arranged. You couldn't fault her. She dealt with the estate agents who sold the bungalow and organized the auctioneers for the sale of his effects."

"Sir Ian had no immediate heir."

"None. But he had a grand-nephew in South Africa. Sir Ian had kept in touch with him. He was the chief legatee."

"Did the housekeeper benefit in any way from the will?"

"Not particularly. I checked up on the will before you gentlemen arrived . . ." He opened a dark green file. "She got £2000 and her wages for the next six months. I think that amounted to another £3000." He checked his notes. "£3750. She received a final sum of £5441.80 after tax and deductions."

"But Sir Ian left a great deal more than that?"

"A great deal more. I suppose it's no harm telling you – after all these years – that he left property and assets totalling over £12 million. Quite a sum."

"And all this went to his grand-nephew in South Africa?"

"Not all of it. Sir Ian left a number of substantial donations to good causes."

"Grasshallows University?" asked Raynes.

Mr Eastwood turned over the pages of Sir Ian's will.

"Yes," he said. "They were included. £250,000 was given to them to assist the work of their Law department. A special prize was set up for the best final year student – the Mallowan Award – carrying with it a sum of £1000. A further endowment of £4000 a year was to be spent on legal books for the departmental library. A very handsome bequest."

Raynes nodded.

"And Sir George got the rest – after all the donations to these good causes?"

"He got about £9 million all told." Mr Eastwood again consulted the final pages of the financial statement. "£8,880,692.18. I hope there is no problem about this, Inspector?"

"Oh, none at all," said Raynes blandly. "We're just making inquiries into the lady who was his housekeeper."

"Mrs Anderson."

"Yes," said Raynes. "Mrs Anderson. Do you remember her quite well?"

"Of course. She was a lady of . . . great character. Full of fun and laughter. A splendid tonic for Sir Ian. Made his last few years much more bearable than they might otherwise have been. She looked after him impeccably."

Raynes pulled a photograph out of his inner jacket pocket. It was a photograph he had removed from Sir George's drawing room on the Sunday afternoon. Judging by Brackles' portrait, it was quite a good likeness. He passed the photograph over to Mr Eastwood.

"Is that Mrs Anderson?"

The lawyer smiled,

"Yes. That's the lady. Looks a bit older than she did. Face a bit fuller. Hair a bit more stylish than it used to be. But that's her."

"Thank you," said Raynes.

He looked at Carlisle.

The young constable whistled silently.

Mr Eastwood noted his reaction.

"There's nothing wrong with this woman, is there, Inspector?"

"Nothing at all," said Raynes reassuringly. "Unfortunately she died about three weeks ago and we're making inquiries into her death. It appears that she answered an advertisement in *The Lady* magazine and became housekeeper to Sir Ian whilst he was at Grasshallows. She looked after him there – and came with him down to Bournemouth. As you say, her behaviour appears to have been impeccable."

"I'm glad to hear that," said Mr Eastwood – much relieved. "How did she die?"

"She was murdered. Poisoned. Died instantly."

"Good heavens!" said the lawyer. "How dreadful!"

Raynes decided that this was the moment to drop a bombshell on the unsuspecting lawyer.

"There's just one point you might like to know . . . "

"And what's that, Inspector?"

Raynes smiled a wry smile.

"She married Sir Ian's grand-nephew and became Lady Mallowan!"

"Good heavens!" said the lawyer again. "Do you mean . . . ?"

Raynes shrugged his shoulders.

"As you say, she did nothing wrong whilst she was looking after Sir Ian. Handled his affairs *impeccably*. But she knew where the money was going – and followed it."

Mr Eastwood pursed his lips.

"No," he said. "Nothing illegal in that."

"So it probably wouldn't have made any difference, her getting only £5441, if she knew she was going to be marrying into the eight million!"

"You think she arranged it?"

"I can't prove it," said Raynes, "but it looks like it."

"Is Sir George all right?"

"In excellent health. I had dinner with him on Sunday. I think he's contemplating marrying again. Wife No. 4."

Mr Eastwood shook his head sadly.

"Such a different man from his grand-uncle. A man of the soil – not of the spirit. I remember him coming in here when he first heard of his inheritance. Couldn't believe his good fortune. He'd spent all his life selling cars and lorries; hiring out building equipment. Never thought his grand-uncle would remember him. He seemed quite overwhelmed."

Raynes agreed.

"They were obviously as alike as chalk and cheese. Sir George is a man who has worked his way from the bottom up. With perhaps a little help . . . from Mrs Anderson?"

The lawyer looked a trifle uncertain at the Inspector's meaning.

"What exactly are you suggesting?"

Raynes put his thoughts carefully in order.

"I am suggesting that Mrs Anderson kept Mr George Mallowan closely in touch with his grand-uncle. Made sure that he wrote nice letters telling him all he was doing. Made sure that all Sir Ian's money didn't go into good causes. Made sure the money stayed in the family. Made sure Sir Ian didn't change his mind – or his will." He looked over at Mr Eastwood's dark green file. He didn't alter it, did he?"

"No." Mr Eastwood looked at the document in front of him. "No," he said. "The will was drawn up and witnessed in November 1971 – long before Mrs Anderson entered his employ."

"Precisely," said Raynes. "It remained unaltered. Mrs Anderson made sure it wasn't changed."

"You could be right," said Mr Eastwood thoughtfully. "I seem to remember there was quite a sheaf of letters from his grand-nephew in Sir Ian's files."

Raynes nodded.

"And presumably Sir Ian sent him some money from time to time?"

"He did. But not a lot. A couple of hundred each Christmas."

Raynes smiled.

"Beautifully handled – from end to end."

Mr Eastwood looked anxious.

"Are you suggesting that Mrs Anderson continued to make sure that all Sir Ian's estate went to his grand-nephew – with the express intention of marrying him the moment Sir Ian died?"

Raynes was quite definite.

"I am. It was in her best interests that Sir Ian did not change his will. That the bulk of his estate stayed in the family. And having done this service for Sir George, she made sure she benefitted too."

"You think it was all arranged?"

"I do."

Mr Eastwood leafed through the pages of Sir Ian's will as if it contained some hidden secret which he had missed. Eventually, he looked up.

"But nothing illegal was done?"

"Nothing," said Raynes firmly. "Sir George has maintained

the family traditions – with great élan. He has a nice country estate, a small stable of horses – and is greatly respected by all the local people."

"I'm glad to hear that." Mr Eastwood sounded much relieved. "One doesn't like to think, Inspector, that one has done anything illegal."

Raynes was charm itself.

"I think you have handled Sir Ian's wishes with complete honesty and integrity. He would have been proud of you. All I am saying is that Mrs Anderson also made sure that she benefitted as well. As the Bible says: 'She has received her reward!'"

"But it hasn't done her much good?"

"No," said Raynes. "Not now it hasn't. But for the past twelve years, she has really enjoyed being Lady Mallowan. Lady of the Manor, with all the perks of being a rich woman."

"And who poisoned her? Her husband?"

"That's what we're trying to find out. Would it be possible to have a copy of Sir Ian's will?"

"Most certainly, Inspector. I'll ask my secretary to copy it right away."

He rang a bell on his desk and a middle-aged lady rapidly appeared – and equally rapidly disappeared at Mr Eastwood's bidding.

There was a long silence. The lawyer stared fixedly at his blotting pad. He twisted his pen backwards and forwards. Something was clearly troubling him. Eventually he raised his eyes and looked at Raynes.

"There's one thing I should tell you, Inspector. It didn't seem important at the time – but in the light of what you have told me this afternoon, it may prove helpful to your inquiries."

Mr Eastwood sighed deeply.

"Two years ago, I had a gentleman in here, asking me the very same questions you were asking – about Sir Ian's will. Because he was not here in any official capacity, I gave him only a brief indication of the facts and figures I have given you. But I told him where he could go and see the will and get the exact details he was interested in."

Raynes felt a sudden glow of excitement flowing through him. This was better than he had dared hope. He leant forward in his seat so as not to miss a word.

"He came from Australia. Australia or New Zealand. I can't remember which. And he said he was a distant relative of Sir Ian."

"Did he give you his name?"

Mr Eastwood opened his desk drawer and hunted through it. He emerged with a black desk diary for 1987. It took him a long time to find what he was looking for.

"Cook," he said at last. "Mr Paul Cook. He seemed a very respectable sort of man . . . "

"Did the information you gave him – come as a surprise?"

Mr Eastwood nodded.

"He looked – how shall I put it? – thunderstruck. He wouldn't tell me what it was that distressed him, but he turned quite pale. He just kept saying: 'I must do something about that!' What he intended to do, he didn't say. I thought perhaps he was in some financial difficulty. Upset at being left out of the will. After all, a few thousands can make a difference to anyone's life."

"Quite so," said Raynes, thinking of what he could do with a few thousands. Pay off the mortgage. Buy a new car. Go on a cruise round the Caribbean with Mrs May. The man must have gone away deeply disappointed.

"Have you heard from him since?"

"No."

"Did he ask you to get in touch with Sir George?"

"No."

"Did he leave a forwarding address?"

"No."

Mr Eastwood looked worried.

"There's more in this than meets the eye, isn't there?"

"A lot more."

"I should have asked him for more details."

"He probably wouldn't have given them. He was playing his cards close to his chest. And there was no reason for you to be suspicious. Especially after all these years."

Raynes was delighted with this final piece of information. Gradually the whole scenario had been revealed before him. He could scarcely believe his luck. His vague hunch had proved incredibly successful. He now had vital information which he was sure had eluded the Sussex police. He might even have found a clue to the murder.

Outwardly, the Inspector remained his calm, professional self.

"I'm most grateful for your help, Mr Eastwood."

"Will you be needing me again?"

"I hope not."

(It was a lie; but who cared?)

The lawyer seemed reassured.

"I'll just go and get you the copy of that will. It should have been done by now."

Raynes looked at Carlisle. There was a glint of triumph in his eyes.

"I can't believe it," said Carlisle.

"It just shows. Whenever you have a hunch, you should follow it."

"All those miserable visits chasing up charladies!"

"100% vindicated! What a day!"

18: *Tea for two*

Whilst they were in the lawyer's office, nothing more was said. But Raynes knew that Carlisle was dying to ask him lots of questions, so he suggested that, before returning to Grasshallows, they should find an old-fashioned tea shop and have several cups of rich, creamy coffee. It would aid their deliberations.

A cafe was duly found and coffee ordered. Carlisle opted for a pot of Ceylon tea which was more to his taste. The Inspector ordered a selection of cream cakes, which his colleague also declined.

Raynes sat back, deep in his chair, with a confident smile

playing over his lips.

"Let's start at the beginning," he said.

"Mrs Anderson answers Sir Ian's advertisement in *The Lady* magazine . . ."

"She has done this sort of thing before."

"Fleecing the elderly and the infirm?"

Raynes nodded.

"We must check up on her past movements – but it seems unlikely that Sir Ian was her first victim."

"But Sir Ian was not the usual sort of victim . . ."

"No. He was as sharp as a razor. Very careful with his money. Very shrewd in business matters. Mrs Anderson couldn't take a penny without him noticing."

"So she looked at his will – and noticed that the greater part of his estate was going to his grand-nephew . . ."

"Who was probably completely estranged from his grand-uncle? Never wrote to him. Never phoned. She could see that as Sir Ian approached his *terminus ad quem*, he would be very likely to revise his will. Cut out the ungrateful nephew and make sure his estate was parcelled out to good causes."

"Bad news for George!"

"Very bad news indeed! He was probably unaware that he stood to gain so much. But Mrs Anderson enlightened him. Wrote to him and told him that eight million would be coming his way. A pleasant surprise. Perhaps she also blackmailed him? Said: 'If you don't agree to marry me, I'll make sure Sir Ian changes his will'."

"So George bucks up?"

"Yes. He starts writing a few letters which Sir Ian reads – and keeps. Perhaps he is impressed with all his grand-nephew's hard work. Not exactly the career he would have chosen; but he has turned out better than expected. Sir Ian even sends him a Christmas present or two."

"And Mrs Anderson speaks up for him?"

"Invariably."

"And keeps a close eye on the will?"

"A very close eye. Because if Sir Ian changes his mind, all is lost. For both of them. Now what is the best way to prevent

Sir Ian changing his will? The best way is to occupy his mind with something else. A change of house. A change of climate. The previous winter in Grasshallows has been particularly grim. Bournemouth is a place renowned for its warmth and sunshine. Geriatrics flock there from every part of the country. What could be nicer than a little bungalow in beautiful Bournemouth? New neighbours. A new doctor. A new lawyer. People whom you don't know all that well. And you are getting increasingly frail, suffering a lot of pain, being pushed around in a wheelchair by the ever-faithful Mrs Anderson."

"Makes you want to cry!"

"Doesn't it? But it is a clever move. Time passes quickly. The will remains mercifully unaltered. Sir Ian dies. George gets his money. Mrs Anderson gets her man. As I said to Mr Eastwood, it is beautifully handled – from beginning to end."

"You think they had worked it all out?"

"I'm sure they did."

"But the lawyer said it was all completely legal."

"So it was. A splendid *quid pro quo*!" Raynes poured himself a second cup of coffee. "All completely legal – *if* Sir George was really the heir to Sir Ian's estate."

"If he wasn't . . .?"

"If he wasn't, that respectable gentleman who turned up at the lawyer's office a couple of years ago . . ."

". . . has been cheated out of eight million pounds."

"No wonder he looked so distressed!"

"Do you think he realized?"

"He most certainly did."

"But what could he do?"

"He could find out where Sir George and Mrs Anderson were living."

"And then?"

"Expose them as frauds and impostors. Take legal action to get his money back."

Carlisle thought for a few moments.

"Why didn't he say anything to Mr Eastwood?"

"He probably thought Mr Eastwood was in it up to his

neck. Some of these lawyers are real crooks. They walk off with big money – especially if it's a large estate. Mr Cook couldn't be sure whether or not Mr Eastwood had taken his cut. Ten per cent of twelve million would have been quite a tidy sum."

Raynes sipped his coffee thoughtfully.

"And why didn't he go to the police?"

"Because he couldn't prove who he was."

Raynes nodded.

"He knew he was the real grand-nephew – but had no proof."

"So he would have to go back to Australia and get proof. He would have to see a lawyer – someone he could trust – to advise him and put his case together. That's what he'd have to do."

Raynes congratulated Carlisle on his deductive skills.

"But," he said, "two years have passed. Sir George and Lady Angela are still living comfortably in their fine house near Rye. There is no sign of legal action being brought against them. Perhaps Mr Cook does not have convincing proof?"

"Perhaps he prefers direct action? He decides to take the law into his own hands and murders Mrs Anderson?"

"But why wait two years? Why not do it right away?"

"Perhaps he did go back to Australia? Perhaps he realized it would be very difficult to prove his case? Perhaps he couldn't afford it?"

"Perhaps," said Raynes. "But suppose he began to blackmail Sir George? Threaten him with exposure? To utter dire threats if he didn't pay up?"

"Have we any proof of that?"

"None whatsoever. But George refuses to play ball and Lady Angela is murdered."

There was a lengthy silence as both men considered the implications of this line of thinking. Raynes was conscious that the case was becoming infinitely more complex than he had first imagined. Was Sir George being blackmailed by the real grand-nephew? It seemed unlikely. Perhaps the poor man had just gone back to Australia in despair? Could revenge have been the motive for the killing? Or was it something completely different?

Raynes decided to help himself to a second cake – a chocolate eclair. He bit deliberately into the soft choux pastry.

"Mr Eastwood has a lot to answer for," he said eventually.

"You mean he didn't check up properly on Sir George's identity?"

"He completely failed in his duty," said Raynes, wiping away the cream from his lips. "He should have made sure Sir George was who he said he was. I imagine he took Mrs Anderson's word for it. The letters. The Christmas cheques. The fact that everything else Sir Ian did was so cut and dried.

"He never thought the grand-nephew was anything other than who Mrs Anderson said he was. After all, if he wasn't the grand-nephew, why was Sir Ian sending him money? Sir Ian's actions suggested that he had no doubt about his identity – so why should Mr Eastwood?"

"George would have had to produce some proof, surely? A birth certificate?"

"These things can easily be acquired. Mrs Anderson would have had all that prepared well in advance. She'd have asked Sir Ian all about his family. His brother and sister-in-law. Their children and grandchildren. Old folk love to talk about the past. She would have found out where the grand-nephew went to school. She would have cast a careful eye over the family photograph album. 'Which one did you say was George?'

"She would have selected a number of useful photos of George as a boy – as a young man. They could have been as much one young man as another. She would have created George's own family album. A few pictures – but enough. His mother's birth certificate. Wedding certificate. Death certificate. Copies if necessary. All carefully set aside for George to produce – to prove he was who he claimed to be."

"You think she did all that?"

"Wouldn't you? It's worth making a bit of an effort to get hold of eight million."

"You seem to be suggesting that Mrs Anderson was the brains behind all this – not George?"

Raynes nodded.

"I think she was. A very unscrupulous woman! Quite determined to get her own way. My friend, Simon – the painter I was telling you about – he said you couldn't help liking her. He said she could wrap men round her little finger. Sir Ian was no exception."

Carlisle poured himself a second cup of tea and helped himself to a strawberry meringue, full of fresh cream.

"Who then is George?"

Raynes smiled.

"An interesting question! Mrs Anderson's lover? Perhaps Mrs Anderson's husband? I would imagine that George must have been living in this country when the plot was hatched. He would have had to change his name by deed poll. Get a new passport. Start a new life in South Africa. Out of sight – out of mind, just like the real grand-nephew. And then he would have to resume contact.

"Typewritten letters, I should think. With suitable letterheads. George Mallowan in strong, bold print – to look convincing. If he did sign his letters, Mrs Anderson would have to be sure they looked like the real George's signature. She might have had to look hard for that."

Raynes sniffed.

"Perhaps she promised Sir Ian to find his erring relative and bring him back to the fold. When she succeeded – great triumph! Perhaps she even wrote the letters and sent them out to South Africa for George to post back? He seems a lazy sort of man – probably couldn't be bothered with all the necessary details – might have mucked it all up! Yes, I think Mrs Anderson probably wrote the letters and made sure they were cast-iron authentic, free from every error. All Sir George had to do was send them back."

"It's very clever."

"Incredibly so. But some people will do anything for money. And remember! They had twelve golden years before anything went wrong. She wasn't nursing Sir Ian out of the kindness of her heart – for £7500 a year. Pushing a heavy wheelchair – and all the rest. She was in it for big bucks – and she got 'em."

"So what do we have to do?" asked Carlisle.

"We have to check that our theory holds water. We have to find out who Mrs Anderson was. We have to find out who changed his name by deed poll to George Mallowan. We have to approach the Passport Office to see when he was issued with a passport. When he entered South Africa. When he left. We have to approach the Australian police to see if they know anything about this man, Paul Cook. Does the real George Mallowan live in Australia – or New Zealand? Is he still there? If not, when did he leave? We have to discover whether our Sir George has been blackmailed – by whom – and for how long. We have to search out Lady Angela's birth certificate – and her wedding certificate." Raynes smiled. "That should be interesting!"

"It'll be difficult digging it all up," said Carlisle cautiously. "It's a long time since it all happened."

Raynes smiled again.

"But these are the things you are good at! You are superb at digging up official documents, phoning people, collecting evidence, getting it all down on paper. Those are things I hate!"

Carlisle finished his tea, put down his fine bone china teacup gently on to its saucer – and wiped his fingers on the elaborate lace napkin. He could see a vast amount of work piling up ahead of him.

"Well, if I'm going to get down to all that," he said, "the sooner we get home the better."

"You can't do anything before Monday," said Raynes realistically. "So you might as well have a decent weekend."

Carlisle picked up the car keys.

"Is this now official?" he asked. "Not private enterprise? No muscling in on anybody else?"

"Absolutely official," said Raynes. "We have reason to suspect that a will has not been fulfilled according to the testator's wishes. A fraud has been perpetrated – on the grand

108

scale. And at least one of those responsible is still living and benefitting from his criminal proceeds. At the moment, it has nothing to do with any murder. It may lead us there . . . It may lead us there very quickly. But this is *our* case. We may seek the co-operation of our good friends in the Sussex police – but that is a treat in store. For the moment, we are concerned with Sir Ian's will. Nothing more."

Carlisle allowed himself one final observation.

"This is going to be very bad news for Mr Eastwood?"

"Very serious. In fact, I'm surprised he didn't see the rocks lying directly ahead."

"You didn't tell him."

"Of course not. If I'd told him, he might cut and run. He might have committed suicide. Most inconvenient – just when we need him."

Raynes stood up – and looked down at the tea table.

"I think I'll take an extra cake with me, just in case I get hungry on the journey home."

"Glutton!" said Carlisle.

Raynes grinned happily.

"One man's sin is another man's salvation! The real Sir George will bless me."

19: *The Awakening Conscience*

It was another week before Raynes could return to matters in Rye. A spate of burglaries had taken place in Grasshallows. Several houses in Ash Lane had been broken into. Two people had been injured. It took the Inspector four days to round up the culprits.

In the meantime, Detective-Constable Carlisle had been following up the leads which Raynes had suggested.

Sir Ian's advertisement for a housekeeper had appeared in *The Lady* in November 1974. It seemed that Mrs Anderson had been employed some time before Christmas that year. A copy of the birth certificate for the grand-nephew, George Mallowan, had been obtained from Somerset House in March

1975. A month later, a certain George Proctor, from Peterborough, had changed his name by deed poll. Two months later, a passport had been issued to that person and in July 1975, South African Airways had transported him to Johannesburg. He had worked in a car rental business in that city until November 1977.

Detective-Constable Carlisle, working on the supposition that if George Proctor came from Peterborough, Mrs Anderson probably did as well, scoured the marriage records of that city and discovered that Angela White had married Derek Anderson in July 1968. She was 21; he was 47. Already, she was showing a preference for the older man.

The marriage had not lasted long; just four years – if that. They had been divorced in December 1972. The grounds for divorce were adultery. The guilty party was accused of committing adultery with a man called George Proctor. The case had not been defended.

Carlisle drove over to Peterborough in the hope of finding Derek Anderson – but discovered that he had died in 1983. None of the White families interviewed knew anything about Angela. It seemed that she did not come from Peterborough. The address on her wedding certificate was a B & B. Carlisle reckoned it would take a lot more digging before he obtained the full facts about Angela White.

However, the Inspector had enough to be getting on with. Two weeks after his return from Rye, Raynes and Carlisle set out to visit Sir George.

They left Grasshallows on Tuesday morning and arrived at the handsome stone gateway at about 2.00pm.

"Hope he's not at the massage parlour!" said Raynes.

Sir George was out – but expected back at about 3.00pm. The two policemen went into Rye for a late lunch and returned at 3.15pm. George arrived a quarter of an hour later.

He seemed delighted to see Raynes.

"Good to see you again, Inspector! Have your brought your lovely lady with you? Beautiful girl! Really set my hormones pounding! No? Well, perhaps we shall meet some other time."

Raynes introduced his colleague.

Sir George looked thoughtful.

"I take it this is an official visit, Inspector? Business – not pleasure? Have you come to tell me who murdered my beloved wife?" He shook his head sadly. "Six weeks on – and we're none the wiser. Come in and have a drink!"

Raynes saw no reason why he should not drink Sir George's whisky – but Carlisle stuck to orange juice. He was driving.

"I'm glad you haven't given up, Inspector. The Sussex police seem to be quite hopeless. They've been questioning young Katie again. Still seem to think she might be involved. Took a statement from her husband too. Apparently he had no alibi either. Left his work at lunchtime, claiming that he had to go home to look after Katie, but wasn't back till 4.00pm. Difficult to explain what he did during those four hours. Doesn't look good, does it, Inspector?"

Raynes decided there was nothing to be gained by rushing. If he took a relaxed approach, the real questions – when they came – would prove even more devastating. He therefore sat back in his chair and asked:

"How is Lesley?"

"Scintillating as ever, Inspector. She was here at the weekend. Of course, she comes down every weekend. But she'll be down again tomorrow. Can't keep her hands off me! Panting for it! I've bought her a lovely gold bangle – specially engraved with her name. Let me show you . . ."

Sir George hurried over with a jewellery case containing the most beautiful gold bangle, resting on red velvet. It must have cost at least £2500.

"You see her name? They've done it so well. She'll love it. She loves fine jewellery. Especially gold."

Raynes wondered whether the bangle would have quite the same attraction coming from a George Proctor.

He and Carlisle duly agreed that it would be a magnificent gift.

Raynes took another sip of his whisky.

"And have you got your picture yet? I don't see it up."

Sir George smiled nervously.

"Well, it's finished. It's been framed. Looks quite splendid. Everyone who's seen it thinks it's a fantastic likeness. Brackles has done a superb job. No doubt about it. But . . ." he hesitated before he spoke " . . . the trouble is – where to put it?"

"You were going to hang it in the front hall. I remember you saying it would be too heart-breaking to have it in here."

"You've an excellent memory, Inspector! Yes, I was going to put it in the hall – but you see . . ." He stared into his glass sadly. " . . . it upsets Lesley. She feels that when we get married, it'll be a bit of an embarrassment. People coming to the house and seeing it. They'll be comparing her and Angela. Still thinking of Angela as my wife. Could be awkward. Lesley suggested we might put it on the staircase or in one of the upstairs rooms. No offence intended. Just more diplomatic."

"And where's the picture at this moment?"

"Brackles still has it. All packed up and ready for delivery. I've paid him £5000 for it – so he's not out of pocket. But it's all a bit difficult at this moment."

Raynes nodded understandingly.

It was just as Debbie had predicted.

Sir George decided that it was time to change the subject.

"Now you gentlemen didn't come here to talk about pictures . . ."

"No," said Raynes, "but I did want my colleague to see your family tree. I was telling him about it."

No subject could have given Sir George greater pleasure.

The light returned to his eyes.

"Of course. I shall be delighted."

He leapt out of his chair and led the way across the room – heading unknowingly to his doom. A false claim uttered in the presence of witnesses.

Carlisle looked suitably interested.

Sir George explained every detail of the family crest. He translated the family motto: "Always fruitful". "Of course people make fun of the Latin words. I do it myself. Leave out

112

the 'r'. Sounds naughty!"

Raynes laughed politely.

He would let Sir George condemn himself out of his own mouth.

"Katie said you were descended from some extra-curricular philandering by Charles II?"

Sir George smiled broadly.

"Great one for sowing his wild oats was Charlie boy! I'm still following in his footsteps! Trying to keep up the family tradition. Of course, not much gets through a rubber sheath! But the idea's there!"

He laughed.

"Now here we have the first baronet – William John Mallowan. He was quite fruitful. Six sons, three daughters. I don't know what happened to the daughters – but five of his sons died.

"Only one heir – James. You'll see he married Sarah Willoughby; she was related to the Duke of Rutland. Their son was the first legal beagle in the family. He made a packet. Invested it wisely. In land. Always a good investment. They had an estate in Norfolk.

"You can trace the line downwards. My great-grandfather – that's him – Sir Ernest. He was a very successful barrister. Made a mint. My grand-uncle, Sir Ian, entered his chambers when he was a young man. Rose to the top. Great chap."

Sir George almost licked his lips as he described the achievements of his forebears.

"Now Ian's brother, George . . . I'm called after him . . . he looked after the family estate whilst Sir Ian was in London." George's voice suddenly changed. "He died in the First World War. At the Somme. Terrible business. Killed the flower of British youth. That's what they say. My father was only a child at the time. Two or three years old. Never knew his dad. His mother brought him up. Sold off the estate in Norfolk. Went to live with her brother-in-law in London. Later they moved to Grasshallows. All very sad.

"You can't help feeling sorry for her . . . Lost her husband in one war . . . her son in the next. I was all she had left – and

113

I lived abroad. Sir Ian, you will see, had no issue. He never married. My father died in North Africa. Sidi Barrani. In tanks. Completely outgunned by Rommel. My mother died in the fifties, my grandmother in the sixties. Sir Ian himself died in October 1977 and I'm the last of the line."

"Not all that *fructus* after all!" said Raynes.

"Not lately."

Carlisle had followed the explanation carefully.

"So all the family fortune came to you?"

"Every penny. All the money from the estates, the legal practice . . . It all came to Sir Ian. Then down to me."

"And where will it go next?"

Raynes' question had a double edge to it – as Carlisle was well aware. But Sir George, naturally, took it at face value.

"That is the 64,000 dollar question, Inspector! Katie refuses to touch it. I suppose it will go to her children. She has two boys. Nice lads." He laughed. "Mark you, I'm not expecting to snuff it – not just yet! Might even father a son or two with Lesley . . . or some other obliging lass. No reason why I shouldn't." His eyes twinkled at the thought. "Of course Lesley's on the pill. Great advantage in one way. Not so good if you're wanting to expand the clan. Trouble is, Inspector, I can't imagine Lesley doing anything that would damage her figure."

Raynes was inclined to agree. It was highly unlikely that she would do any such thing.

"How old is she?" he asked out of curiosity.

"I believe thirty-two is the official figure."

Sir George chuckled.

"Nearer thirty-five, I should think."

"So, if Lesley doesn't come up trumps – and if you don't find some other . . . 'obliging lass', the line goes extinct?"

"'Fraid so."

Sir George shook his head sadly.

"Fortunately, time is on my side."

"Not for much longer," thought Raynes.

"You must be very proud of your family history," said Carlisle – painfully aware that the moment of exposure was

114

rapidly drawing near.

"Great tradition! Great heritage!" Sir George's whole body radiated pride. "Part of old England! That's what it is. Part of old England!"

Raynes decided that this was the moment to puncture the balloon. "Great pity then, it's not yours!"

He said it quietly – so quietly that Sir George did not immediately catch on to what he had said.

"What's that, Inspector?"

"I said it's a great pity it's not yours."

Sir George looked at Raynes with a blank expression.

"Did I hear you right, Inspector?"

"I said it's a marvellous family history – but it belongs to the Mallowans – and you are George Proctor."

It was clear that Sir George found it difficult to adjust to the sudden change in the conversation. The blow had caught him off balance – as it was intended to do. For so many years he had thought of himself as Sir George Mallowan, it was difficult to think otherwise. He had so totally immersed himself in his new role that he had completely forgotten the real person underneath. For twelve years, he had lived a life that was more real than anything else which had gone before. Adjusting to the truth did not come easily.

Raynes understood this.

"Why don't we sit down?" he said in a kindly fashion. "This has obviously come as a tremendous shock to you."

But George was not giving up without a fight.

"I simply cannot understand what you are talking about, Inspector." He sat down heavily in his winged chair. "What on earth are you suggesting?"

"I'm suggesting that you are not the rightful heir to Sir Ian's estate. That you have usurped the title by deceit. That you are guilty of a colossal act of fraud and that you are embezzling money on a massive scale, involving many millions of pounds."

He said it quietly – but firmly, because he was not sure how George would react.

"I thought, Inspector, that you had come here in connection

with Angela's death. I hoped you might have some good news about the investigation into her murder."

"That is the job of the Sussex police," said Raynes. "I am here on a completely different matter. The fraud was conceived and prepared in Grasshallows – or perhaps in Peterborough – fifteen years ago."

"So your questions have nothing to do with the murder?"

"No."

It was not entirely true, but Raynes did not want to confuse the main issue. He felt that George was still trying to wriggle away from the truth.

He continued: "Like my colleague, I was immensely interested in your family tree. When you first showed it to me, I was greatly impressed. And then you mentioned your connection with Grasshallows. Sir Ian lived there and Katie went to university there. When I got back to Grasshallows, I asked a few questions about Sir Ian. I discovered that before his death, he moved to Bournemouth. I made inquiries with several law firms in that town and discovered that it was Mr Eastwood of Miller & Duckworth who handled his estate. I think you met Mr Eastwood . . . ?"

Raynes looked at George.

George stared back.

Raynes wondered if he was taking in what was being said.

"Mr Eastwood told me that you were working in South Africa at the time Sir Ian died. Is that right?"

George nodded.

"You were in the rental business? Cars and lorries?"

George nodded again.

"You were not expecting to receive anything from Sir Ian and the legacy came as a surprise. You returned to England and went to see Mr Eastwood. There was no difficulty about you inheriting the title – or receiving the money. You obtained just under nine million pounds. Is that right?"

Raynes was trying to keep strictly to the facts and avoid any element of accusation.

George nodded glumly.

He could not disagree.

116

"Once you had got the money, what did you do?"

"What d'you mean?"

"You didn't buy this house immediately?"

"No, we went for a holiday."

Raynes was glad that George was once again willing to speak.

"You went to Mexico?"

"Yes."

"Is that where you and Angela got married?"

A tear rolled down George's cheek.

"That would have been in December 1977?"

"Yes."

Raynes noted that the line of George's mouth had begun to grow harder. He was getting angry.

"Before you married her, what was Angela's surname?"

George said nothing.

"She was called Anderson, wasn't she? Married in July 1968 to Derek Anderson? Divorced in December 1972? Is that true?"

"You tell me."

"I am telling you."

"The co-respondent in the divorce case was a certain George Proctor."

George remained impassive.

"After her divorce, Angela became housekeeper to a number of elderly people – including Sir Ian Mallowan. She went to work for him in November 1974."

Raynes hoped that Detective-Constable Carlisle had got all his facts correct. If he made a mistake at this point, he would be in big trouble.

George continued to stare at the Inspector like a large owl. He wondered how Raynes had managed to gather all this information.

"In March 1975, Mrs Anderson obtained a copy of a birth certificate from Somerset House. All quite legal. And in April 1975, Mr George Proctor changed his name by deed poll to George Mallowan. Again perfectly legal. And in July 1975, the said Mr Mallowan flew to South Africa, where he worked for two years in Johannesburg.

"So far so good! Nothing wrong there. But the George Mallowan in South Africa was *not* Sir Ian's nephew. At some point between July 1975 and October 1977, an attempt was made to convince Sir Ian that the George Mallowan in South Africa was his grand-nephew. Letters were sent to Grasshallows and Bournemouth. Handy evidence. Cash was sent to Johannesburg.

"Not much. But enough to suggest that Sir Ian thought he was dealing with his long-lost grand-nephew. So that, when he died, this George Mallowan slipped naturally into his shoes. Into a substantial inheritance. Beautifully done. But an act of fraud and deception, because you knew full well that you were no relation to Sir Ian."

If Raynes expected any confirmation of the truth of these statements, he was disappointed. All he received was an icy stare from his victim.

"Now I realize," said the Inspector, "that it was Angela who arranged all this. She did the planning. She handled all Sir Ian's business affairs with Mr Eastwood. He trusted her. She seemed no more than a faithful retainer who would receive her own modest bequest. £5441, I believe.

"So, Sir Ian's will was carried out – to the letter. You received the residue of the estate and you've been enjoying it for the past twelve years."

Raynes decided that this was now perhaps the moment to thrust in the final banderilla.

"I must apologize for removing from your house a photograph of Lady Angela. I picked it up whilst you were showing us over the house. I don't know why I took it – instinct, I suppose. I showed that picture to Mr Eastwood and he confirmed that she was the Mrs Anderson who looked after Sir Ian, who married you in December 1977 and thereafter masqueraded as Lady Angela Mallowan – supposedly Sir Ian's legitimate daughter-in-law, when in fact she was nothing more than a common thief."

Raynes' final words stung George as they were meant to do.

"You'll have to prove that in a court of law, Inspector."

Raynes coolly overrode George's objections.

"No problem. Detective-Constable Carlisle has already checked all the facts and I have not the slightest doubt that they are correct. We have a copy of the will. Statements from witnesses in Grasshallows who knew Sir Ian. Somerset House and the Passport Office have confirmed their information in writing. The lawyer, Mr Eastwood, will testify against you. The case against you is cut and dried. I think the best advice I can give you is to blame the whole thing on your late wife – and plead guilty. That way, you should minimize your sentence. Otherwise, you could be put away for several years. No more Lesley . . . no more 'obliging lasses'. Just cleaning out your own lavatory pan in a dark cell."

In a matter of ten minutes or so, Raynes had reduced the proud scion of a great family to a prospective jailbird, serving time in some hideous Victorian prison. He had done it using undeniable facts, accurate dates and with simple precision. It was a superb demolition job, calculated to shatter Sir George. And it had visibly done so.

George held out his glass.

"I need another drink, Inspector. A large whisky. Neat. The Macallan."

Raynes nodded to his colleague.

Carlisle put down his notepad and went over to the cocktail cabinet. George sat in his chair, looking dazed. He drank half his whisky before he spoke.

"There's no alternative, Inspector?"

"None that I can see."

"It's such a long time ago . . ."

"One gets used to acting a part?"

"Second nature."

George sighed deeply.

"I wish I had Angela here to help me."

"She got you into all this."

But George was unwilling to let his late wife take all the blame.

"No. I knew what I was doing. We both went into this together." He drank a little more whisky. "Well," he said philosophically, "we had twelve bloody good years. Twelve bloody good years! And it isn't much fun without her."

"Empty?"

"Bloody empty! Lesley does her best. So does Katie. But there's no motor in the machine. No tiger in the ruddy tank. People didn't come to see me; they came to see her. I knew that. I just deluded myself that they liked both of us."

He looked at Raynes.

"I'm getting sentimental."

"I understand your feelings."

"I think you do." George downed the rest of the whisky. "I like you, Inspector . . . yes, I like you. You've rumbled me; but I trust you. What should I do now? Do I have to get out of my home? Move to some miserable flat? Sell the car? Or are you going to arrest me on the spot? Is this where the handcuffs come out? Or are you saving them till later?"

Seeing that George showed every sign of co-operating, Raynes was at his most gentle.

"If you're willing to make a statement, I shall require nothing more from you at this point. You will not be taken into custody. You can remain in the house. Keep your car and your bank account. At this stage, there is no need to tell your friends – unless you want to. Only when the matter comes to court – and sentence is passed – will things change down here. I'll make it as easy for you as I can. It'll give you time to adjust. I shall have to take your passport – and other personal documents – but you can carry on your normal life for the time being. It could be many months before the case comes to court."

George appreciated the friendly way Raynes had spoken.

"You're a good egg, Inspector. I used to expect this sort of thing happening. At the beginning, I wondered when the law would catch up on us. But as the years went by, I forgot all about it. Perhaps it's as well Angela isn't here to see all her dreams shattered."

Raynes nodded his agreement.

"Tell me, Sir George . . ."

The accustomed title tripped off his tongue.

George laughed.

"Old habits die hard!"

"They certainly do. But tell me – have you at any time been approached by the real George Mallowan – Sir Ian's grand-nephew? I've been wondering whether he might have threatened you – or submitted you to blackmail?"

George looked surprised.

"Never heard from him. Never thought about him. Not once all these years. He could be dead for all I know." A crafty look came into his eyes. "If he's dead, Inspector, would it make any difference?"

"It could."

Raynes was prepared to be charitable.

"If he's dead – and is completely without any surviving family, I would be willing to leave things as they are. I shall still take a statement, but in those circumstances, I would not proceed to court."

Carlisle looked up – surprised at Raynes' rash offer.

George visibly brightened.

" . . . But I have to tell you that a gentleman who might have been George Mallowan approached the lawyer, Mr Eastwood, about two years ago – and made inquiries about Sir Ian's will. He didn't give his real name; but if he was Sir Ian's grand-nephew then the chances are that he will have some family connections. We're making further inquiries in Australia and New Zealand at this moment."

George's spirits fell.

"Bugger'll probably have half a dozen sons!"

"Probably. But in the unlikely event of his having no issue – and being certifiably dead . . ." Raynes smiled " . . . I should be willing to leave you as you are."

"That's very kind of you, Inspector. But I presume you're not being as generous as you sound?"

"No," said Raynes. "For all I know, you could be facing serious charges from the Sussex police."

George looked blank.

"What sort of serious charges?"

"Well, they're still trying to find out who killed your

wife."

George looked amazed.

"Well, it wasn't me. Good Lord! Why would I want to kill her?"

Raynes shrugged his shoulders.

"Well, you know how things are. So often, when you have a murder, it's a close friend or someone in the family who does the dirty."

"George Mallowan!" said George smiling.

"Yes," said Raynes. "But which one?"

20: *Madame Cezanne*

Raynes was determined that George Proctor should provide a full statement of his misdoings. He settled him down in the dining room with Detective-Constable Carlisle and made sure that the fullest details of the fraud were recorded and signed. Whilst the statement was being prepared, he conducted a full search of the house and took charge of George's passport – just to make sure his bird did not fly to distant lands. Fortunately, all George's private papers were kept in a large dispatch box. Raynes went through its contents with great care. It seemed to contain all he was needing. Rather than take out selected documents, it seemed better to take the entire box. He locked it into the boot of his car.

That should clip George's wings!

From Blake House, they moved on to Katie's home. Raynes made George mark the location of her house very clearly on his map. It was not far away – about four miles – on the other side of Rye.

"But," he said, "there's no point in rushing round. She doesn't get home till 5.45pm. Sometimes later."

Carlisle was exuberant with the success of their visit. The speed with which Raynes had got the confession out of George and the ease with which the statement had been drawn up and signed.

"His lawyer'll be furious when he finds out."

"I don't think he'll say a word to his lawyer. I think he'll keep his exposure very much to himself. I think he'll say as little as possible and enjoy his remaining days of freedom to the full. The massage parlours in Brighton'll be working overtime!"

"Don't you think he'll say something to Mrs Travers?"

"Would you? Once she knows that he's just a plain old commoner like the rest of us . . . And once she knows he'll be losing his house and all his money . . . she won't want to know him. She'll drop him like a brick."

Carlisle smiled.

"I think you were very kind to him. Perhaps too kind? Would you really let him off if George Mallowan turns out to be dead? And to have no family?"

"Well," said Raynes, "you've got to give people like George some hope. Otherwise he'll probably top himself. Remember! He's got that gun room. Pistols, sporting guns and such like. It wouldn't take too much to push him over the edge. And the Sussex police might be annoyed if we destroyed one of their prime suspects."

"D'you think Katie'll look after him?"

"I think Katie'll be a great help."

"But she's going to lose her horses – and the stables?"

"Yes. Katie's going to lose quite a bit. But she's a strong character. More than her father, that's for sure."

* * * *

Katie arrived home just after 6.00pm.

She seemed surprised to find the Inspector parked outside her front gate. Raynes introduced her to Detective-Constable Carlisle.

"This must be an official visit," she said.

"I'm afraid so."

"You'd better come in. My husband's away playing golf. He normally plays nine holes and then ends up in the club house for a little light refreshment. He won't be back till nearer 7.00pm."

She opened the front door.

The first thing that Raynes saw was a large picture of a horse.

"Jo'burg?" he asked.

"Near miss," she said. "Natal."

"Has he recovered from his bereavement?"

"Getting a little better. Still a bit unpredictable. I've taken him for a couple of runs. It'll take time. He's a lovely horse."

Raynes and Carlisle were ushered into a large untidy sitting room which seemed to reflect Katie's homespun personality.

"Would you like anything to drink?"

"No. We had a drink with your father."

"Oh, you've been there. Was it something to do with the murder?"

"No."

"It wasn't a social visit?"

"No."

Katie looked puzzled.

"Well, what can I do to help?"

"Just one small thing. I should like to see your marriage certificate."

"My marriage certificate?" Realization began to dawn on Katie's face. "I think I can guess what you're after."

"A very simple request," said Raynes.

Katie went off into her bedroom. There were sounds of drawers being opened and shut. A rustle of paper. Then she re-appeared with the document.

"I knew I had it somewhere."

She handed it over to the Inspector.

He ran his eyes over the certificate.

Maiden surname: Proctor.

He showed it to Carlisle then passed it back to Katie.

"That's all I wanted to know."

"You've caught up with Dad at last?"

"I'm afraid so."

Raynes explained how his suspicions had first been raised

when George had shown him the family tree. The contrast between the pedigree of his illustrious forebears and the sheer earthiness of his host. Something did not ring true.

"I know what you mean," said Katie. "Dad's a bit of a peasant."

"If it hadn't been for that family tree, I wouldn't have suspected anything."

Katie nodded.

"Pride comes before a fall."

"Very much so."

Raynes told her about his inquiries in Grasshallows and Bournemouth. His visit to the lawyer. The incriminating photograph and his discovery of how the fraud had been committed.

"I presume it was Angela's idea?"

"Who else? She had this hold over Dad – like she had over everybody else. She could get people to do what she wanted. Especially men! She had this bright idea of redirecting her boss's wealth. 'Five million!' she said. 'That's what he's worth. And with a little bit of luck it can be ours.' She sold the idea to Dad. He was a bigger sucker than most because he actually loved her. They'd been lovers on and off for years. She was longing to hit the big time and this was her way of doing it. 'Just a simple piece of impersonation,' she said, 'and it'll be a piece of cake.' Dad told me how she'd planned it. He was sent off the South Africa to play his part and when Sir Ian died, back he came. I think he was terrified he'd be found out, but Angela planned it so carefully that it went like clockwork.

"Of course, Dad had to tell me. Otherwise I wouldn't have known why he'd changed his name or got so rich. I didn't like what he was doing – but I would never have split on him. He worked so hard all his life – especially all that time in South Africa. I felt he deserved to have some good luck – however long it lasted. And it's lasted a long time. He promised me that when they settled down, he'd get me some horses – which he did. So I benefitted from the scam. That helped to keep my mouth shut."

Raynes smiled.

"Every woman has her price!"

"And every man! Look at Brackles and that blasted picture! £5000 Dad paid him; and £500 when he was in custody. Just to keep him sweet. And now he can't even hang it anywhere – because Lesley won't have it in the house!"

Raynes smiled mischievously.

"You're not thinking of hanging it in here?"

"Certainly not! I never want to see her again. She's caused our family enough trouble and scandal. And now Dad's going to pay for it – and lose everything. That's what's going to happen, isn't it?"

"Eventually," said Raynes.

He explained to Katie the arrangements he had made with her father.

Katie wept quietly.

"And I'm going to lose Jo'burg and Natal – and it's all her fault!"

Raynes wondered what he could say.

"I'm sure the person who buys the house will keep the stables – and maybe the horses. It may work out better than you think."

"It's so unfair," said Katie. "All these years, she kept reminding us that it was her idea, her brains, her money . . . We were all supposed to feel indebted to her for everything. And she was very tight with her money – despite appearances. She did very little to help us."

Katie wiped her face with her sleeve.

"Mark you, it could have been worse; but Max wouldn't take her money. He said: 'We'll paddle our own canoe.' And we have. Paid our own mortgage. Bought our own cars. Thank God we did. Otherwise, we'd be losing our home as well." She shook her head in disbelief. "The misery that woman's caused!"

"D'you think Lesley's any better?"

"No. Worse."

"Perhaps if your dad loses all his money, she won't want him?"

"That's a thought. Either way, she's in for a shock."

"She is."

"I wonder if Dad'll tell her?"

"Probably not. I think his pride'll prevent him. I got the impression that he'd try and live it up till the last minute."

"I don't blame him." She paused. "Well, I do blame him. For marrying Angela in the first place. And then for bringing a creature like Lesley down to Rye."

Katie looked at the Inspector.

"I'm sure she's up to something. That's why she brings Janet along. Not just for sex – but to distract Dad. Mrs Beaton told me that she'd caught her nosing around in the kitchen."

Raynes raised his eyebrows.

"My friend also noticed her nosing about."

"Did she?"

"Well, she saw her in one of the bedrooms. Moving a picture . . . opening a cupboard . . ."

"Well, that proves it."

"What d'you think she's looking for?"

"Work it out for yourself!"

Raynes worked it out quite quickly.

"A safe?"

"She'll never find it where she's looking."

"You think she has the key?"

"It's gone missing."

"Since when?"

"Since Angela died."

"No spare?"

"No. There was only one key – and it was in Angela's pocket the day she died."

"So if Lesley got that key . . .?"

"She had to be involved in the murder."

"I thought you blamed the anti-hunting brigade?"

"I do. They're still my No. 1 suspects."

"You may not know this – but Philip Royle was in Rye the afternoon Angela died. He was supposed to be at the dentist, having his teeth fixed."

Katie looked into the middle distance.

She took a deep breath.

"So he might have seen Dad dropping her off in town – and then followed her to the studio?"

"It's quite possible. Anger can do strange things to people."

"Especially to fanatics like that!"

Raynes wondered how much he should say.

"My friend and I went to the pub at Winchelsea . . ."

"I hope he didn't try to poison you?"

"He didn't know who we were. But we had an interesting chat with him."

Katie looked surprised that anyone could have a civilized conversation with such a miserable rat.

"Did he admit to it?"

"Not to the murder. But we got him to admit to the threatening letters and the phone calls."

"It's only a step away from murder. I think he's mentally ill. How anyone could do the things he did to an animal?"

Raynes listened carefully to what Katie said.

"So Philip Royle remains your chief suspect?"

"Yes, but Lesley comes a close second. There's one thing I didn't know when I last spoke to you. Apparently Lesley was also in Rye that afternoon."

"Are you sure?"

"Pat says that when Dad came back to the house – after dropping Angela off – she was there. They were laughing and joking. Spent the afternoon together. I think Mrs Beaton told him. So . . ."

Raynes was left to draw his own conclusions.

But he was still intrigued by the safe.

"Do you know what Angela kept in that safe? Money? Jewellery?"

Katie hesitated before she replied.

"I've no idea."

Raynes looked at her sadly.

It was a pity she had to lie.

21: *Of this Men shall know nothing*

Their conversation was interrupted by the sound of a car pulling into the driveway.

"That's Max," said Katie. "He's home earlier than usual."

The front door crashed open – then the sitting room door.

Max did not seem to be in a good mood.

"Who are you then?"

"They're the police."

"Not again! Why can't you leave us alone?"

He glared at Raynes and Carlisle. Then back at Katie.

"And where are the kids?"

"They're still at your mother's. I haven't had time to collect them."

"Well, go and get them! Now! I'll deal with these gentlemen."

Katie muttered a few apologies, put on her sheepskin coat and rushed out to the car.

"Well, gentlemen!" said Max. "Time's up. Off you go. We've had more than enough of you lot."

Raynes did not move.

"Have you been drinking?" he asked. "Drinking and driving?"

His question punctured Max's self-confidence.

"I'm under the limit."

"Are you sure?"

Max instantly grovelled.

"I'm sure you gentlemen are concerned with more serious things than drunk-driving?"

"You're quite right," said Raynes. "Fraud, theft and murder. And we've caught up with George Proctor."

"George who? Oh, Sir George?" He laughed contemptuously. "About time too. He's been living a lie for too long."

"You don't like your father-in-law?"

"He's just a dirty old man. The life he leads is an absolute disgrace. I've told Katie to keep away from him but she still goes down there. We don't let the boys go anywhere near him. We don't want them getting corrupted."

Raynes was inclined to agree with Max that George was a bad influence – especially on the young.

"And how long have you known about this masquerade?"

"Right from the beginning. Couldn't understand why Katie's dad was living in such a large house. When I first knew her, he was away in Africa. Came back loaded. New name. Fancy title. 'Come into money,' she said. 'Whose money?' I asked. I was sworn to secrecy. Made to sign a special document saying I promised to keep quiet. In return, they bought us this house."

Raynes could not let that pass.

"Your wife said you paid your own mortgage."

Max laughed.

"Did she? You don't want to believe everything Katie says. She's her dad's daughter. Very much a chip off the old block. Not quite as ugly as he is, but she's got all his wiles. I see it more, the older she gets."

Raynes raised his eyebrows.

"What was your reaction to Lady Angela's death?"

"Good riddance! Pity they didn't get both of them."

"They . . .?"

"Mr and Mrs Travers."

"You think they did it?"

"Don't you?"

"We've quite a number of suspects."

"Including old George?"

Raynes nodded.

"Don't let him off the hook. He wanted to get rid of her. I know he did. Two . . . or three months ago. Just after Christmas. Asked me if I could lay my hands on some cyanide. He said he'd asked Katie but she refused. He knew I had access to chemicals at the college, so he turned to me."

"Did you give him any?"

"Did I hell! I wasn't wanting to get involved in murder."

"What did he want the cyanide for?"

"Pigeons! I ask you. He said they'd been messing up his

stately home so he wanted to polish them off. I didn't believe him then. I certainly don't believe him now. I told him that bread soaked in whisky would be equally effective. When I heard that Angela'd snuffed it, I said to Katie: 'That's your dad!' She didn't like that. She sticks up for him. We had one hell of a row. Miserable old bugger!"

By now, Max had sat down in a large armchair. He was fairly red in the face and stank of whisky. Raynes reckoned that he must be well over the limit.

But on the other hand, he found Max refreshingly honest. He hoped Carlisle was getting all his comments down.

"So you think he got the cyanide from somewhere else and polished her off?"

Max waved a reproving finger.

"I didn't say he polished her off. Don't misquote me. That's the trouble with you policemen. You jump to conclusions. I said Mr and Mrs Travers did it. You haven't met them."

"I've met Mrs Travers."

"Well, you should meet him. He's an out-and-out crook. Knife you as soon as look at you. Gave Angela the creeps. She hated Lesley but she was frightened of Tom. Anyone would be. Bloody psychopath. I think she had some hold over him. I don't know what it was, but she managed to keep him at arm's length. Eventually, of course, they got to her. You don't escape those sort of people."

"You think George was trying to get the cyanide for them?"

"They probably put the screws on him."

This was a new theory. Raynes considered it.

"You don't think it was any of the anti-blood-sports brigade?"

"Nah."

"Your wife seems to think it was."

"She can't see further than her bloody horses! She thinks that if they're capable of injuring a horse, they wouldn't hesitate to kill a human being. She's wrong. I know some of those people. Philip Royle used to be a student at our college.

Dropped out of course!" Max laughed sadly. "Not one of nature's great achievers. Chip on his shoulder. Likes to think he's someone important. Wants to lead a crusade against the ungodly. In this case, the idle rich."

Raynes was interested to hear that Max knew Philip Royle.

"Where is this college where you work?"

"Hastings. Technical college." He smiled a bleary smile. "Pat's wife works there too. I got her the job. Nice bit of crumpet. Better not say that in front of Katie. She'd go off her head."

Raynes laughed.

"It's a small world."

"It is. But I could've told Katie that. Philip's a coward. He gets into bad company – and then he tries to show off. To be a big guy. Mark you, he paid a high price for it last time!" Max laughed. "Lost half his teeth! He'll probably think twice before he causes any more trouble . . ."

"You mean after what Angela did to him?"

Max grinned.

"Slashed him right across the face. Then kicked him in the pusser! I think she likes using her whip." Max laughed. "Katie tells me she offered Pat a bit of sado-masch in the stables, but he refused. He refused! More fool him! If I'd been given the chance, I'd have really given it to her!"

Various wicked thoughts passed through the Inspector's mind. He suppressed them. Instead, he looked at the large blank space of wall beside the door.

"I did suggest to your wife that Lady Angela's picture might go quite well in here. I gather it's not acceptable to Mrs Travers."

Max almost had a fit.

"You must be bloody joking! I wouldn't have any picture of Angela in here. Not even a photograph."

Raynes looked at him thoughtfully.

"You hated her that much?"

"She was a bitch. And that's all I'm saying."

Raynes was at his most gentle.

"What did she do to you?"

"Nothing."

It was clearly a lie.

Raynes was quite used to people not answering his questions. He was in no hurry. Katie's husband would spill the beans in due course. If there was some secret in Max's past, Raynes would wait patiently for his confession. He didn't think it would take long. Max was sweating profusely. Something was eating away at him.

Raynes kept looking at him.

The silence became oppressive.

Max eventually burst out: "It's no use sitting there all silent. I'm not going to admit anything to you – especially not with that git sitting on the sofa taking notes!"

Raynes looked across at Carlisle.

He was sorry his colleague's best efforts were not being appreciated.

He looked back at Max.

"So there is something to admit?"

"I'm not saying anything."

"Off the record?"

Carlisle put away his notepad and put his pencil into his inner pocket.

"Would you like a glass of water?"

"Water! What would I want with bloody water? You can get me a Carlsberg. It's in the fridge."

Carlisle went off into the kitchen.

Max looked at the Inspector. There were tears in his eyes.

"Why should I tell you anything?"

"Because I'm a complete stranger. You may never see me again. And anyway, I can guess what's troubling you. Lady Angela had some hold over you; like she had over Tom Travers. Blackmail? Has she been blackmailing you? Is that why you hate her so much?"

After having heard so much about Lady Angela, it seemed a fairly straightforward guess, but Max was quite amazed that the Inspector should see the problem so clearly.

"I'm afraid you're right."

"Has it been going on for some time?"

"Several years."

"And now she's gone?"

Max wiped his face with his sleeve.

"I can't tell you what a relief it's been."

Carlisle returned with the beer.

"Thanks!" Max took a quick gulp. "Ah, that's better." He looked at the Inspector. "You're a man of the world. You know the sort of things people get up to . . ."

Raynes nodded in a friendly fashion.

He had heard the same introduction a thousand times before. Normally it presaged the revelation of some grubby little sin, better taken to a priest and spewed out in a confessional.

Max stared at the floor.

"Photographs, Inspector. That's what it was. Photographs of a few lads I've known over the years. Kept them as a sort of souvenir. Plus a few letters. Nothing particularly bad. Nothing pornographic. Just poses. People having fun together. I had them hidden away, but she found them . . ."

He paused.

" . . . I don't know how, but she found them. She threatened me. Said she would tell Katie. I'd get thrown out. Divorced. Never see the kids again. Might even lose my job."

Raynes nodded sympathetically. It didn't surprise him.

He felt that Max would feel all the better for getting it out.

"So when she raised her little finger, you had to jump at her beck and call?"

"Something like that."

"And when she asked you to get the cyanide?"

Max's face was a study.

"*She* asked you to get the cyanide? It wasn't George. It was her. Who was she going to kill?"

Max shook his head.

"Mrs Travers?"

Max was silent.

"Philip Royle?"

Raynes noticed that he had scored a direct hit with his second shot. Max's face crumpled and tears ran down his cheeks.

"She wanted to kill Philip?"

Max summoned up the courage to speak.

"She hated him. He was sending her all those letters and phone calls. Katie told me."

"So she put the screws on you? Get me the poison – or else!"

Max nodded.

"Did you get it for her?"

Max laughed sarcastically.

"Yes. But it didn't work."

"Didn't work?"

"No. I got her a bottle from the chemistry lab. I'd seen it sitting there for years. Potassium cyanide. She used it – but it didn't work. She got someone to slip it into his drink. But nothing happened. She tried it on a stray cat. Put in some milk. It was useless. It was the right bottle but somebody must have poured it down the sink and filled it with something else. Probably quite a sensible idea. Dangerous leaving stuff like that on an open shelf."

Raynes' voice had a more cutting edge.

"I would say that you have been very lucky. If it had been the right stuff, you would have been guilty of murder. Of providing a substance with intent to kill."

"I know. But what could I do? She had me by the balls." He finished off his beer. "Mark you, if she had killed him, I'd have had no hesitation in shopping her to the police."

"Bit late then," said Raynes.

Max shrugged his shoulders.

"When did this happen?"

"The end of January."

"About a fortnight before the murder?"

"Yes, it would be."

"Trial run," said Carlisle quietly.

"Looks like it."

"There's one thing that worries me like hell," said Max. "Those photographs and letters. Where are they? They must be somewhere in that house. I'm terrified they'll be found."

135

"Is that why you're drinking so much? Fear?"

"Probably."

Raynes had a very clear idea where the photographs would be. In Lady Angela's safe – wherever it was. And Lesley had the key!

He looked at Max in a more kindly fashion.

"If we find them, we shall put them out of harm's way. They have no relevance to the case. There'll be no chance of Katie seeing them."

"You won't say anything to her?"

"Not a word – unless I discover that you're the murderer. If you are, the deal's off."

Raynes found himself repeating what he had said to George Proctor. Two offers of clemency in one day! He must be getting soft.

There was a sound of another car drawing up outside the house. Katie had returned. There were children's voices on the steps – in the hallway . . . The sitting room door burst open.

"Dad!"

"Your dad's not very well."

Katie rapidly shepherded the children into the kitchen.

"Are you still here?" she said. "I thought you'd have gone by now."

"We've been looking after your husband. He's had far too much to drink. The sooner he goes to bed the better."

Katie's face fell.

"Why does he do it? Why can't he stop?"

Raynes got to his feet.

"Well," he said, "we have to get back to Grasshallows. It's a four hour journey."

Max looked up, bleary-eyed.

"You're not the Sussex police?"

"No. Grasshallows."

He looked at Katie.

"Some of our happiest days . . . on the river . . ."

Raynes said: "Don't be too hard on him. It's a difficult time – for all the family. Affects different people in different ways. As for your father . . . I'm worried about all those guns. Is there anything you could do?"

Katie nodded.

"Don't worry. I'd already thought of that. I've removed all the cartridges and ammunition. All that's left are blanks."

Sensible girl! Raynes began to admire her – thinking of all the problems she had had to face, as well as the possibility of losing her beloved horses.

"Perhaps you could ask the police to withdraw his gun licence?"

"He wouldn't like that."

"There's going to be a lot of things happening your dad won't like."

"I know. But it could have been one way out. At least the two of them would have been happy together."

The suggestion was too much for Max.

He was violently sick all over the sitting room floor.

"Now look what you've done!"

Raynes and Carlisle decided it was time for a sharp exit.

22: *At the Casino*

On their return to London, they called in at Gatwick and made enquiries about the accident which Mrs Travers had reported. As Debbie had suspected, no accident had occurred that Sunday morning in March. Lesley was a liar. And if she was capable of lying about that, she was capable of lying about anything.

Whilst they were in the police station, Raynes outlined his plan for staying the night in London whilst Carlisle drove his car home. Naturally, his colleague asked him what he planned to do in the city. The Inspector said he intended to visit Mr Travers' gaming club – not with the thought of making or losing any money – but with the object of confronting Lesley and Tom.

Carlisle looked at his watch. It was already 9.50pm. He was going to be home very late; certainly after midnight. Would it not be a good thing if he made a phone call to Mrs Carlisle saying they had been delayed – and they could then visit the club together?

Raynes wondered if Carlisle was trying to cramp his style; but on mature reflection, he decided that it might be safer for them to visit the club together – on the basis that if things turned rough, four fists might be more useful than two.

They left the car at New Scotland Yard and completed the journey by taxi.

* * * *

The *Nightflyers* gaming club was on the first floor of a building in Bruton Street. The club was brightly lit and an expensive red carpet covered the stairs. The bouncer at the door was impeccably clad in evening dress with a scarlet cummerbund.

The Inspector and his colleague were asked if they were members. When it transpired that they were not, they were ushered into a small office where cards were issued. It was just a matter of filling in a form and paying a fee. As a member, Raynes was entitled to bring in one guest. Filling in the form, he described his occupation as "Undertaker" and his colleague as "Mortuary Assistant". He was issued with a purple and grey membership card and directed towards the bar, where they would receive a welcome drink on the house.

"Seems quite respectable," said Carlisle, looking round.

"Perfectly respectable," said Raynes. "As one would expect. It's what they get up to behind the scenes – the stacking of the cards, the number of times the roulette wheel lands on a given number, the gentle persuasion of the hostesses, the strong arm tactics on people who fail to pay their dues, the laundering of dirty money – such things might go on. But for sheer comfort and pleasure, it seems to have little to fault it."

The bartender was geniality itself.

"What will you have?"

"A Manhattan," said Raynes.

"And a lager and lime."

The drinks rapidly appeared.

"The Caisse is on your left as you go through the door."

"Thank you," said Raynes.

There were two main rooms, offering a wide variety of games. All but two of the tables were being used. Altogether, the Inspector estimated that seventy or eighty members were present. Not all were playing. Some were sitting chatting to their friends. Others were leaning over the tables watching the gentle brush of the cards against the green baize, the fatal roll of the silver ball around the wheel, the elegant click of dice and the rise and fall of the coloured chips. There was a quiet hum of activity, occasional laughs and a feeling of intense concentration as people watched their fortunes wax and wane.

The croupiers were all attractive girls in white blouses and short red skirts. They had sharp eyes, lithe bodies and moved their hands with speed and grace. Their movements were a pleasure to watch.

Raynes cashed £100 in chips and felt ready for anything. He and Carlisle slowly made a round of the tables to see how play was going – before they joined in. Raynes decided they should try their luck on the roulette wheel but he did so without any expectation of success.

However, almost from the first spin of the wheel, good fortune seemed to be his.

Gingerly, he placed a small bet on the black – and black it was. He let his stake accumulate – but then withdrew. He watched the ebb and flow for a few minutes before he made any further move. Once again, he stuck to the black, doubled his stake and won again.

"I'm not normally lucky," he said apologetically. "My guardian angel must be working overtime."

As he said that, he suddenly noticed Lesley at a nearby table. It was her dark red hair that caught his eye – and then the expensive gold choker around her pale neck. She was wearing a dark green velvet dress. It seemed that Lesley was helping an elderly man with a bald head and a large cigar to improve his game.

Raynes stayed at the table until his accumulated winnings had more than covered his costs. He then gave a small heap of chips to Carlisle and told him to go easy and not get carried away.

Knowing how deeply concerned his colleague usually was about money, he was aware that there was little chance of Carlisle going wild. If he lost, it didn't matter; if he won, he might pull in enough to buy his infant a set of building bricks or a plastic duck. He wondered how Mrs Carlisle would react to the thought of her husband spending the night in a gambling den!

Leaving Carlisle to fend for himself, Raynes moved to a corner of Lesley's table to see how her escort was faring. His bets did not seem all that large – but the night was young. Judging by the colour of his chips, he seemed to be loaded. His game – and hers – might last for some time.

Whilst Raynes was watching Lesley, he himself was being watched by at least two other people in the room. Bernard had cast his eye over the new members' forms and noticed Raynes' declared occupation. It was not unknown for funeral directors to come in and have a flutter, but the inclusion of his guest as "mortuary assistant" suggested that someone was taking the mickey. Bernard liked to keep his eye on such "comedians". They could bring the club into disrepute.

The other person who was watching the Inspector was Janet – Lesley's friend. She had just come back from the ladies' room and saw him standing beside her table with a very intense look on his face.

She knew she had seen him before – but she could not remember where. She went over to Bernard and asked: "Who's that man in the dark suit with the blue tie?"

Bernard looked down his nose.

"Never seen him before. He claims to be an undertaker."

"Oh, he's not an undertaker!"

"Well, find out who he is."

Janet took her time before approaching Raynes. He was suddenly aware of a woman with a very strong perfume and a dark red dress standing at his side. She was smiling nervously.

"I think we've met before."

Raynes recognized her immediately.

"You're quite right."

"I see so many people."

"And you've forgotten who I am."

"I'm afraid so."

"It was a rather unpleasant lunch party. You broke a glass."

Janet blushed with embarrassment.

"You're the policeman. Richard . . . Richard somebody?"

"Richard Raynes."

"I'm sorry I couldn't remember your name."

Raynes looked her over with a friendly eye.

"You're looking very attractive this evening. Have you been doing well at the tables?"

"The night is young. I've only just arrived."

It sounded better than saying that she was still searching for some gullible punter who might respond to her fading charms.

"And what are you doing here?" she asked.

"I've just come up from Rye – with my colleague . . ."

He nodded towards Detective-Constable Carlisle who seemed to be doing unbelievably well at the roulette table. "We've been seeing Sir George this afternoon."

"We're going down there tomorrow. At least, I think we are."

Raynes smiled.

"More of this three-in-a-bed stuff?"

Janet blushed again.

"He is a terribly naughty old man. But very athletic for his age. For him, one woman is just not enough."

"Not even Lesley?"

"I think he's probably a bit too much even for her. That's why she needs my moral – or rather, immoral – support."

"Do you like it down there?"

"It's beautiful. I'd love to live in Rye. It's just a fairytale place – all the little streets and houses. I couldn't believe it when I first saw it."

Raynes decided to tease her a little more.

"Perhaps it would be better if you married Sir George?"

"I don't think he'd be interested in me. He likes glamour. Lesley matches the house. Green and gold. She'd make a superb hostess."

Lesley heard her name being mentioned.

She looked up.

Shit! It was that police inspector she had met at George's a couple of weeks ago. The one who kept asking her awkward questions. What the hell was he doing here?

Whilst she was distracted, her partner suddenly won a whole heap of expensive chips. That would never do! Concentrate on the job in hand!

Raynes and Janet moved over to a corner seat.

"Can I get you a drink?"

"A glass of champagne."

"Two."

It would probably cost a packet but he could always claim it back on expenses.

"Are you still following up Lady Angela's murder?"

"Yes."

"Are you any nearer an arrest?"

"Well, I think we've found who supplied the cyanide."

A look of relief passed over Janet's face.

"I thought you suspected me?"

Raynes laughed.

"I still do."

"Why should I do a thing like that?"

"Well, if it was Lesley who murdered Lady Angela – and let's face it, she stands to gain most from her death – then the source of the cyanide is probably via the jewellery trade. You therefore seem the most likely choice."

"But Lesley didn't kill Angela."

"She was down in Rye the day she died."

This seemed to come as news to Janet.

"Was she? Are you sure?"

"I'm told that she and Sir George were seen together in the house – or on the steps – shortly after Lady Angela died."

Janet looked puzzled.

"I'm sure she said she was in Paris at the time. I remember her saying: 'Well, they won't get me. I've got a perfect alibi. I was out of the country'; I think it was Paris."

"I always distrust people who have perfect alibis."

"You probably distrust everyone."

"It helps. So many people tell me lies."

"I suppose they do."

Raynes' eyes twinkled.

"People who claim to have been held up in a traffic jam near Gatwick airport! 'A terrible accident! Bodies everywhere!' I think that was Lesley's excuse for being late for lunch that Sunday. And you backed her story!"

"Did I?"

Janet decided to appear coy.

"There was no accident at Gatwick that day."

"You checked?"

"Of course. I check everything. So where was Lesley that Sunday morning?"

Janet looked embarrassed.

"Well, if you promise not to say anything . . . I don't think it's important . . . she was in a pub on the outskirts of Rye, chatting up a young farmer. It's not important. She was just being . . . Lesley. I don't know why she lied."

"Presumably to keep Sir George happy? She wouldn't want him to think his future fiancée was being too generous with her charms."

Janet laughed.

"Well, he knows what she does for a living! She's always chatting up someone. I think she does it instinctively."

Raynes looked at Janet more seriously.

"Do you honestly think Lesley loves Sir George? Or is she just interested in his house, his money, his title?"

"You'll have to ask her. All I know is that she's bitterly

unhappy with Tom. She wants to get out."

"Don't you think she seems more interested in the house?"

"The house?"

"Mm. She seems to spend a lot of time peering into dark corners . . ."

"It's a beautiful house."

"Yes. But she's looking for something, isn't she?"

Janet was beginning to feel uncomfortable. The conversation had taken a nasty turn. She wondered if she should just throw back her champagne and go. But the Inspector still seemed to be entranced by her company. His eyes twinkled with warmth. Very few men treated her quite so nicely. She decided to put up with his questions a little longer. So, after some hesitation, she said: "I'm not aware of it."

"People have told me that she's been looking behind pictures, inside cupboards . . ."

"I expect she wants to know where things are."

"No," said Raynes. "That won't wash. People who do such things are looking for something. Probably a safe. Lady Angela's safe. Isn't that what she's doing?"

"I don't know."

Janet did not know what to say.

Raynes moved closer and put his hand on her arm. She appreciated the intimacy of his gesture. He looked into her eyes.

"Why not tell me the truth? You've not been invited down to Rye just to entertain a dirty old man. You're there to distract him – to occupy him whilst Lesley explores every corner of the house. If Lesley was on her own, she'd never have a moment's peace. Sir George would be right behind her. But you can kiss and caress – and for a few minutes Sir George will hardly think of Lesley." He smiled. "Isn't that so?"

There was very little Janet could say.

Raynes took her silence as confirmation that what he was saying was true. He had no doubt it was.

"So what's in that safe? Jewellery? Money? Valuable

144

papers?"

Janet's eyes moved rapidly away from Raynes' face.

There was someone behind him.

"Oh, Lesley?"

Janet's face crumpled with anxiety.

What had she overheard?

"Mr Raynes," said a cold voice, "if you want to ask questions, you should ask me."

Raynes turned. Even though he knew he was facing a very angry woman, he continued to exude charm and warmth.

"If you're not too busy, I will."

23: *Bar at the Folies Bergere*

Lesley Travers was not having a good evening. Her partner was not as dumb as she had thought. He had been very responsive to her charms, but when it came to placing his chips, he had shown himself quite independently-minded. Although she had thought he had drunk enough to reduce his powers of concentration, he still appeared capable of placing his bets wisely – and winning. At the present moment, he seemed likely to go on winning for the rest of the evening. She was wasting her time.

Lesley herself had lost interest in the game. She was wondering what Raynes was doing at the club. What was he saying to Janet? And, more significantly, what was she saying to him? She uttered her apologies and left the table – only to hear the word "safe". She had arrived not a moment too soon.

She asked Janet to take her place.

Then she turned on Raynes:

"What are you doing here? You're not a member."

"I am now."

"Have you come here to cause trouble?"

Raynes noted that Carlisle had turned away from his game and was watching them. He also noticed that a tall, bald-headed man who looked like King Edward VII was staring at him in a hostile manner.

"No. I just came along to keep you acquainted with our investigations into the death of Lady Angela."

"You don't belong to the Sussex police."

"We're approaching it from a different angle."

The bald-headed man intervened.

"Are you needing help, Ma'am? Would you like me to call the bouncers?"

"No. I can handle this."

"Is there somewhere else we can talk?"

"The bar?"

"All right. The bar."

Lesley swept across the room in her beautiful green velvet dress. Raynes followed her.

Carlisle wondered if he should follow; but his game was still going so well that he was loath to leave it.

Lesley entered the bar.

"Put on some music, Sam."

"Yes, Ma'am."

"And bring me a Cinzano."

"Yes, Ma'am."

Raynes noted that he was not being offered a drink.

"Well," she said, sitting down in a red leather chesterfield. "What are you here for?"

"I think you heard me talking to Janet about safes. It seems to me that one of the chief attractions of Sir George's house is a certain safe. You have been looking for it, but cannot find it."

Lesley's face was inscrutable.

"I believe you also have the key?"

"I do not have the key."

The answer flashed back.

"But you concede there is a safe?"

"I concede nothing."

Her drink arrived.

"Thank you, Sam."

"What I want to know is what is in the safe?"

"Nothing to do with you!"

Raynes smiled.

"It's certainly nothing to do with me – but you have taken a great deal of time and effort trying to find it. I even suspect that's one of the reasons why you've been taking Janet down to Rye. So that she can distract Sir George whilst you're searching the house room by room."

"Did she say that?"

"No. But it's easy to guess. Why else would you be going down to Rye?"

Lesley looked surprised at his question.

"Obviously to see George. After all he is my fiancé. We shall be getting married, Inspector. My divorce is only a matter of days away."

Raynes immediately registered a lie.

He looked her squarely in the eye.

"Can you tell me honestly that you love George?"

"Of course I do. He's sweet."

Another lie.

"You wouldn't be marrying him for his money or his title?"

"That's what Brackles thinks. And you know what I think about Brackles!"

She spat out the words with contempt.

"He thinks you're just an unscrupulous little gold-digger."

"He's just jealous!" Lesley Travers was looking cold and angry. "He's entitled to his opinion – his jaundiced opinion. And I am perfectly free to marry George."

"When the divorce comes through!"

Lesley downed the rest of her drink.

"Now perhaps you will go?"

Bernard put his head round the door.

"Are you still all right?"

"He's just going,"

"I think," said Raynes, "that before I go, you might like to hear one further piece of information which affects you personally."

Lesley looked unmoved.

"The reason why I asked you whether you were intending to marry Sir George for love – or for his money . . . or for his title, was because you could be making a grave mistake." He paused before dropping his bombshell. "You see. . . Sir George is *not* Sir George."

Lesley looked confused.

"I'm afraid my investigations into this case come from a different angle. I am involved in a fraud case concerning the will of the late Sir Ian Mallowan – the fourth baronet – who once lived in Grasshallows. As you know, Sir George claimed to be his grand-nephew. He inherited the estate. You've seen his family tree."

Lesley nodded.

"He's very proud of it."

"Indeed. But I'm afraid it's proved his downfall. Sir George is not Sir Ian's grand-nephew. He's an impostor. His name is George Proctor."

An unpleasant man with dark eyes, black greasy hair and a sallow face, crossed the bar.

"Bernard tells me you're having trouble with this bloke."

"No. I'm all right."

"If he's causing any trouble, Emile's ready to throw him out."

"No. Everything's under control."

She obviously wanted to hear the rest of the story.

"Who is he? Bernard says he's some sort of policeman."

"Inspector Raynes. He's a friend of Brackles."

"Brackles?"

"I met him down in Rye a few weeks ago."

Tom Travers looked at Raynes with undisguised hatred. He hated policemen. He didn't like them in his club. It would give him infinite pleasure to see Emile boot him out.

"Could you please leave us?"

"He's got his chum on the roulette table, making a heap."

Raynes was glad to hear Carlisle was doing well. He'd probably lose most of it before the night was over. Raynes took his remaining chips out of his pocket and piled them on the table.

"If I'm about to leave, perhaps you would be kind enough to cash these for me?" Raynes reckoned that he'd made about

£150 from his brief time at the table.

"Change them yourself!"

Tom turned on his heel and walked back to his office. Once there, he re-directed the closed circuit TV to the bar and watched Raynes and Lesley continuing their conversation. He didn't trust the policeman one inch. If he stayed much longer at the club, he'd be the one needing an undertaker.

Back in the bar, Lesley was trying to adjust to what Raynes had just told her.

"You're not having me on?"

"No. I've been up to my neck in the case since I last saw you. I saw Sir George this afternoon and broke it to him."

"What's he feeling?"

"Devastated, naturally. After twelve years, he thought he'd got away with it. But charges will have to be preferred and George will have to give up the estate. Probably in a few months' time."

A flicker of relief passed over Lesley's face.

Raynes smiled.

"Still time for you to find that safe!"

"Don't be ridiculous! I'm not looking for anything."

"Whether you are or not, I fear your marriage prospects in Rye have been greatly reduced. George may be moving to a council house. More likely, he'll be going to jail."

Lesley sighed deeply.

"Can you explain to me exactly how you have come to this conclusion?"

"Certainly."

Raynes explained briefly and simply the steps he had taken to uncover the fraud. His visit to Bournemouth. The contents of the will. The steps George had taken to impersonate the grand-nephew.

"Of course," he said, "it was Angela's idea. She arranged the whole thing. She was Sir Ian's housekeeper – Angela Anderson. She married George in December 1977. That was part of the deal. His daughter, Katie, knew all about it. That's why she wouldn't have anything to do with her. She was frightened Angela would get her dad into trouble. Which she

149

has. But, fortunately for Angela, she won't have to face the music. Whoever killed her spared her that."

Lesley was not sure she blamed Angela entirely.

"But," she said, "this was your doing! If you hadn't come to lunch that Sunday, nothing would have changed, would it? If you hadn't seen that family tree . . . If you hadn't made enquiries . . . everything would have been all right?"

"I have reason to believe that the real grand-nephew has been over from New Zealand. I'm hoping to make contact with him so that he can inherit what's due to him. At least, what's left."

"Oh, stuff him!" said Lesley. "It's you we have to thank for all our misery! For mucking things up. You and your friend, Brackles!"

"I wouldn't blame him."

"I blame him for lots of things! He's a piss-artist in every sense of the word. It'd have been much better if he'd drunk that brandy – not Angela. Then we wouldn't be in this fucking mess!"

Raynes raised his eyebrows.

"Second time lucky?"

"You bet!"

From the bitter tone of her voice, it was clear that she meant it. Brackles had better watch out.

"It seems such a shame . . ." said Raynes, twisting the knife a little further, " . . . such a shame that after all these years of storing your brandy, you should dispense with so faithful a servant."

Lesley snapped.

"That's nothing to do with us! Don't you ever say it has!"

"Could leave a nasty dent in your profits!" Raynes added. "You might even lose your licence."

"That brandy has got nothing to do with us."

Her protestations sounded a little thin.

"It's no use denying it," said Raynes. "Someone who knows your husband told me he had seen him loading up boxloads of the stuff down in Rye and shipping it back to London. Brackles has said nothing to me, but it's common knowledge down in Rye. They described your husband as a slimy little crook. Now I've seen him, I think I know why."

Lesley very much wanted to see the back of the Inspector. She needed time on her own to mull over all the things he had told her – and to reshape her plans. She was determined to leave Tom, but if George was for the high jump, there was no way she could even think of marriage. But she still had to find that safe. And she had to protect the club against the charges of smuggling. It seemed unlikely that Raynes would do her any favours. He knew she was a bitch. It was no use offering him her body. It was too late to think of blackmail.

Lesley looked at the Inspector hopefully.

"Can we do a deal?"

Raynes was surprised at her sudden change of direction. He must have touched a raw nerve. A very raw nerve indeed.

"What did you have in mind?"

"I help you. You help me. I know you've got most of the cards in your hand. You've smashed up my wedding plans. But perhaps I can rescue something from the shipwreck."

Raynes said: "Try me!"

He was wondering what she was thinking of offering him. A night of passion – after which he might end up with a bullet in his brain? Even now, he would be lucky to leave the club without getting a stiletto in his back.

Lesley looked at him appealingly.

"Forget about the brandy . . . please!"

Raynes was honest with her.

"The brandy's not my baby. It's the Sussex police who are dealing with that. There's no reason why I should say anything to them. But if they catch up with you, it won't be because of me – or Brackles."

(He must try to protect Brackles.)

Lesley looked suitably grateful.

But there was more.

"You're perfectly right. There is a safe – somewhere in George's house. I've been looking for it for weeks. I've looked everywhere. I'm going to keep looking. It doesn't have a key. Whoever told you that is leading you up the garden path. It has a combination lock. I have the number. I am willing to give you that number." She leant forward. "Whoever finds the safe – and gets into it first – shows the other one what's in it. There's something in it I'm after. That's what I want. You can have the rest. But Angela kept something in that safe which I must have."

Raynes looked at her.

"The price of your divorce?"

Lesley looked at him with amazement.

"You are a remarkable policeman!"

"So they say."

Lesley looked a little happier.

"Will you do that?"

The Inspector reasoned that he had nothing to lose from the deal – and much to gain. Access to the safe as and when she found it.

He smiled cheerfully.

"I will – on two conditions. One – that you do not turn out to be the person who killed Lady Angela. In that case, all deals are off. Secondly, that my colleague and I get out of this place alive with all our winnings intact."

Lesley laughed.

"Oh, don't be ridiculous! No one'll hurt you."

Raynes shrugged his shoulders.

"Having seen what sort of person your husband is, I'm quite sure he's capable of murder."

Lesley understood his anxiety. Seeing Tom Travers for the first time could be a little unnerving.

"I'll come down to the door with you. You'll be perfectly safe."

"Those are my conditions," said Raynes.

"We are agreed then?"

They shook hands on the deal.

Tom Travers was still watching them on his closed circuit TV. He noticed the smiles and the handshake. There was a sour look on his face. He turned to Bernard who was watching over his shoulder.

"What's she doing now?"

"She's pulling off some deal – to keep the bastard quiet."

"I don't trust her one inch."

"She's saved your skin plenty of times. You should be grateful."

"She's as treacherous as hell."

"Give her the benefit of the doubt. The sooner we get that sod out of the club the better."

Back in the bar, Lesley was giving Raynes the combination number of the safe: 718364. He repeated it twice.

"And remember! If you find it first, you let me see everything – and take the documents I need."

"I have made a promise," said Raynes, "and for once I'll keep it."

"You'd better. Or I'll put Tom on to you!"

Raynes winced.

"Spare me!" he said. "He's probably watching all of this."

"I'm sure he is – and he's going to be very jealous."

Raynes looked at his watch.

"So you'll be going down to Rye today?"

"Yes, I shall. I'll keep going till I find that safe."

"And you won't say anything to George?"

"Not until he says something to me."

Raynes chuckled mischievously.

"Well, at least you won't have to worry about that blasted picture."

"I think Brackles should keep it as a personal souvenir."

Carlisle burst through the door into the bar. He looked excited and slightly flushed.

"Ah, you're still here! I thought you might have gone."

"No. I'm chatting up this charming night club queen." He looked at Lesley in a more friendly fashion. "This is my colleague, Detective-Constable Carlisle. He's never been in a gaming club before. I think he's had beginner's luck."

Raynes pointed to the pile of chips lying on the table.

"You might as well cash these while you're at it."

Lesley stayed with them whilst Carlisle collected his winnings and escorted them down the steps. At the entrance, she gave the Inspector a cool, fond kiss.

"Thank you," she said. "You've been a great help."

Raynes hailed a passing taxi. Once inside, he breathed a sigh of relief.

"I'm glad I'm out of there."

"Were you frightened?"

"Just a little," Raynes conceded. "Her husband's been watching us all evening. He's a complete psychopath. I remember his face. I'm sure I've met him before. A brutal murder in South London. Bermondsey, I think. But he got off. Dangerous swine. He'd shove a knife in you as soon as look at you."

He turned to Carlisle.

"So how much have we made?"

Carlisle counted the notes again.

"£1800 . . . £1850. And we had a float of . . .?"

"£100. Plus the membership. I think you're due me £150."

"Gosh," said Carlisle, "£1700 for nothing!"

Raynes smiled.

"But how are you going to explain it to your wife? She thinks you were on police business. How are you going to explain that you spent the whole night in a gaming club? I think she might have something to say about that!"

24: *Voice of evening*

When the Inspector returned to Grasshallows, he spent an interesting two hours examining the contents of George Proctor's dispatch box. He was pleased to note that Angela and her husband had kept all the documents relating to their previous lives, so that from birth certificates, wedding schedules and divorce papers, he was able to reconstruct their history quite easily.

Angela had been born in west London – Hammersmith – in 1947. She had been born Angela White, married in Peterborough in July 1968 and divorced in December 1972 – as Carlisle had already discovered. Her second marriage was to George Mallowan in Acapulco five years later.

George was born and brought up in Peterborough. He was

now fifty-nine. He had been married twice and it seemed that Katie must have been a child of George's first marriage. Both his previous unions had ended in divorce – adultery being the grounds on each occasion.

Raynes was delighted to see a copy of the birth certificate of the real George Mallowan, which Angela had obtained from Somerset House. It seemed that he had also been born in London – in Hampstead – in April 1939 which would make him nine years younger than the impostor.

At the time of Sir Ian's death, the real George would have been thirty-seven whilst his impersonator would have been forty-seven. The difference might not have been all that obvious to Mr Eastwood.

Raynes cast his eyes over the details once more – and stopped suddenly. How interesting! He thought about it for several minutes. It could be a coincidence. On the other hand, it might not. He made a mental note to contact Mr Eastwood again in the near future.

Carlisle, having recovered from his recent burst of good fortune, was busy getting his notes typed and photocopied. Soon he was able to give a copy to Raynes who went through them, searching for points he might have missed.

"The Sussex police seem quite interested in Katie. George says they've questioned her several times. And her husband – who has no alibi."

Raynes underlined the point in red biro.

He read on.

"George didn't say much, did he?"

"You did most of the talking."

"Smashed him into little pieces!"

"Well, he made up for it in his statement. Couldn't have been more co-operative. Signed it all like a lamb."

"And Katie confirmed it. That's useful."

"She told us quite a few lies."

Raynes skimmed through the second interview.

"Especially about her house. Did they pay the mortgage or not? Was it a gift? A bribe to keep their mouths shut? I rather think it was the latter, but she didn't like to admit it. Tried to put us off the scent."

"It was quite an expensive house. But not very well looked after."

"An absolute tip."

Raynes read through the script more carefully.

"That's what I was looking for. The bit about the key."

"The key to the safe?"

"Yes. Katie claimed that it went missing after the murder."

"Didn't she say that the person who took the key did the murder?"

"Yes, she did. But that was a blind."

"Was it?"

"Lesley tells me it has a combination lock. She even gave me the number." He paused. "Let me get this right. 718364."

Carlisle promptly wrote the number down.

"Why did she tell you that?"

"Because she loves me!" Raynes laughed. "No," he said, "it's not that. She did a deal with me. I was to keep quiet about the brandy. No prosecution. At least, not from this end. In return, we pool forces on the safe. We both look for it. Whoever finds it will show the contents to the other. There's something in that safe which she wants rather badly. She's determined to get it. Thinks that if I get in on the act, we shall find it more quickly. Hence her generosity in giving me the number."

"I see," said Carlisle. "So you weren't just having an idle chat?"

"Good heavens, no!" said Raynes. "It was high politics with her husband, Tom, watching my every move. I alerted her to Sir George's fallen state. He probably won't tell her. But it may suit her to maintain the fiction. She was going down to see him this afternoon. Janet told me."

"So the search goes on?"

Raynes returned to Carlisle's notes.

"Katie said: 'She'll never find it where she's looking'."

"Suggests it's not in the house?"

Raynes smiled broadly.

"That's the most helpful thing you've said all week."

Carlisle looked surprised at the unexpected compliment.

"Obviously," said Raynes, "the safe is in the stables!"

"The stables?"

"Yes. Lesley'd never think of looking there. She'll comb through every room in the house – where she would expect to find it. But Angela doesn't trust anyone. She had her stable block specially built. That's her world. A world where she feels most at home. She loves her horses. It'll be hidden down there. Katie must have seen it. She's another horsey lady. That's where it'll be."

He smiled.

"We're getting there."

"Are we?"

"I think so."

Carlisle returned to his notes.

"What do we do about Max?"

"Place question marks all the way through!"

Which he promptly did. Various words like "cyanide" were underlined and crosses placed against all references to Angela.

"It'll be interesting to see whether those photographs appear in the safe."

"I can't imagine where else they'd be."

Raynes read on.

"Angela was frightened of Tom."

"So were you."

"Yes – and I can see why. Max thought she had a hold over him."

Raynes looked up. "That could be it. Angela had some information about Mr Travers; something that could put him away for a long time. Tom knows that. He demands the stuff back. Angela refuses. Lesley is sent down to Rye to get her claws into Sir George. In the process, she is expected to dig up the dirt."

"But she doesn't find it."

"No. So Tom threatens Angela. Either you hand it over or I bump you off. Angela refuses to play ball. Tom murders her . . ."

"Making sure he involves Brackles?"

157

"Whom he also hates. They both hate Brackles. I don't know why. He seems quite harmless to me." He sighed deeply. "But Tom still needs to recover the stuff. Lesley continues her forlorn search, getting steadily more desperate. D'you know what she said to me last night? She said that finding it is the price of her divorce. If she gets the stuff out of the safe, she can escape from Tom. No wonder she's so desperate."

"So the safe becomes the key to all this?"

"It's absolutely vital that I get into it before anyone else."

Carlisle could see that the Inspector was concentrating his mind on this one thing. He asked the obvious question.

"When were you thinking of going?"

"Tonight," he said. "I cannot afford to wait a moment longer."

25: *The Nightmare*

It was dark. Very dark. Raynes was a "townie". He was used to the city lights. He had almost forgotten how dark the countryside could be at night. But he had with him a large torch – and several batteries in his coat pocket.

His car had been left in a lay-by on the main road about half a mile away from Sir George's house. He had found the gates wide open and had walked round the side of the house, keeping to the shadows and making sure he avoided the noisy gravel.

The stables were down a narrow lane at the back of the house. In daylight, it had not seemed all that far. But in the darkness, the track seemed long and treacherous – rutted and uneven. He used his torch all the way in case he slipped and broke his ankle.

Eventually he reached the stables. The small, concrete yard and the two rows of loose-boxes with their bright green doors. He felt that the horses were aware of his presence. There were sounds of snorting and shifting, a shaking of heads and the nervous clip of horseshoes against the concrete floors. He had the strange feeling that they were following his movements – as he was listening to theirs. Up be that moment, he had thought of horses as inanimate objects, but now he was very conscious of them being alive – and alert. He realized that they were large, powerful creatures. He must be careful not to get kicked or hurt.

Raynes walked across the stableyard, flashing his torch to left and right. This was not going to be as easy as he had thought.

He did a complete tour of the two blocks, noting the fresh white paint. Apart from the ventilating bricks, there was nothing to suggest any hidden box or door.

At the far end of the loose-boxes there were locked store rooms. He took out his set of keys and a piece of tough plastic. Within a minute or two, he was into the tack room – with all the saddles, bridles, ropes and hard hats. The other room contained wooden chests filled with sacks of barley, coarse mix, HorseHage and pony nuts. There were buckets, bales of hay and straw; bags of sand and wood shavings; forks and shovels and a couple of wheelbarrows for mucking out. It was all very tidy and well organized. But no sign of any safe. Raynes went out and locked the store room doors behind him.

It was now that he had to face the unpleasant fact that if the safe was hidden in the stables, it must be hidden in one of the loose-boxes. It was a natural hiding place. The horses provided a constant guard and very few people would dare to venture into a narrow, confined space occupied by a large and possibly hostile beast. If the need to find the safe had not been so compelling, he would not even have dreamt of doing it.

But he was determined to to follow up his hunch. His instincts told him that if the thing was anywhere, it would be in Natal's box. That was Angela's favourite horse. But Katie had told him that Natal was restless and temperamental. He could be vicious.

Raynes felt that it might be foolhardy to tackle Natal first. He decided to have a trial run with Durban – a horse with a good nature who didn't try to fight his rider. Raynes hoped he would give him a friendly welcome.

He unlocked the padlock on the green door.

A large inquisitive head immediately popped out.

"Hello, Durban," said Raynes. "Good boy!"

For all he knew, it might be a gelding just as much as a mare. He patted the horse's neck as he had seen Katie pat him.

He pulled the lower flap open a fraction and put his foot behind it in case the horse tried to push his way out. But Durban retreated.

"More frightened of me than I am of him," said Raynes to himself.

He realized that it might have been diplomatic to have brought with him a bucketload of feed. That might have distracted him.

Durban stepped back even further as Raynes slipped into his box and switched on his torch.

Amongst the bedding straw, there were two sizeable heaps of dung. There was a smell of urine – but it was by no means overpowering. He bolted the lower door behind him and walked across the straw to look at the metal rack on the further wall which contained a supply of hay for Durban's midnight snack.

Raynes shone his torch around the ceiling, walls and floor. There was nothing that looked like a safe. No door, no metal knob, no picture or appliance that might hide anything. The walls were clean and bare. His observations were constantly interrupted by Durban who swung his great head back and forward as he sniffed at the Inspector's coat and tried to lick his face.

Now and again, he seemed about to deliver a hefty blow, but Raynes kept his hand on Durban's neck and patted him reassuringly. It seemed to work. The animal remained friendly. But Natal might be a different prospect.

He moved towards the door and let himself out.

Before he tackled Angela's horse, he returned to the store-room and poured some pony nuts into a bucket. He thought it might help.

He went over to Natal's loose-box, but even before he shot a bolt, he was conscious of an atmosphere.

Natal was in a restless state. As he put his hand on the lower door, the horse's head shot out and there was a very formidable snort and a distinct flash of teeth. Raynes rattled the bucket. The horse could smell the food. He offered a small handful which was greedily seized.

Raynes flashed his torch and Natal, like Durban, immediately recoiled. Raynes stepped forward and put the bucket on the ground. The smell in this box was stronger and the floor seemed to be quite wet.

Natal was busily exploring the bucket as the Inspector turned his attention to the walls.

At first sight, they seemed as bare as those in Durban's box – and his heart sank. All that journey for nothing! But as he flipped at the hay in the rack, he saw a flash of green behind it. A small green steel door was flush with the wall behind the feeding rack. The horse could not reach it – and for most of the time, it would be effectively hidden behind the hay.

Raynes smiled broadly.

His instincts had proved correct. He went over to the far wall and reached up to the small steel door. Before he could even touch it, he was flung violently sideways. Natal had now finished his feed and turned to deal with the interloper. The shoulder of the horse had caught his shoulder – and he slipped on a heap of brown dung. His torch went out. Natal bent over him – vengefully.

He rose slowly to his feet.

One of his hands seemed to be covered in soft, squelchy muck.

"Easy, Natal. Go easy. Not so rough! Good boy!"

He bent down to pick up his torch. It would not work. Perhaps the bulb had been broken. Then he noticed that the end had come off the torch and two of the batteries had fallen out. He found the spring cap on the floor – but not the batteries. He put his clean left hand into his right hand pocket – an awkward manoeuvre – to pull out a couple of new batteries.

He was conscious that the horse had moved away and was now beside the door. He was glad of a few moments respite before he returned to tackle the safe.

Suddenly, the lights in the loose-box snapped on. A powerful fluorescent strip light. Raynes was dazzled. But only for a few seconds.

There in the doorway was a shadowy figure holding a double-barrelled shot gun with two black holes of cold steel pointing at his head.

"Put your hands up! And come out slowly. If you make a false move, I'll blast your head off!"

26: *The Scream*

Raynes was suddenly conscious of his vulnerability. He had no weapon. He had been caught on private property without a search warrant. He was trespassing. He had opened a lockfast building. And the man with the gun had the law on his side.

He was aware that he must look a ridiculous sight. His coat was covered with straw – and, under the glare of the bright light, he could see that his right hand and the arm of his coat were smeared with excrement. There was no way of wiping it off. He had been told to put up his hands. He would have to come out, looking a complete mess.

He didn't think that the man – whoever he was – would shoot. The bullet might ricochet off the walls and hit Angela's horse. Still, one could not be sure. Firearms were a dangerous game. One false move and anything could happen.

He put up his arms.

Not all that far – but enough to show willing.

"Come out of the stable."

The figure with the gun moved out further into the yard, still keeping him covered.

"Shut the lower door . . . and bolt it."

Raynes did what he was told.

He had little option.

But as he shot the bolt back into place, he realized who the man was. Pat . . . Pat Baxter. Angela's groom. The reluctant lover. The affectionate father whose wife and daughter were having a picture painted for his birthday. On April 28th. The man who didn't like talking to policemen.

Raynes turned round to face his captor.

He was about to remind him of their previous meeting, but Pat didn't seem to be in the mood for conversation.

The shotgun waved to the right.

"Move."

Raynes decided to say nothing. If he was taken to the police station, he was sure he would be able to talk himself out of it. At least, he would be amongst friends. It was out here, in the middle of the night, that nasty things could happen. A shot could be fired. A body disposed of. And the only person who knew where he was, was two hundred miles away. By the time he was reported missing, all trace of his existence could have been swept away. A small pool of blood in the middle of nowhere. No one would even hear the shot.

Raynes reflected that there was nothing else for it but to co-operate.

"Turn left!"

It seemed that they were making their way back to the house. What would George say? Would he relish this delicious moment of *schadenfreude*? Or would he see this as an opportunity for revenge? For the humiliation he had suffered on Tuesday afternoon?

Raynes could not ignore the fact that he was in the hands of murderers. One or more of these people had killed Lady Angela. If they knew all that he now knew, it would be in their best interests to get rid of him – quickly and quietly. It seemed that Pat had mistaken him for one of the anti-hunting fraternity It was as well to keep up that fiction as long as possible.

Raynes stumbled up the lane.

Without the help of a torch, it was not easy. He fell twice. On the second occasion, he managed to "lose" the ring of keys which had been in his pocket. He still had the piece of plastic, but that could be disposed of later.

They crossed the gravel to the main front door of George's country home.

"Ring the bell!"

The shotgun continued to point ominously at his groin.

Raynes rang the bell.

There was a long, depressing wait. He was ordered to ring the bell again. There were no lights, no sounds from within the building; but suddenly an upper window opened with a clatter.

"Yes? What is it?"

"I've caught one of those bastards. Caught him in the act. He'd broken into the stables. He was interfering with Natal."

An amusing picture came into Raynes' mind.

He suppressed it.

If Pat had hoped to stimulate George's interest by mentioning Angela's favourite horse, he failed. George was in a bad mood. Not surprisingly . . . for it was now 2.00am and he had probably been drinking a prodigious amount of whisky before he went to bed.

George was brief and to the point.

"Have you got a gun?"

"Of course."

"Well, shoot him! Dump the body on the Marsh."

The advice seemed unnecessarily extreme. Even to Pat.

"You said you wanted the next one handed over to the police. All you have to do is phone."

Raynes was heartened by the obvious disagreement. He wondered if this was the moment to cut and run. Could he be sure that if Pat fired, he would miss? No, he couldn't. The groom was a countryman – born and brought up in Norfolk, he had said. He'd probably been shooting ducks and pheasants all his life. Even though it was a dark night, he might still hit him. Better to wait for the police.

There was a further silence.

George had gone to phone.

Pat looked at the Inspector more closely. The face was vaguely familiar but he couldn't place it. Perhaps he had seen him during the fiasco on Boxing Day? He felt an intense hatred for those who had caused all the mayhem. He was just thankful that he had caught this rat before he could do any damage to the horses.

George re-appeared at the upstairs window.

"They'll be here in ten minutes."

He slammed down the window.

Raynes breathed a quiet sigh of relief.

At least there would be no embarrassing confrontation.

Pat had clearly guessed that Raynes was thinking of escape. He ordered him to lie flat on the front door step. It was cold and humiliating – but it seemed that he would survive.

The groom maintained his distance – never closer than ten feet – ready to shoot at the slightest false move.

Raynes edged the piece of toughened plastic out of his right-hand coat pocket and left it on the doorstep. He coughed loudly to cover his manoeuvre.

It was a long ten minutes.

More like half an hour.

They heard the car coming along the road, the brakes being applied at the entrance gates – then the approaching crunch of gravel. Headlights lit up both captor and victim.

Two policemen got out of the car.

"What've we got here?"

"One of those anti-hunt campaigners!" said Pat in a tone of utter disgust. "I caught him in the stables. He was planning mischief against her ladyship's horse."

Raynes stood up.

The policeman looked him over.

"Looks as if he's been rolling in shit. Smells like it too."

"What's your name?" asked the other policeman.

Raynes said nothing.

"Playing hard to get? Don't worry! We'll get him talking. We have ways of dealing with people like you."

Raynes had heard these macho claims many times before. He had every intention of speaking – but not whilst Pat was standing so close – with a loaded gun.

The gun also attracted the attention of the police.

"Have you got a licence for that gun?"

"Of course."

Raynes immediately registered that Pat was lying.

Probably it was one of George's guns – but if it wasn't, Pat could be in trouble.

Pat was more interested in blackening the Inspector's reputation by accusing him of other crimes.

"It's probably him who came here the other night and sprayed paint all over the stables. You could charge him with that as well as molesting the horses."

Raynes remembered the fresh white paint on the walls of the stables. Obviously, Philip Royle and his gang had already attacked them. Pat had taken precautions and he – Raynes – had fallen into the trap. There must have been some alarm system which he had triggered off.

The first policeman was speaking:

"What exactly was he doing to the horses?"

"I think he was in the process of letting them out. He'd got into one loose-box – but the horse was being a bit frisky. I think he knocked him down. But if he'd let him out, there's no saying what would have happened. He could have broken a leg. Had to be put down. They're expensive animals – Thoroughbreds. They don't come cheap."

The policeman was not particularly interested in the horses. They'd got the suspect; it was for someone else to prefer charges. He asked his colleague to handcuff Raynes and put him in the back of the car. He didn't exactly relish the smell of horse dung which would doubtless linger long after Raynes had been deposited at the police station.

Raynes heard his final words to the groom.

"I'd be careful if I were you, mate. Threatening people with guns. Could be a nasty accident. Then you'd be sorry."

There was a sound of the gun's breech mechanism being opened.

"It's not loaded!"

Raynes gritted his teeth in anger.

Hell's teeth! He could have escaped!

27: *The Escape Ladder*

Half an hour later, Raynes was sitting in a very soulless waiting room. He reflected that a similar room in Grasshallows had pictures and curtains; but here there was only blue lino and grey plastic chairs. A policeman sat with him, trying to make friendly conversation. He soon gave up.

After another long wait, he was escorted into an interview room. A sergeant was seated at the other side of a broad, black table, picking his nose.

"Name?"

"Raynes. Richard Raynes."

"Date of birth?"

The Inspector gave him the information he wanted.

"Address?"

"5 Greenway Gardens, Grasshallows."

"You're not a local?"

"No."

"I thought they said you were a member of the local anti-hunt campaign?"

"They may have said that; but I'm not."

The sergeant looked mildly curious.

"Well, what are you doing down here?"

"I've been accused of molesting a horse."

The sergeant looked down at his notes.

"It doesn't say that here! It says: 'breaking and entering a lockfast property, thereby endangering and putting at risk livestock belonging to the owner of the said property, Sir George Mallowan . . .'"

Raynes was glad to hear that the molesting of horses was not contained on the charge sheet. Fisting a pony was not an item which he wished to see on his C.V.

"I certainly entered the stables, but I did not break in," Raynes lied happily. "Nor did I put at risk any of the animals. When I went into the loose-box, I bolted the door behind me."

"So you admit you were in the stables?"

"I do."

"And what right had you to be in those stables?"

Raynes smiled disarmingly.

"I happen to be a friend of Sir George. I had lunch with him two or three weeks ago. I was shown over the stables by his daughter, Katie. Being in the district again, I naturally decided to call on Sir George and renew my acquaintance with his stud."

The sergeant looked at Raynes through half-closed eyes.

What a load of balls!

"Mr Baxter says that you were probably one of those who sprayed the walls of the stables with coloured paint."

Raynes shook his head.

"I didn't."

"He also says you were carrying a torch."

"I was – and the horse knocked it out of my hand. It also knocked me on to the floor. Hence the . . ." He indicated his hand and arm still plastered with smears of dried excrement.

The sergeant smiled.

"Well, you deserved that! But it still doesn't explain what you were doing on someone else's property at that hour of night."

Raynes was at his most convincing.

"I came down from Grasshallows to see Sir George. I set off rather later than I intended and I got lost in all these country lanes. Things look so much different in daylight. I couldn't find the house. When I got there, everything was dark and locked up. I rang the door bell – several times. I reckoned Sir George must be asleep. He does drink rather heavily – as you probably know. Well, I remembered that his daughter, Katie, had told me that they kept a spare key to the house down at the stables. So I thought perhaps if I could get the key I could let myself in. As a family friend, I'm sure Sir George wouldn't have minded . . ."

It all sounded eminently plausible.

The sergeant began to look at him with a little more respect.

"So you're a friend of Sir George?"

"Yes."

"Is that a professional relationship – or personal?"

"A bit of both."

The sergeant seemed uncertain as to what he should do next. He looked at the few objects which had been taken out of Raynes' pockets and were now in a plastic bag; a set of car keys and several batteries. Why should Mr Raynes be carrying a torch and so many batteries if he was expecting to be put up by Sir George?

Raynes could guess what he was thinking.

The sergeant looked up.

"Are these your car keys?"

"Yes."

"And where is your car?"

"In a lay-by on the A259 just outside East Guldeford."

"What kind of car is it?"

"A Rover. Top of the range . . . walnut burr, all mod cons."

He provided the registration number.

"And why did you leave it in a lay-by?"

"Because I was still searching for the house. I knew it was somewhere nearby so I parked the car and just walked. I found the house just a few minutes later. I didn't bother to go back for it."

"Is the car still there?"

"I hope so."

"And do you have any means of identification in the car? Information that would corroborate the details you have given me?"

Raynes nodded seriously.

How petty bureaucrats loved jargon!

"We shall arrange for the car to be brought in."

"That's fine."

"And you will be held in custody overnight."

Anything was better than facing a man with a gun.

The Inspector was suitably grateful.

The sergeant explained: "We shall have to keep you in custody until we know why you broke into the stables."

Raynes was mildly annoyed.

"I've already told you. I was looking for a key. I didn't

break into the stables. If you care to go down and examine the locks, you will see that they have not been tampered with. And there was nothing wrong with the horse. It has been very unsettled since Lady Angela died . . ."

A twinkle of interest came into the sergeant's eyes.

"You know about that?"

"I think everyone does. I read it in the national press."

"And where were you at the time her ladyship died? Were you down in Rye for another friendly visit? Putting your head in where you're not wanted?"

"No. I was in Grasshallows."

"But can you prove it?"

"I'm sure the local police authority will be able to supply you with the precise details of where I was on that day."

The sergeant was about to make some sarcastic comment that Mr Raynes was obviously well known to the police; but a more sobering thought suddenly occurred to him. He had not asked the suspect his occupation.

"Do you work for the police, Mr Raynes?"

"Detective-Inspector. Grasshallows Constabulary."

The sergeant looked somewhat embarrassed.

Why hadn't the man said it before? Had he been stringing him along? Pulling his leg?

"And where can I find proof of your identity and occupation, *Mr* Raynes?"

"It's all in the car . . . Sergeant."

28: *Release*

By 5.00am, the Inspector's Rover had been brought into the police compound. It had been fully searched and, as Raynes had said, it contained ample proof of his identity – even though there was no identification badge. The Inspector told them that he had left it in the top drawer of his desk.

Raynes had been allowed to have a wash – and brush down the sleeve of his coat. He had been given a cell with a blanket and a pillow; he had drunk a mug of tea – and fallen asleep.

His problem was now in the hands of others.

The day staff came on duty at 8.00am and a young inspector read through the charge sheet – and the sergeant's report.

"He was threatened with a gun?"

"That's what the beat man said. A Mr Patrick Baxter. Sir George Mallowan's groom."

The inspector nodded.

"Had he a licence for the gun?"

"He said he had. But apparently it wasn't loaded."

"Not loaded?"

"No."

"It all seems very peculiar. What's a police officer doing entering a stable at 1.00am? Why doesn't he sleep in his car? Surely it would be more comfortable?"

"Do you think we should send someone out to see Sir George? Make sure his horses are all right?"

The Inspector picked up the phone and dialled.

"Sir George? This is Inspector Appleton of the East Sussex police. You remember me? Yes, I thought you would." He smiled. "I believe you had a break-in at your stables last night?"

Sir George was suffering from a considerable hangover. Memories were vague and elusive but he thought he might have heard something during the night, but he couldn't be sure.

Inspector Appleton asked him if he knew a detective called Raynes. Sir George laughed. Of course he knew him.

Had he had him to lunch? Shown him the stables?

Sir George confirmed that he had.

"What's all this about, Inspector? Not in any trouble, is he?"

The Inspector smiled.

"No. He's fine. Just checking up. What's your groom's telephone number? Mr Baxter? Yes. Thank you . . . Thank you very much."

He dialled a second number.

Mrs Baxter was just getting Cherry ready for school.

Yes, her husband was the groom up at the stables. Yes, he

had caught a man in the stables early that morning. No, the horses were all right. None of them had been injured – none of them escaped. They were all safe and well. Her husband? He was back at the stables mucking out. He would be home at lunchtime.

The Inspector thanked her for her information.

He looked at the duty sergeant.

"Not much of a case, is it? Over-zealous groom jumps to wrong conclusion . . . Holds family friend at gunpoint . . . Doesn't give him any chance to explain . . . Hands him over to the police. Turns out to be a bona fide citizen – a police-inspector, no less!"

"So you won't be preferring charges?"

"I don't see that we could make them stick. But I'd like to meet this Inspector Raynes. Has he had breakfast?"

* * * *

Raynes was ushered into the young inspector's office at about 9.00am. He was feeling much more confident. Both men looked at each other with some curiosity – bemused at the strange turn of events which had brought them together.

"There seems to have been a misunderstanding?"

"Very much so," said Raynes. "But it's all been handled quite faultlessly by your staff."

If in doubt, flatter.

Inspector Appleton smiled.

"Must be a bit odd; seeing it from the other side?"

"Bit of a shock. Yes."

"So what were you doing at that hour of the night in Sir George's stables?"

"I think I said . . ."

"I know what you said, but I don't believe you. If you had wanted to sleep anywhere, you'd have slept in your car."

"I would've preferred to sleep in the house."

"Would you?" said Appleton sarcastically. "And what would a senior police officer like you be doing – staying with an an old rogue like Sir George? You know his wife was

172

murdered?"

"He told me."

Raynes was unsure as to whether he was being charged or not. The policeman who had brought him his breakfast told him that when he had seen the inspector, he would be free to go. But Appleton was a suspicious man. And Raynes knew he was right to be suspicious. The story did not hold water. But it would be difficult to make anything stick.

The two men looked at each other.

"Are you working on the Mallowan murder?"

"No."

Raynes had no hesitation in denying his involvement.

"You haven't been brought in on this by Sir George?"

"No. I met him through an artist friend of mine."

Inspector Appleton raised his eyebrows.

"Simon Forbes. He's a painter. Lives next door to Brackles."

The Inspector put down his brown file.

"That man is a complete crook!"

"Yes, I know. The body was found in his studio."

"Not just a body!"

Raynes shrugged his shoulders.

"I don't know about anything else."

"In that case, Mr Raynes, you are a liar!"

"Well, you don't expect me to admit that I'm a friend of someone whose been storing vast quantities of booze in his cellar?"

"Has he employed you on this case?"

"No."

Inspector Appleton was beginning to get annoyed. This detective was proving a very slippery customer.

He was clearly up to his neck in all these matters. He'd been caught red-handed. Now he was trying to wriggle out of it.

Appleton was determined to get to the bottom of it.

"You're not going to tell me that you don't have a professional interest in this case?"

Raynes looked across the Inspector's desk. His eyes were

173

as cold and as forceful as they normally were when he was confronting a tricky suspect.

"It is – I grant you – a fascinating case. I've been told all about it – naturally. But that's not why I came down to Rye. I came down here to collect a picture. Simon Forbes and I were at university together. We're old friends. When I first came down to Rye, Brackles had just been released from custody. Naturally, I was told the whole story from his point of view. I met Sir George. I met his daughter. I was shown round the stables. Therefore, I have quite a detailed knowledge of the case. But I assure you – I have strenuously avoided getting involved."

"So why come back?"

Raynes could see no way out of the conversation without revealing his hand – even to some small degree. He weighed the pros and cons.

Appleton mistook his silence for non-co-operation.

"You cannot just walk in on our patch!" he said. "You'd be furious if we'd done something like this to you. Breaking into a lockfast property without a search warrant. It was bound to lead to trouble. My boss . . ."

Raynes put out a reassuring hand.

"You don't have to tell me. I'm perfectly aware of it. The truth is I've been investigating a case of fraud up in Grasshallows. The trail has led me to Bournemouth, to London; and now down here.It does not involve Lady Angela's murder – but it may cast some light on it. I cannot be sure. But I've been working on this case for the last fortnight and I was hoping to wrap it up before the weekend." He took a deep breath. "I had thought something might have been hidden in the stables but I was wrong. It's in Katie's house. I was misled."

Appleton looked over his desk.

There was a glint of sudden curiosity in his eyes.

"In Katie's house?"

Raynes nodded.

"Yes. I believe it was her husband who supplied the cyanide."

"Her husband?"

"Yes. I know everyone thinks it was her. But he has access to the poison as well."

Appleton's mind went into top gear.

Raynes could imagine the thoughts that were racing through his mind. He hoped his statement would distract the young inspector.

"But surely that's got nothing to do with your case?"

"No. But it's one of the things I've come across in the course of my investigations. I may have to ask you for a search warrant to examine Katie's house."

"Not today?"

"No. Not today. I need to go and get tidied up. To have a bath. A change of clothes. And time to think."

Inspector Appleton looked at Raynes coldly.

"I think the best thing you could do, Mr Raynes, is to get into your car and drive straight back to Grasshallows. If you wish to obtain any more information down here, please let *me* know. We shall conduct all necessary inquiries – as we have been doing. If you must come down here again – at least have the courtesy to let us know. So that next time – if there is a next time – you will not have the humiliation of getting arrested and brought in here."

"It has been very embarrassing," said Raynes meekly.

"Well, let it be a lesson to you! Avoid East Sussex! Avoid Sir George. And above all, avoid Brackles! And if you have any ideas about the murder, let me know. And we'll handle it – through the correct channels."

Raynes was tempted to observe that the "correct channels" had had nearly six weeks to come up with a solution and had manifestly failed. But this was not the moment to point out his colleague's failings. He had already caused Inspector Appleton sufficient irritation. A formal complaint could easily be made against him. It was a time to let sleeping dogs lie.

"You get my point?"

"I do."

It seemed that there was little more to be said. Raynes thanked Appleton for being so understanding. He apologized once again for putting him in an invidious position.

Within five minutes, he was out on the street.

Free!

But Appleton had not yet finished with the Inspector.

He called in a plain clothes man and pointed out the interloper as he reclaimed his keys and climbed into his car.

"Follow that man!" he said. "And make sure he gets out of this county without causing us any more trouble!"

29. *The Little Painter*

The front door was open. Raynes walked in. There was no one in the kitchen, but there was a sound of music from the studio upstairs. He climbed the rickety steps.

"Bloody hell!" said Simon, 'Fancy seeing you again!"

"I've just escaped from the police. I was arrested last night. Spent a night in the cells."

"Dog eats dog?"

"Seems like it."

Simon put down his palette and brush. He was doing a painting of Henry James' house. It was one of his stock items. He had done it so many times that he could polish off a creditable copy in less than two hours – without even thinking about it. Tourists always snapped them up. He could sell at least three a week in summer. This morning's painting was a moonlight scene, full of dark blue shadows and cream-coloured walls. Raynes' memory of the house was that its frontage was of red and brown brick.

Simon looked at his friend anxiously. He had never seen Richard quite so uptight.

"What happened?" he asked.

Raynes told him the full story.

"Inspector Appleton's warned me off his patch," he concluded. "But I've still got to get into those stables; and my keys are somewhere on that rutted track leading down from Sir George's house."

"No problem!" said Simon, wiping his hands on a piece of

grey towelling. "We'll find those keys and get you in."

"But what about the groom? I don't want to be held at gunpoint a second time – and then handed over to the police again. Appleton'd be sure to put in an official complaint."

Simon thought for a few moments.

"I could phone Liz."

"Who's Liz?"

"Cherry's mum. She's on holiday this week. She'll tell me what her husband's up to. If he's coming back to the house for lunch, she could delay him. How long d'you need?"

"Just a couple of minutes. It won't take me more than a few seconds to get into that safe. I know the combination . . . at least I did." He thought carefully for a few moments. "Yes, I've still got it. But it's dealing with those horses that worries me."

"Probably out in the field during the day."

Raynes brightened.

"That'd be a great help."

"And you want Pat well out of the way?"

"I don't want him to see me going into that safe."

"It's that important, is it?"

"I think so. Lesley's been looking for it for weeks; but she still thinks it's in the house. I saw it last night – just before that horse knocked me down." He laughed sadly. "What a mess! Covered in shit!"

Simon said: "D'you want to go there now?"

Raynes shook his head.

"No. First of all, I should like a bath. I feel absolutely filthy. Next, I would like a really strong gin and tonic. After that, a change of clothes . . . you should have something that would fit me. We're both about the same size."

Simon smiled.

"You could probably do with a bite of lunch. I was going to have a quiche and a baked potato; but if you like, we could go into the town and have something more elaborate."

"Why not?" said Raynes. "Even though he told me to get the hell out of Rye, he can't stop me going into a restaurant and having a bite of lunch."

"Of course not," said Simon. "I'll put the immersion on. It'll take about half an hour to heat the tank. You can have your gin and tonic whilst you're waiting; and I'll finish this painting."

* * * *

By the time they had had a couple of steaks and some decent claret, Raynes was beginning to feel more like his normal self.

As they walked past the Martello Bookshop, Simon said quietly: "Don't look round; but I think we're being followed. Grey-haired chap. Noticed him a few weeks ago keeping tabs on Brackles. I'm sure it's the same bloke."

"Appleton doesn't trust me. Can't say I blame him!"

Raynes and his friend continued to amble along the pavement. As they crossed the road, the Inspector looked to left and right.

"I see him."

As they neared the studio, Simon said: "I'm sure that's his car. The blue one. Left it just round the corner from the house." He laughed. "It's a dead giveaway! No parking ticket! If any of us parked there, we'd have been booked in five minutes."

Raynes smiled.

"We shall have to give him the slip."

"No trouble in these country lanes. We'll soon shake him off."

"Shove a brick under his front wheel!" said Raynes, feeling increasingly aggressive. "I'll walk over and look at that charming little house. He won't dare to come any closer till I move."

A large lump of stone was duly wedged under the nearside front wheel and the two men walked back to the studio.

Simon phoned Liz.

"Is Pat there?"

"No. He's still at the stables. But he's due back at 3.30pm. He's got a doctor's appointment. Why are you asking?"

"Richard wants a word with him."

"Richard who?"

"Richard Raynes. You remember . . . The man who commissioned that picture."

"Oh yes! The Inspector? Is he down here?"

"Just arrived," Simon lied happily. "We've just had lunch together. Can we pop round later?"

Liz did not sound all that keen.

"Pat won't be back from the doctor's till nearly five. Then he'll have to go back to the stables."

Simon looked at his friend.

Raynes shrugged his shoulders.

"Oh well, never mind. Perhaps we can fit it in another time. See you soon! Love to Cherry."

* * * *

At 3.20pm, they left Rye.

Neither of them looked at the blue car as they passed it – but they were very conscious that it was there. However, there was no sign of it following them and they went through two sets of traffic lights without any other car visibly on their tail.

Raynes didn't rate their chances of escape all that highly. His destination was so obvious – and so close – that it would not take Inspector Appleton long to find him.

As they covered the short distance to Blake House, Raynes rehearsed with Simon what he was to do. He should go over to the house and invite George to a meal. He should engage him in conversation for as long as possible whilst Raynes went down the lane and hunted for the keys.

Seeing his car parked at the front door, Appleton would assume that the Inspector was inside. (At least he hoped he would make that assumption!)

"When am I supposed to be having this meal?"

"Next Sunday – or the week after. You can always cancel it."

Simon looked thoughtful.

"Actually, it's quite a good idea. It would be a nice way to

179

round things off for Brackles."

"In what way?"

"Didn't I tell you? Brackles is going back to New Zealand. Leaving whilst the going is good. One of his friends in London has got him a passport. Forged, of course. Otherwise, he wouldn't be able to get out." He paused. "I shouldn't be telling you this."

Raynes smiled grimly.

"It's nothing to do with me – but it won't please Inspector Appleton. He'll go ballistic!"

"I'll make sure Brackles leaves him a bottle or two. Perhaps give him one of his canvases . . ." Simon returned to his more immediate problem. "And what do I do if George says: 'No'?"

"Keep talking – about burglars, about horses, about things which go bump in the night . . ."

"And you just walk in – casual like – clutching Angela's emeralds and say; 'I just happened to be passing'?"

Raynes laughed.

"Something like that."

"And if George isn't in?"

"Talk to his housekeeper, Mrs Beaton. She does wonderful Yorkshire puddings. Ask her for the recipe."

For once, the best laid plans of mice and men went extremely smoothly.

The car drew up outside the house. Raynes sprinted down the lane. Simon ambled over to the front door and rang the bell.

The door was opened by the housekeeper who informed him that Sir George was in Brighton, but due back within the hour. Mrs Beaton invited him to join her for a cup of tea in the kitchen. Simon accepted.

Raynes walked rapidly down the rutted track – and soon saw the tell-tale flash of silver in the grass. His keys were wet but intact. He put them in his coat pocket.

He went on down to the stables. He could see the horses grazing in a nearby field. He counted them. Six. And breathed a sigh of relief. He entered the stableyard. The doors of the loose-boxes were wide open but the store rooms were locked. The Inspector checked that there was no one in sight. He looked at his watch.

3.38pm.

It was now or never.

He went into Natal's box, tramped through the fresh straw and reached for the small green box he had noted the night before. Even in daytime, it seemed well hidden.

He looked over his shoulder nervously.

He flicked open the box. Inside, there was a much more solid steel door with a brass knob. It would be very difficult to prize it open without demolishing part of the wall.

Fortunately he had the number.

718364.

He paused to make sure he had got the number quite correct.

Then he pulled the brass knob towards him. It opened.

Raynes again looked over his shoulder.

Still undisturbed.

He reached into the safe. There was no jewellery box. No money. Just a series of thick white envelopes – about seven of them. Raynes slipped them into the inner pocket of his coat.

He closed the safe. Rang up a different series of numbers. Tugged again at the knob. Locked – rock solid. He shut the green outer door. Looked again at his watch.

3.41pm.

He took a deep breath and walked cautiously towards the door. It was ominously quiet. No clatter of hooves. No menacing figure wielding a gun. No police sirens.

He shut the lower flap of the loose-box and walked out of the stableyard, expecting at any minute to be challenged. But, unbelievably, he walked free.

He made his way up the rutted track to the house; went over to the front door and rang the bell.

Simon answered the door.

"Sir George is not in."

"Oh, what a pity!"

"He won't be back till 4.00pm."

Mrs Beaton also appeared at the door.

"He's in Brighton."

"Visiting the massage parlour," thought Raynes.

The housekeeper looked at him closely.

"I know you, don't I? I recognize your face."

The Inspector smiled.

"I expect so. I was at a dinner party here about three weeks ago. A Sunday lunch. You made the most excellent meal. Seafood *en croute*; roast beef and Yorkshire pudding, followed by a summer fruit dessert . . ."

"Oh, yes, I remember. And someone smashed a glass."

"That's right. Janet. Lesley's friend."

Mrs Beaton had no time for either of them.

"Disgusting pair!"

"So I hear."

Raynes allowed a look of severe puritanical revulsion to flicker across his face. Simon wanted to laugh. What a hypocrite! But his friend managed to keep a straight face.

"I'm afraid we shall have to go. Can't wait any longer. We had hoped to invite Sir George to a meal." He smiled graciously, "Another time?"

Mrs Beaton looked distressed.

"He'll be very sorry to have missed you."

* * * *

"Did you get it?" asked Simon.

"Whatever it is – yes."

"You mean you're not sure?"

"There's just a series of envelopes."

He pulled one out of his pocket.

"Doesn't look very exciting."

"I expect the contents will be quite lethal."

Simon pointed ahead.

"There's our friend."

The blue car was parked at the side of the road. The grey-haired man was relieving himself beside a tree. Raynes could not resist waving as they passed by.

"I'm going to drop you on the outskirts," he said. "Will that be all right?"

"Fine. I suppose I'll get my clothes back?"

"I'll have them dry-cleaned, ironed and returned as quickly as I can. You may expect a delivery before the weekend."

"As soon as that?"

"As soon as I've put the final pieces of the jigsaw together."

He pulled up at a sign which said: "Rye 1".

"You'll appreciate if I don't linger?"

"No. This is O.K. You go up the road to Tenterden. Take the A 28 to Ashford. Then you're on to the M 20."

"Thanks," said Raynes. "You've been a great help."

Simon smiled bravely.

"I'll try to mislead the opposition!"

30. *Next!*

It had taken remarkable self-control for the Inspector not to look at the contents of the safe until he was back in Grasshallows. He could easily have stopped in a lay-by or in some hotel car park and read them there. But he felt a compelling need to return to base, to be surrounded by familiar objects and by people whom he could trust. He still had the feeling that he might have been followed and all this vital evidence snatched away. In the cold light of day, such fears seemed spineless and stupid, but after his experiences in Rye, he felt a need to withdraw within his own protective shell.

He laid the pack of envelopes down on his desk, made himself a cup of sweet black coffee and settled back to see what Angela had hidden away.

Each item had been carefully labelled. He flicked through the pack till he came to **TOM TRAVERS**. This was the one Lesley had been looking for.

On the envelope, there were clear instructions:

IN THE EVENT OF MY DEATH, THIS ENVELOPE
SHOULD BE DELIVERED UNOPENED TO THE

Raynes sliced the envelope open. Inside, there were two photographs and several sheets of blue airmail paper, handwritten in blue biro. Instinctively, he turned to the photographs.

One was of a dark-haired girl sitting on a low stone wall. In the background were boats and masts – a harbour somewhere. The young girl was smiling. There was a shyness in her eyes as if she had never been photographed in a bikini before.

The other picture was clearly of the same girl – but several years later – now glamorous and sophisticated. She was lying on a golden divan, smoking a cigar. The cigar probably belonged to Tom Travers, because her left arm was round his neck and her buttocks firmly ensconced in his lap. One leg lay flat upon the yellow cushions; the other was raised to show a long scarlet dress slashed to the hip, displaying an elegant brown leg.

Raynes looked at the back of both photographs. The first one said: "Found in Helen's flat after her death." The second: "Taken in *The Blue Diamond* night club, 4th June 1967."

The Inspector unfolded the thin sheets of blue paper.

"Helen Dimitriades was born in Athens. She came to work in London as an au pair girl. It was a summer job to help her improve her English. I believe she wanted to become an air hostess. So she got this job with a family in Wimbledon – but it didn't work out. She said that she didn't like the responsibility of looking after young children – but I think she preferred the bright lights.

"Even before she gave up being an au pair girl, she had found her way to *The Blue Diamond*. Tom was quite taken with her. Of course, he was quite taken with any new face – so long as it was female! Helen had a sort of loose-limbed Mediterranean charm which got to him. He employed her as a barmaid-cum-bottle-washer but very quickly she graduated to being a croupier on one of the tables. He bought her a few slinky dresses. He found her a flat. He probably screwed her. He screwed most of the girls who came his way.

"She was certainly the flavour of the month – but then she did something stupid. She came to work wearing a rather nice gold bracelet. I think she said it had belonged to her grandmother. Anyway, it was quite obviously antique – probably about a hundred years old. The moment Tom clapped eyes on it, he knew it was worth a packet. He offered to buy it from her – but she just laughed at him. Helen probably thought he was joking, but Tom had a key to her flat. One day, she came to the club in tears. Her flat had been burgled and her bracelet had gone.

"We all assumed that Tom had taken it. We knew what he was like. I told Helen that Tom normally took any jewellery that came his way to a shop called the *Cloche d'Or*. So she went to the shop – and there it was in the window – priced at £1800. She was livid.

"She went into the shop and told them it was her bracelet. It had been stolen. They said they had bought it from a very respectable and long-established customer. She told them not to sell it or she would put the police on to them. She came back to the club and accused Tom to his face of having pinched the bracelet. I heard the row. She threatened to go to the police if he didn't go down to the shop and get it back. He eventually agreed. They went out – about 4.30pm. She never came back. And I never saw her again.

"Tom returned about 7.00pm. I asked him what had happened to Helen. He said he had sacked her. I asked him if she had got her bracelet back. He told me to mind my own business. I went round to Helen's flat a couple of days later. The lock wasn't up to much. It didn't take more than a few seconds to get in. The whole place had been cleared out – except for this photograph, which I found at the back of a drawer.

"I questioned Janet about the bracelet. She denied all knowledge of it but I could tell she was lying. Nothing more was said but, about six weeks later, the police came to the club. I didn't see them – but Bernard did. Helen was missing.

She hadn't returned home to Greece and her parents were looking for her. Tom said he couldn't help them. She'd only worked in the club for couple of weeks – then moved on. I began to wonder if he'd bumped her off.

"It wouldn't have been the first time. He told me he'd drowned one of his ex-girlfriends. She had been pregnant and wanted him to marry her. He was only nineteen and didn't want to be tied down. He didn't say much. Just took her on a holiday to Bulgaria, filled her up with cheap wine, went down to the swimming pool and held her head under the water for a couple of minutes.

"He used to boast that if any woman got in his way, he'd soon deal with her. 'Happy accidents' he called them. That's why people didn't mess around with Tom. You never knew what he might do.

"I couldn't be sure about Helen. But a few months later, one of the waiters at the club told me what had happened. It was during a New Year's binge – he'd had a lot to drink. He told me that Tom had taken Helen back to her flat; given her a Mickey Finn. Whilst she was knocked out, he'd put a plastic bag over her head and Sellotaped it tight round her neck. Riccardo – he was the waiter – had helped Tom move the body. They buried her in an inspection pit under a garage in Theydon Bois.

"They did it at night. He remembered going out to Theydon Bois – but he couldn't remember where the garage was. He said it was a private house – not a factory. I would have asked him for more details but, a couple of days after the party, he vanished. We never saw him again. I think Tom must have got wind that Riccardo was blabbing – and dealt with him. He's probably in the same inspection pit as Helen.

"It was about then that Tom became suspicious of me. He came up to me one night – as we were clearing up. He seemed quite calm.

"Did Riccardo speak to you?"

"I was very brave."

"Yes," I said. 'He told me about Helen."

There was a longish silence.

"You wouldn't be as foolish to say anything?" he said quietly. His voice really gave me the creeps.

"Of course not," I said.

"I wouldn't want anything to happen to you. Bernard might get upset." (I was having an affair with Bernard at the time.)

"His words sent real shivers down my spine because I knew he meant it. I decided that the only means of defence was attack. So I said to him, cool-like:

"If anything happens to me, chum, the police will get the full story. I've written everything down – chapter and verse. So long as I'm alive, I'll say nothing about Helen. But if I die, the full story goes to Scotland Yard."

"Tom believed me – which was just as well because I hadn't written a thing! But that night, when I got home – and Bernard was asleep – I wrote down the whole story and put it in a sealed envelope and sent it to my aunt.

"Tom did nothing – I said nothing. Soon afterwards, he had a nervous breakdown and went into hospital. Guilt, I should think. Whilst he was away, I left Bernard, moved out of London and covered my tracks. My aunt died last year and her daughter sent me back the sealed envelope.

"I have not heard from Tom these past fourteen years. I do not know if he is still alive. Certainly, he has not tried to contact me. I have re-written these facts – just in case anything ever happens to me. I enclose a full list of those who worked in *The Blue Diamond* whilst I was there. I have checked on Helen's family through the Greek consul. And I have made inquiries about properties in Theydon Bois.

"An estate agent was able to tell me that the houses No. 85 - 91 Morgan Drive all had garages with inspection pits when they were built in the 1930s. I expect Helen's body – and perhaps other bodies – are still there. I think the police should investigate these addresses and also, if I die in suspicious circumstances, the finger of blame should be pointed first and foremost at Tom Travers.

Signed: Angela Mallowan
19th June 1982."

There was an addition to the statement – written in black biro:

"Just recently I have discovered that Tom is still around – and so is Bernard. They are running a gaming club called *Nightflyers*. A friend of theirs – a painter called Brackles – has settled in town and has been storing booze for them. A fisherman – I think it is someone called Ernie Thompson, or Johnston – has been bringing it across from France, and Brackles is storing it in his cellar. Tom comes down to collect it. Stupidly, I told Brackles that I knew Bernard, not realizing he was still working with Tom. Now, after all these years, Tom knows who I am and where I live. His wife has made contact with my husband. It seemed a coincidence but I cannot really believe it. Her name is Lesley. She and her husband are dangerous . . ."

At which point, Angela reached the bottom of the page. Her additional statement was undated.

Raynes put down the flimsy sheets of paper. He felt a deep debt of gratitude towards Angela. She had opened a hidden door and revealed a world of corruption and murder which he had never suspected. The whole background to the case was laid bare. Her affair with Bernard; her escape from the London club world; her desire for anonymity. A new name. A safer life shielded by money and a title.

Raynes admired her bravery in recording the misdeeds of Tom Travers, which might well have cost her her life. It explained a great deal. No wonder Lesley's husband wanted to get hold of this document! No wonder he was willing to give her the divorce she wanted! No price would be too high. The man must be absolutely desperate.

But now that the Inspector had seen the document, Tom was doomed. Two murders at least; perhaps many more. If he instituted a search of the garages in Morgan Drive – and if he found bodies – then Angela's statement should be sufficient to put him away for life.

The question arose as to whether the most recent murder was connected with the past. Was it revenge? An attempt to silence a witness? Now that Tom had discovered where she lived – and who she was – had he been responsible for the murder in Brackles' studio? "If any woman gets in my way, I'll soon deal with her!" Angela had certainly been a major obstacle in Tom's life.

Raynes wondered what he should do about his promise to Lesley. He had agreed that if he found the document, he would hand it over to her so that she could get her divorce. And yet it was *prima facie* evidence of murder; which would have to be presented in court. If he gave her merely a photocopy, Tom would know that the original was in the hands of the police. He might escape. He might kill Lesley. Another "happy accident".

The Inspector knew that he could not let her down. If she had not given him the combination number, he would never have been able to open the safe. He would never have obtained the crucial evidence. He would have to show her what he had found. Surely she would understand? Surely she would be willing to wait? Once Tom was arrested and jailed, she would have no difficulty in getting a divorce.

Raynes put the papers back in their envelope.

He turned to the other packages. There were three names he recognized: Max Middleton and Philip Royle he had expected to see – but the third one he had not.

Out of curiosity, he opened the package marked **CHARLES EASTWOOD**.

Angela certainly had no hesitation in recording her misdeeds; she did it with gusto and good humour. The story of how she had tricked Sir Ian's grand-nephew out of his millions was lovingly recorded – as was her affair with Charles Eastwood.

Once Sir Ian had moved to Bournemouth and chosen Miller & Duckworth to be his lawyers, and Mr Eastwood had been appointed to look after this important client, Angela had set out to win over the lawyer, to seduce him body and soul. He had immediately been ensnared.

Instead of posting Sir Ian's letters, she had delivered them personally to Mr Eastwood's office. They had chatted; had coffee together. He had taken her for a drink. Gone to Lyme Regis on a summer's afternoon. A memorable afternoon on the Undercliff. Sunshine and kisses – and perhaps more! Perhaps much more?

There appeared to be no Mrs Eastwood. So Charles – "your loving Charles" as he signed himself in his letters – nurtured high hopes that Angela Anderson might become his châtelaine. Certainly she was efficient and caring. She was good fun. Discreet. And judging by his letters, she had agreed to become his wife, but not whilst Sir Ian was alive. Her chief duty was to care for him.

Mr Eastwood said he understood this. And not only understood . . . he deeply admired her for her devotion to Sir Ian. The dedicated servant faithful even unto death. As Carlisle had said: "It made you want to cry."

Raynes read through Mr Eastwood's love letters to Angela. There were about eighteen of them. He seemed utterly besotted with her. There was no evidence of collusion on his part. He had not been bribed or blackmailed into deceit. But he had certainly been softened up before the crucial interview with George.

It seemed that she had agreed to marry Mr Eastwood the moment the estate had been wound up. Once the bungalow had been sold, she would move into his flat. They had talked about getting married in the spring of 1978. She had suggested a honeymoon in Mexico! But Charles preferred Greece. He had given her one or two of his mother's rings. An emerald brooch. A necklace. He had even loaned her £1000 to improve her wardrobe!

Raynes laughed out loud.

He could imagine that Angela would have enjoyed teasing the staid, old-fashioned lawyer. "I shall need some new shoes, some black lace nighties for my trousseau!" And, of course, he fell for it.

The later correspondence was painful. She had not replied to his letters. Had she ditched him? How could she leave him after all their hours of happiness together? He could not believe that she would break her promises. Did she not care about his feelings? He had never loved anyone as much as he loved her. How could she do this to him?

He had felt betrayed. Then he became angry. Especially when he discovered she was using an accommodation address. Why was she not being straight with him? Had she met someone else? He accused her of stealing his money. He could not believe that she would do something like that to him.

Then he had received the £1000 back – with interest: £1500. He was reduced to a grovelling apology for doubting her. He loved her. He missed her. He begged her to write. Just one letter to say she was all right. He would not be the last to feel cheated or deceived. What was amazing was that Angela had kept all these dreadful, whingeing letters. Why?

Raynes could imagine that his visit to Bournemouth must have brought back all sorts of bitter memories. When he had produced that photograph of Angela and told him that she had married Sir George, that must have reopened a very painful wound. If he had not realized it before, he would have discovered that she had used him – as she had used every man she had ever met – and then cast him aside. The Inspector found himself wondering whether the visit of Paul Cook had set the alarm bells ringing. Had Mr Eastwood perhaps made his own enquiries and tracked her down to Rye? It was a distant possibility but it could not be ignored.

He turned to the other envelopes. He opened the one marked **PHILIP ROYLE** and emptied the contents out on to his desk.

As Katie had said, they were a series of poison pen letters – some typed, some written in capitals – all threatening dire things.

It was not hard to identify the author. There were frequent references to broken teeth and the costs of dental treatment. These were referred to in the third person – as if someone else was making the complaint; but every now and again, the word "my"appeared instead of "his". Raynes noted the various punishments the writer intended to inflict on Lady Angela. Several of them involved death. Philip might have wanted to save foxes, but he had no intention of sparing Lady Mallowan or her horses.

Raynes put the letters back in their envelope. They hadn't taught him anything he didn't already know. Philip was bitter and twisted; and he wanted revenge. Was it just words? Or did his words betoken action? He still could not be sure.

He opened the envelope marked **MAX MIDDLETON**. It was surprising that Lady Angela should target her own son-in-law, but she had obviously learnt that the best form of defence was attack.

Inside were more letters in handwriting he now recognized as that of Philip Royle. But the content was very different. These letter were humble . . . begging . . . grateful. Favours were sought; cash was needed; assignations were made. Reading between the lines, it was easy to see that Max was Philip's fairy godfather. He supplied him with cash, wrote references for jobs; sustained his morale. Having dropped out of college, Philip apparently dreamt of becoming a male model. The photographs illustrated parts of Philip's anatomy not normally visible to the public eye. "Beefcake" was a word that came to mind.

The young man obviously thought Max would relish these intimate pictures. But Philip had not become a male model. He had become a barman at the *Windmill* in Winchelsea.

A man of disappointed hopes. However, a man still sensitive about his appearance. Being slashed across the face with a whip and having broken teeth would not improve his looks. Raynes felt that he must have had a strong personal bitterness towards Lady Angela, quite apart from his stand on hunting. Philip himself was a wounded animal.

Raynes looked inside the other envelopes; but their contents did not seem to have any relevance to the case. He put them all away in the office safe and sat back to think about what he had learnt.

As he tried to focus on the details, he kept yawning and rubbing his eyes. He realized that his mind was tired and unresponsive. From a professional point of view, it had been a very demanding three days – a lot of driving, constant interviews – quite apart from the emotional drama of being arrested and held in custody by the police.

He realised that he would have to call it a day. He thought of food; and he thought of sex. He wondered if Debbie was busy. One never knew quite what she was up to. He picked up the phone and dialled her number.

"Not before eleven," she said. "And when you come, bring an Indian. A lamb kadie would be nice." The line went dead.

Raynes looked at his watch.

10.15pm.

Time for a shower and a change. He was glad she was not booked all night. He didn't really want to be on his own.

He bought the Indian meal along with a couple of garlic nans, and headed for her basement flat. 11.15pm.That should be all right. He walked down the steps and rang the bell.

Nothing happened.

When he rang the second time, the door was wrenched open by a rather drunken-looking policewoman. Her white blouse was open to her waist – no bra. Her jacket was loose and her black and white chequered hat was perched at a jaunty angle on her head. She seemed to be wearing black, high-heeled shoes and dark blue tights. One of them was laddered.

"You're arrested!" she screamed.

For a moment, Raynes was taken aback.

"You're drunk!" he said.

"On the way there," she said. "Come in."

Raynes followed her into the kitchen.

"The last trick wanted to be thrashed by a policewoman. Hard work. I needed a couple of gins to get me going."

Raynes put the carrier bag on the kitchen table.

"Was he satisfied?"

Debbie laughed.

"Red hot, I should think! I didn't let up. Gave him the works – till he bled." She shrugged her shoulders. "He wanted sado-masch. He got it! Two hundred lashes at a pound a time. Bloody hell! I earned it."

She tore off her hat and jacket and kicked off her high heels.

193

"Some people think I get my money for doing nothing. Just lying on my back and thinking of England! But sometimes, it's bloody hard work! Now what have you got?"

She emptied the carrier bag on to the table.

"Oh good! You've got the kadie. And the nans. No booze?"

Raynes looked at her with a faint smile.

"O.K. I've had enough. But I'm going to have another."

"I'll have a whisky."

"Pour your own!"

As she left the kitchen, she pulled off her white blouse. He could see red weals on her back.

She went off into the shower and was away for ten minutes.

Raynes got out the plates, knives and forks. He put the foil trays in the oven to keep them hot. He poured her another gin and himself a whisky.

Mrs May returned in her white silk dressing gown, tied with an elaborate bow. Her hair was now brushed and she had repaired her face.

Raynes was thinking how different the real Debbie was when compared with her picture. There was no serenity, no gentleness, no real beauty. So much was contrived. But at least she was a genuine person – and she was fun.

She took a hefty swig of her gin and started opening the foil trays and spooning the contents out on to the plates.

Raynes looked at her busy fingers and her almond-shaped nails.

"So then," she said, "what have you been up to since I last saw you?"

Raynes sighed and picked up his fork. It was difficult to know where to begin.

"I went into Angela's stables. I found her safe. I was attacked by a horse. I got covered in shit. I was then held up at gunpoint. Frog-marched up to the house. Handed over to the police. Spent the night in a cell. Would that be enough to be going on with?"

Mrs May smiled wickedly.

"And you've come here for more? You want another fifty lashes from a policewoman?"

Raynes shook his head.

"I was looking for something a little less energetic. The milk of human kindness . . ."

Debbie finished her gin.

"You won't get that round here!"

"I live in hope," said Raynes. "I think an all-over body massage would be nice. Something that would send me straight to sleep. Stop me thinking about the case." He looked at the slightly demented figure across the table who was tucking vigorously into her pilau rice. "And I think you could do with some massage as well. I saw those marks on your back."

Mrs May did not immediately reply. She ate another couple of pieces of lamb before she looked up.

"I enjoyed it," she said. "I won't deny it."

Raynes said quietly:

"What happened to the Archangel Gabrielle? The fair prospect of Rye?"

A slight look of remorse flickered in Debbie's eyes. Or was it the gin?

"She was a fake," she said. "Just another fake."

Raynes reached across the table to touch her hand.

"I prefer the real woman," he said.

"More fool you!"

31. The Morning After

When he awoke the following morning, Raynes was glad to find he was sleeping in a large, comfortable bed – rather than on a narrow bench in a police cell. The sight of Debbie sleeping peacefully beside him was reassuring. Life had returned to normal. He listened to the distant rumble of traffic outside the flat and watched the second hand of the bedside clock silently ticking away.

There was no hurry to get up. If there was any crisis, his

195

mobile phone would have been bleeping before now. He shut his eyes and enjoyed another relaxing half hour before he got up. When he had had a shower – and dressed – he went into the kitchen to find Mrs May making one of her cholesterol-rich breakfasts, throwing everything into the frying pan.

She seemed to have recovered from her drunken excess and was feeling more tenderly disposed towards the Inspector. She could not remember all that much about the night before but suspected that she had been sad, mad and bitchy.

"How's the back?" Raynes asked.

"Bit sore. I'll feel better when I've had a shower."

Raynes felt a great deal better himself when he left the flat and drove the few hundred yards along the road to Grasshallows police station.

He dealt with the overnight business quickly and efficiently and then opened the safe, took out Angela's envelopes and dumped them on Carlisle's desk.

"Have a look at that!" he said. "Start with the one on Tom Travers."

Carlisle picked up the envelope and drew out the sheets of blue airmail paper. He read the statement through slowly – and then looked at the photographs.

He turned to the Inspector.

"That finishes him!"

"Completely. But we shall need proof."

"A couple of bodies?"

"The more the merrier. I suspect that this may be Mr Travers' private graveyard. There could be quite a few corpses waiting to be exhumed."

For a moment, Carlisle looked anxious.

"You weren't thinking of doing this on your own?"

"No," said Raynes, thinking of his most recent piece of private enterprise. "I think we've already ruffled enough feathers. We need help. We need manpower. We need search warrants. In short, we need the Metropolitan police. They wouldn't thank us if we barged in. We'd get more than a thick ear."

"So we call in the U.S. Cavalry?"

"Yes, but we must make sure we direct them to the right spot."

Carlisle looked back at Angela's statement.

"She doesn't seem very sure which house it was . . . It could be any one of four garages . . ."

Raynes took a sip of sweet, black coffee.

"I think we shall have to do a little research into who owned which house. The estate agents will help us. The voters' register. The rates department. Perhaps even a personal visit. We need to find out who owned the various properties since 1960. Which house had an open inspection pit – and when. Once we have a few names, we can check with Criminal Records to see if any of them was a friend of Tom Travers. I don't think it'll be all that difficult."

"You're expecting me to do that?"

Raynes showed a hint of exasperation.

"Don't complain! You've got the easy part!"

He told Carlisle about his experiences in Rye. His colleague was vastly amused by the scene at the stables; the Inspector rolling around in the straw, covered in dung.

"It was no joke," said Raynes. "And then I got stuck in a police cell – all night. They thought I was an anti-hunting fanatic! I thought you might have to come down and bail me out."

Carlisle laughed.

"I missed the chance of a lifetime?"

"You did."

"But I suppose it was all worthwhile?"

"Well, you see what Angela had stashed away. A damning indictment. No wonder Tom Travers was going up the wall."

"Is the rest as lurid?"

"Well, it's not quite so exciting – but it explains a great deal. Try Philip Royle next – then Max . . ."

" . . . and Charles Eastwood?"

Raynes nodded.

"The one who got away!"

"Lucky him!"

The Inspector continued writing his report for the next half hour whilst Carlisle ploughed through the letters and. photographs – occasionally whistling with amazement.

He put down the final envelope.

"Quite a haul!"

"Yes. We shall need copies of all the documents. I shall phone New Scotland Yard once you've identified the house and the garage. I shall have to give a copy to Lesley – I promised to show her what was in the safe. That'll mean another visit to London. I'll drop in on the Commissioner and show him what we've found. It's useful having friends in high places! It'll probably take a few days to arrange. We'll not get the pit opened till Wednesday or Thursday at the earliest. Depends what else they're doing."

"But if I get it wrong?"

"You won't. And anyway, I'll double-check."

Raynes smiled reassuringly.

Later that morning, there came a further piece of good news – a fax from the police in New Zealand. Sir Ian's grand-nephew had been living in the South Island for twenty years. He had been working on a farm. The police sent all his personal details including his passport number. However, the police reported that George was no longer living in New Zealand. He had returned to Britain in 1987. It was believed he was still there.

Raynes was delighted with the news. It was most encouraging to see his seeds of inspiration bearing fruit.

Everything was steadily falling into place.

He showed the fax to Carlisle.

"Explains a lot, doesn't it?"

"Living right on the doorstep!"

"Under an assumed name!"

"Makes one think."

Raynes reached for his diary.

"I wasn't intending to return to Rye till later in the week. But I think this calls for action. I shall go there on Monday."

* * * *

Raynes decided that it was more than his life was worth to enter the *Nightflyers* club a second time. He therefore parked his car round the corner in a nearby street and walked the short distance to the club's front door. He asked the doorman if he would let Mrs Travers know that someone wanted to see her. Instead of giving his name, he gave the man the combination number of Angela's safe.

The doorman looked reluctant to oblige but a £20 note did the trick and Lesley arrived at the door in a long purple dress with a white silk shawl.

"I presume," said Raynes, "that you would like to speak to me in private. My car is just round the corner."

They walked to the car.

"I found the safe."

"Where was it?"

"In the stables."

"The stables? I'd never have thought of looking there."

"It was quite a good place to hide it. You have to get past the horses. Then there's a groom with a double-barrelled shotgun."

"Pretty scary?"

"It was. I got knocked to the ground by Lady Angela's horse. I was covered in shit. Then I was marched up to the house at gunpoint and handed over to the police."

Lesley laughed.

"You? Handed over to the police?"

"They thought I was a member of the anti-hunting brigade."

"But you found what was in the safe?"

"I have it here."

He tapped his breast pocket.

By this time, they had reached the car. As they settled into the front seats, Raynes switched on the overhead light. He pulled Angela's envelope out of his pocket and handed it over to Lesley.

"I'm afraid I couldn't give you the original. It'll be needed in court. But I've done a photocopy; but even that's pretty hot stuff. I wouldn't advise you to keep it. If Tom knew you had it, it would be certain death."

"As it was for Angela?"

"As it was for quite a few people. Read it and you'll see what I mean."

Whilst Lesley read through Angela's statement, Raynes kept an eye on his mirrors. He also put on the central locking. Once or twice the doorman from the club came and looked down the street.

Lesley finished reading, folded up the sheets of paper and stared out through the windscreen. She said nothing.

Raynes passed over the original photographs of Helen Dimitriades. She looked at them and sighed deeply.

"A professional murderer," said Raynes. "Been killing people for years – but you probably knew that."

Lesley nodded.

"I think he's more careful these days. Threats are enough. But if he was really pushed, he wouldn't hesitate."

"Well, you see now why he wanted to find the safe."

"Was there more?"

"Not about Tom – but there was plenty of other stuff about people Angela had a grudge against."

"What are you going to do with this?"

Lesley flicked through the sheets of paper and then handed them back to the Inspector.

"Well, I think we shall have to arrest him. The Metropolitan police will do that. Later this week, they'll start digging up the bodies. If one of them happens to be this Greek girl, he'll get life." Raynes smiled. "And then you'll be able to get your divorce. I don't think Tom'll be in a position to trouble you any more."

Lesley seemed grateful.

"Thank you for helping me. You've gone to a lot of trouble."

She gave him a quick kiss.

Raynes looked at her thoughtfully.

"I wonder," he said, "if you could do something for me? I wonder if you could get some fresh crystals of potassium cyanide from your friend, Janet, as quickly as possible. I would like you to put them in an envelope and hide them in Tom's safe – or in a drawer in his desk. Make sure there are definitely no fingerprints and that the stuff is one hundred per cent genuine."

"You want me to plant it on him?"

"Yes," said Raynes. "To make absolutely sure he gets convicted. With a man like Tom, I daren't leave anything to chance."

32. *The Beguiling of Merlin*

Liz Baxter was as warm and cuddly as ever. She was once again wearing a soft, white jumper and figure-hugging, plum-coloured trousers.

She welcomed the Inspector perhaps more warmly than he had expected. He was offered a cup of coffee and followed the plum-coloured trousers into the kitchen, where he inspected a selection of Cherry's own paintings which were plastered all over the kitchen wall.

"Has your husband got his picture yet?"

"No. His birthday's not till the twenty-eighth."

"Are you having a big party?"

"Of course. It's not every day we commission a painting."

"I take it's a special occasion?"

"The big five-0. I don't think he really wanted to celebrate his birthday this year – but we just couldn't let it pass by. It's also a sort of thank-offering for our marriage; for surviving all we've been through this past year."

"Angela?"

"Yes. Angela."

She sighed deeply as she poured out the coffee.

"Just sugar, please. Two spoonfuls."

They sat down at the kitchen table.

"She did her best to drive us apart."

"But your husband resisted her?"

"It might have been better if he'd given way. She'd have played around with him for a while and then moved on to someone else."

She stirred her coffee sadly.

"Instead, his refusal just provoked her. She decided to spread stories. Bare-faced lies. Made out she was having a great time with her groom. And everyone believed her."

"Including you?"

"Yes. Including me. People kept coming up to me and saying how sorry they were. Day after day. Pat denied it till he was blue in the face. Then he got angry – and hit me. In front of Cherry. I know I shouldn't have said all I did. I'm sorry now, but at the time, I was livid."

"Why didn't he just resign?"

Liz shrugged her shoulders.

"We needed the job. It gave us a roof over our heads. And Pat loved the horses. He always loved horses. He didn't see why he should go when he'd done nothing wrong."

"So you went?"

"Just for a fortnight. Last November. Cherry and I went to stay with friends."

Something inside Raynes told him that he should ask who the "friends" were, but he didn't want to appear too nosey. So, instead, he turned to the peacemaker.

"Katie told me that she went to see you."

"She was a great help. She told me what her stepmother was like. She told me how she'd lied about Pat – just to get her own back on him. I couldn't really believe that she could be as wicked as that."

"So you returned home?"

"Well, it was coming up to Cherry's birthday. December 4th. She was beginning to get very upset – missing her dad. Crying a lot. Playing up. So we came back for her birthday. Then we both decided we should do something nice to celebrate his birthday. Hence the picture."

"Are you pleased with it?"

"Very. Pat'll be really chuffed."

"When I last saw it, it wasn't quite finished."

"It is now. And Simon's hunting for a suitable frame."

Raynes did not miss the obvious point.

"Why didn't you ask Simon to do the painting?"

202

Liz looked at the Inspector.

A slightly mocking look.

"Do I need to explain? I'm sure you've already gathered that Simon and I are good friends. Nothing intimate. Just very good friends. He helped me out during the separation. But after all that's happened, I didn't want any more tongues to wag. It was safer going to Brackles." She smiled sweetly. "Anyway, at that time, Simon was far too busy. He spent hours on your picture."

Raynes finally caught up with his inner voice.

"You stayed at the studio?"

"Didn't Simon tell you?"

"Never said a word."

"Good for him!"

"It must be true love!"

Liz smiled.

"It may be . . . on his part. Anyway, we lived with your picture. Cherry kept asking: 'Why has the lady got no clothes?' And Simon said: 'It was a very hot day'. I think that's what gave us the idea of getting one of our own. And Brackles is terribly fond of children."

"And brandy!" Raynes said to himself. To Liz, he said:

"You must have wondered whether Brackles would be still around to finish it?"

"Well, of course, he was arrested. And no one was allowed into his studio for two weeks. The police were everywhere. The questions they asked!"

"They came to see you?"

"The very next day. They wanted to know exactly what I'd seen and done when I turned up with Cherry. I told them. In fact, I told them several times. Pat got absolutely fed up with them."

"He doesn't like policemen."

Liz twisted up her face.

"The thing is – he doesn't have much faith in them. All his life, they seem to have put obstacles in his way. Just yesterday, they came round to ask him about a gun licence. They went on and on about it. And yet, when there was an attack on the stables the other night, they refused to send anyone."

"An attack on the stables?"

"Well, there've been two this week. The first was on Easter Monday . . . everyone was away at the hunt. They came and sprayed the walls with graffiti – and slogans. Pat had to clean it all off and re-paint the walls. He also put in a small alarm . . ."

Raynes managed to keep a straight face.

" . . . And it was just as well he did. Another thug broke into the stables on Tuesday night; but Pat caught him and handed him over to the police. But what happened? Did he appear in court? No, they let him go."

"Infuriating!" said Raynes.

"It does make you wonder," said Liz. "They spent a whole hour going on about his gun – but they let these people off scot-free. On Monday, they said all their men had been on duty at the hunt – to make sure there was no protest – not like there was on Boxing Day. They said all their staff had gone home." She shook her head. "They don't seem to have got anywhere with the murder either."

"Your husband told me that he thought it was those people up in London."

"I wouldn't be surprised. Simon thinks they had it in for Brackles. Wanted to kill two birds with one stone."

"But why should they want to get rid of Brackles? He was doing a good job for them, storing all that booze."

"Perhaps Lesley was getting impatient?"

Liz spoke more truly than she knew.

Raynes looked at her thoughtfully.

"And where were you on the day of the murder?"

"Working."

"At the College in Hastings?"

Liz nodded.

"With Max?"

"Yes. He's a senior lecturer."

"And you?"

"I'm a technician."

204

"In a laboratory?"

Liz flushed visibly.

"Yes."

"With access to poisons?"

She smiled bravely.

"We have some nasty things locked in our cupboards."

"Potassium cyanide?"

"I've never looked. But there's sulphuric acid and hydrochloric acid; they're dangerous enough. But you'll be glad to hear the head of department, Mr Bayliss, keeps all the keys in his pocket. Not me."

"Do you see Max much at the college?"

"Sometimes. When I go in for coffee."

"You meet him there?"

"Occasionally. Most days I spend the coffee break setting up the equipment for the next class."

"Do you leave work early? Do you collect Cherry from school?"

"I work part-time. Sometimes morning – sometimes afternoon. When I'm working Pat collects her."

"And which shift were you working on the day of the murder?"

"The police have already asked me that."

Raynes smiled.

"I'm asking you again."

Liz looked sad and disappointed.

"I thought you were a friend," she said reproachfully. "A friend who came down all the way from Grasshallows to have a cup of coffee . . ." Her eyes twinkled. " . . . and to admire my figure."

"It's certainly worth admiring," said Raynes gallantly. "And worth a trip all the way down from Grasshallows! But you're right. I find it impossible to keep my nose out of a juicy case."

Liz laughed.

"Well, if you want to know what I was doing, I was buying a Valentine card for my husband. He'd already got a Valentine card that morning – which he thought came from me. But it didn't."

She grimaced.

"It came from Angela."

"How did you guess? Even though she was hard at it with Brackles, she couldn't let go."

"So you were in town that afternoon?"

"I was."

"And who did you see? Brackles? You must have seen someone."

"I saw Max."

"Really?"

Liz nodded.

"With someone I never expected to see him with."

"Philip Royle?"

"You knew?"

"No. It was an intelligent guess. Max has a soft spot for Philip. Felt sorry for what Angela did to him at Christmas. Just as Katie felt sorry for you."

"Pat would have been horrified."

"Sleeping with the enemy?"

"I don't know what they were doing."

"Actually," said Raynes, "they were probably going to the dentist's. Philip Royle told me he was in Rye that afternoon getting his teeth fixed."

Liz looked frankly disbelieving.

"They both seemed incredibly cheerful. They were laughing and joking. Makes one think."

"It does."

There was silence for a few minutes. Raynes looked at her engagement ring. Quite a small one. Not expensive. And a wedding ring. Very plain and simple. But she had beautiful hands. He could imagine them softly caressing him. He revelled in the fantasy for a few seconds and then decided to get back to business. There had been enough small talk. It was time to disclose why he had come down from Grasshallows to see her.

"Tell me," he said, "why did you come to live here?"

"In Rye? Because it's a beautiful place."

"And Pat got offered a job here?"

Liz nodded.

"I think you said he originally came from Norfolk?"

"He did."

"Is that where you were living before you came to Rye?"

Liz looked hesitant.

"No. He had a job in Suffolk."

"And before that?"

"We lived abroad."

"In New Zealand?"

"How did you know that?"

Raynes pointed to Cherry's artistic endeavours.

"She seems to have an affection for Mount Cook. And the only Mount Cook I can think of is in New Zealand."

Liz visibly relaxed.

"You're quite right. We were in New Zealand. She was very happy there. Didn't want to come to England."

"And you yourself are from New Zealand?"

"I am. I was born in Christchurch."

Raynes smiled. A dangerous smile.

"Where you married Pat?"

She nodded.

Where was all this leading?

She soon discovered.

"I imagine it must've been difficult changing your name?"

"Changing my name? Most people do it when they marry."

"So they do," said Raynes. "But I think you've changed it more than once. You were born Elizabeth Baxter . . .?"

"I was."

There were red patches on both her cheeks. She looked extremely flustered.

Raynes put a finger to his lips.

"You were Liz Baxter. You married. And yet, you are still Liz Baxter. How do you explain it?"

Liz had no intention of explaining it. Her mouth was drawn in a firm, hard line.

"I think," said Raynes, "that your married name is Mallowan. Am I right? In fact, Lady Elizabeth Mallowan?"

Liz was speechless.

She could not think how to answer. She had been happy to talk about Simon, about her job – and about the murder. But she had never expected the Inspector to ask her questions about *that*. Never for one minute. He had caught her completely off guard. As he had intended.

"Yes," he said. "Lady Mallowan – in very reduced circumstances. Why?"

Liz recovered her voice.

"I'm not saying anything. You'd better ask my husband."

"Sir George?"

"I'm not saying anything." She looked at the clock. "He's due back in about ten minutes. You can ask him."

"I will," said Raynes. "But I must say that I find it surprising that the heir to Sir Ian's wealth should be working as a groom on the estate of the man who deprived him of his heritage. His rightful heritage. Why? And for what reason?"

Liz still felt numb with shock. It was difficult to think of anything to say. She must stall – stall for time. Warn Pat. But how could she warn Pat? The moment he walked in, the Inspector would pounce. And Pat would blame her for blabbing. He would say it was her fault.

She looked at the Inspector.

"You bastard!" she said to herself.

Raynes could almost see the words forming on her lips. He knew what she was feeling. There would be no kisses from those lips; no caresses from those hands.

She took a deep breath.

"Would you like another cup of coffee?"

"That would be most kind," said Raynes. "But spare me the hydrochloric acid!"

"If I had it, I'd use it!" said Liz.

Raynes smiled.

"I bet you would!"

33. *The Last Man*

The minutes ticked by; no one spoke. Raynes looked out of the window – a beautiful spring day. Liz drank her coffee sip

208

by sip – very slowly. The Inspector knew that whatever he said, she would remain silent and tight-lipped until her husband returned. She had expected him home at noon, but he did not return till 12.15pm. So it was a long wait.

They heard Pat's pick-up truck stop at the gate, the sound of heavy footsteps coming up the path, then the door crashed open. Pat was carrying a large sack of potatoes. He seemed surprised to find they had a visitor.

He put the potatoes down and looked at the Inspector.

"Haven't I . . .? Aren't you . . .?"

Raynes quickly took out his identity card.

"Inspector Raynes. Grasshallows police. Friend of Katie Middleton. We met at the stables last month."

But Mr Baxter felt that they had met more recently than that. He looked closely at the identity tag and then at Raynes' face.

"I remember you . . ."

" . . . And I remember you. But my visit today is about something quite different."

Pat looked at his wife.

"This is the man I caught at the stables."

"The thug?"

"Yes. The one who set off the alarm."

Raynes smiled a faint smile.

"You threatened me with a double-barrelled shotgun."

Pat laughed coldly.

"You deserved it. Breaking into the stables in the middle of the night. Frightening the horses . . ."

Raynes stopped him there.

"Did you find any damage to the locks? Any broken woodwork?"

Pat looked at him with hard grey eyes.

"No. I can't say that I did."

"I used keys. Official keys to get in. Katie . . ."

He decided it would do no harm to incriminate George's daughter.

"She never said."

"Of course not. It was a police matter."

"You were after that safe?"

Raynes nodded.

"Did you know what was in it?"

Pat turned away.

"I knew the safe was there; but I didn't know what was in it. She wouldn't have told me. But I knew it was important to her. She kept her valuables in it."

Raynes decided to allay Mr Baxter's suspicions.

"That safe has a combination lock. How d'you think I'd have got into it if I didn't have the number?"

"Why didn't you come in daylight," Pat snapped, "like any honest person? Why come like a thief in the night?"

"I knew that other people were looking for that safe. I wanted to get there first."

Pat sniffed contemptuously.

"I can see now why the police let you off. Dog doesn't eat dog."

"Quite so," said Raynes, glad that Pat would never know the unpleasantness of his arrest and his uncomfortable half hour with Inspector Appleton.

"Anyway," he added, "that wasn't the reason why I came to speak to you and your wife . . ."

Liz intervened.

"Be careful what you say. He knows . . ."

"Knows what?"

"I didn't tell him. But he knows."

Pat looked at the Inspector more closely.

Raynes took a deep breath.

"I have discovered from the police in New Zealand that you are George Mallowan, the grand-nephew of Sir Ian Mallowan of Grasshallows – now Sir George Mallowan – and you have been cheated out of an inheritance which is rightly yours."

Pat continued to stare at the Inspector.

His face was pale.

Raynes said: "Shall we sit down; then I can tell you what has been happening."

They sat down.

The Inspector reminded Pat of the afternoon he and Debbie

had met him at the stables. How they had had lunch with Sir George, who had proudly showed him his family tree.

Raynes explained that he had had some inner doubt about the document. Something had nagged him. He described how he had gone back to Grasshallows and set enquiries in motion. How those enquiries had taken him to Bournemouth.

Pat looked at Liz.

"Mr Eastwood."

"The lawyer."

"Yes," said Raynes. "The lawyer. He was the one who cheated you out of your inheritance. But not deliberately. He was misled."

Pat snorted.

"He was a crook. All lawyers are crooks." He turned to his wife. "I told you he was up to his neck in it."

Raynes smiled pleasantly. It was nice to see all the details clicking into place.

"You were Mr Cook?" he said. "Mr Paul Cook?"

Pat looked a trifle embarrassed.

"You went to see him?"

"He was tight as a clam. Wouldn't say anything."

Raynes explained. "I think you have to understand. He too had been led up the garden path. We all were. The housekeeper, who had been looking after Sir Ian's affairs, arranged the whole thing. She even made sure there was a pile of letters from his grand-nephew in South Africa . . ."

"South Africa?"

"Yes. That was the story. You were working in Johannesburg, writing quite regularly to Sir Ian, telling him how you were getting on with your business, renting out lorries and equipment."

Pat and his wife looked blank.

"When the time came for Sir Ian's will to be executed, the grand-nephew was summoned back from South Africa; he signed all the necessary documents and inherited the nine millions. The rest you know."

Pat shook his head with amazement.

"He gave the money to the wrong man?"

"Yes," said Raynes. "But he didn't know it was the wrong man. He was led to believe that this was the real Sir George. He acted in good faith."

"Good faith!"

"The person who led him up the garden path was the housekeeper. As I said, she arranged all this."

"But why did she do that?"

Raynes laid his ace on the table.

"Because she intended to marry Sir George. They got married shortly after he received the money." He paused. "It will probably help you to understand the situation more clearly if I tell you that his housekeeper was a Mrs Angela Anderson."

It was clear from the stunned silence around the table that neither Liz nor Pat knew this part of the story.

Raynes hoped that perhaps, now they knew where he was coming from, they might be more co-operative. He waited a few more moments till the facts had sunk in, then he said: "Why don't you tell me your side of the story – from the beginning?"

Pat was silent.

Liz said: "We've got nothing to lose."

Pat looked at the Inspector.

"Are you going to deal with Sir George?"

"Most certainly. He's going to be charged with fraud."

"He's not going to be able to wriggle out of it?"

"No. I've told him he's been rumbled. But I've also told him it may be some time before the matter reaches court. Once he is charged, all his accounts will be frozen."

Pat sighed.

"It's been a long business. A long, long business. I grew up in the shadow of Sir Ian. My father died in the war, when I was two. I never knew him. Sir Ian looked after all our family affairs. He was a great man – but he had his faults. He could be mean and interfering. Not very generous – especially if you didn't do things his way. He'd got my life mapped out even before I'd reached primary school. Told me I should go to university – even which college. He would pay for it. But

212

I'm afraid I didn't like being dictated to. Never have . . ."

He smiled sadly at Liz.

"I much prefer to paddle my own canoe. I liked working with animals. With horses. I worked on a farm in Suffolk for many years. Occasionally, I asked Sir Ian for help. He helped – but he seemed to grudge every penny. Sent me long, sanctimonious letters telling me I should better myself. I got rather tired of it.

"I married – but it didn't work out. I decided to emigrate. To clear out of the country. To go as far away as possible. New Zealand seemed a good choice. Very British – and yet unspoilt, Plenty of land; forests and mountains. So I went there. When was it?"

"1968."

"Yes, 1968. Cut all links with Britain. Didn't want my ex-wife chasing after me! I sent Sir Ian the odd letter – the odd card; but I didn't give him my address. In fact, to be honest, I forgot about him. I was so busy with my new life. Managed a large farm in the South Island. Enjoyed it immensely.

"It wasn't till I met Liz that I began to think about things back here. She asked me about my family. I told her about Sir Ian. She thought I ought to write to him and tell him about us. So I wrote. No reply. I wrote again."

"Three times you wrote."

"You sent your letters to Grasshallows?"

"Yes. And all I got back – after the third letter – was 'Not known at this address'. So I realized he had moved."

"Or died!" said Liz

"Quite," said Raynes. "What year would that have been?"

"1979."

"Then Cherry was born . . ."

"We thought we ought to tell him about her; but by that time, he'd been dead three years."

"He died in October 1977."

"Yes, I discovered that. I wrote to the Law Society about him and they told me when and where he'd died. They also told me who his lawyers were; but when I wrote to them, they gave me a very dusty reply."

"So you came over yourself?"

"Eventually. I must confess I didn't rush. I had more important things on my mind; but Liz said I might be due some money. We were thinking of buying a farm of our own. So I came over – when would it be? Late '85 – early '86? And I went down to Bournemouth to see that lawyer.

"He was very unhelpful. Told me the bare bones of the situation. Wouldn't show me the will. Told me where I could see it. He led me to believe that the bulk of Sir Ian's money had gone to good causes. That was what I had expected. I was quite shocked when I did see the will. £12 million! And only £3 million to good causes. I'd never thought he was so rich. I imagined that he'd perhaps left a million – at the most. Perhaps given me £100,000. That would have been nice. But £9 million!"

"So what did you do?"

"Well, I couldn't prove I was the grand-nephew. I had no documents with me except my passport. I had no other family living in England. I couldn't afford any expensive lawsuit. I didn't know any lawyers. So I went back home and discussed it with Liz.

"She suggested we should hire a private eye and track down the impostor and also check up on Mr Eastwood. It took time. More money. When the information did come back, it was devastating. Sir George and Lady Angela were respectable members of the county set; they had a large mansion, land . . . friends. It seemed that it would be difficult to shift them.

"We took it to our lawyer in Christchurch to see what he could do, whilst we came over here as a family. We stayed with old friends of mine in Suffolk – and then we heard, from the private eye, that Sir George was wanting a groom for his stables. It was an ideal opportunity to get our foot in the door!"

"Pat applied for the job. Got it immediately. And they gave us the house."

"When was that?"

"Just before Christmas 1987. We celebrated Cherry's birthday the first week we moved in."

"Bare boards!"

"It's improved a bit since then."

"So you were eyeball to eyeball with the enemy?"

"Yes. It was very interesting watching them at such close quarters. We dispensed with the private eye. But we urged our lawyers in New Zealand to get on with things – but they were very slow chasing up documents. Then the person handling it fell ill . . ."

"And later died!"

"Yes. He died."

"So you have still made no claim?"

Pat reached up to the second shelf of the kitchen dresser and handed Raynes a letter. The Inspector read it – and looked up.

"Another three months?"

"That's been the story all along. I can't think why they've been so slow."

"I can," said Raynes.

"Money," said Pat. "The longer they take, the more they charge, I've no time for lawyers."

"Or for policemen!" said Raynes to himself.

To Liz and Pat, he said: "We had great difficulties ourselves. It wasn't till we got to Mr Eastwood that we began to see what had happened."

"You began at the other end. You met Sir George; you saw the family tree."

"Quite right. But we had a terribly frustrating time in Grasshallows trying to find anyone who remembered Sir Ian."

"And now?"

"Well, things are obviously going to come out into the open. But so is the murder inquiry."

"What difference does that make?"

"Well," said Raynes, "technically, none at all. From all my investigations, I can prove that you are the real Sir George Mallowan – and the gentleman in Blake House is an impostor. We can get him chucked out. And we can get you what money is left. But, in revealing your identity, you become the number one suspect."

Pat looked alarmed.

"Whilst you were just the groom, looking after the stables, there was no reason why you should have wanted to kill Lady Angela. I know she made sexual demands on you . . . tried to break up your marriage . . . and perhaps you may have wanted to hit back. But that was three months ago. Why wait so long? And there were other people who hated her more . . ."

"The people in London?"

"Precisely. But if it emerges that you are the rightful heir to Sir Ian's estate; if Sir George and Lady Angela have defrauded you of your inheritance – and have been living it up for the past twelve years. Twelve years! And then you appear on the scene, living under an assumed name. If you had discovered that Lady Angela was personally responsible for the fraud – then you might have had every reason for hating her . . . for wanting to kill her. You therefore become a leading suspect. Had you never thought of that?"

Pat stroked his chin.

"If I'm to be honest with you, yes. That's why we used Liz's family name. Didn't want people to know who we really were. After the murder, we were frightened it would come out. The police would look into our background – and everything. But they didn't."

"We assumed that our secret was safe."

"It was – until I saw Cherry's pictures."

Pat looked at the display on the kitchen wall.

"It's not all that obvious."

"Not unless you know what you're looking for."

Raynes returned to the murder investigation.

"So on the afternoon of Monday 14th, you were in the stables?"

"I was there most of the day. Two of the horses were sick."

Pat did not seem to be hiding anything. All he seemed to care about was horses.

Raynes stood up.

"Well," he said, "we'll keep your secret for a little longer. But when the murder enquiry becomes public, it'll have to come out."

As he left the house, Raynes cast a final glance at the kitchen dresser. There, on the top shelf, were the two Valentine cards sitting side by side. It was perhaps a good thing that Pat did not know that one of them had come from Angela. It might have put him off his lunch.

34. *Beelzebub*

It took Philip Royle some time to realize who his customer was. One saw so many new faces. Over the Easter weekend, the pub had been full of visitors. Perhaps he was one of them.

It was only when he laid his identity card down on the bar that Philip realized that he was once again facing the Inspector who had so unnerved him two weeks before.

"You remember me?"

"Very well."

"Letters sent to a lady?"

"Oh, yes?"

Philip seemed relieved that it was only letters that were being mentioned.

"I have them in my possession." Raynes paused. "I don't think the Sussex police have seen them yet. Otherwise, you might have been charged before now."

"I was very angry."

"I know you were. But your letters provoked Lady Angela to thoughts of murder . . . *your* murder."

Philip wiped the bar with a cloth.

"I'm still here," he said.

"You've been very lucky," said Raynes. "From what I hear, she arranged for someone to get her the cyanide – with a view to silencing you once and for all."

"She didn't succeed."

"No. Because you have friends."

Philip said nothing. Max had told him about his conversation with the Inspector.

"It seems that someone changed the contents of the cyanide bottle to something less dangerous. Did you eat or drink something that made you sick?"

Philip nodded.

"I had a violent case of dysentery at the end of January. It was very unpleasant."

"It could have been worse."

Philip nodded glumly.

Raynes moved to more delicate matters.

"I believe it was your friend, Max – Mr Middleton – who supplied Angela with the 'cyanide'?"

"He was being blackmailed. He told me."

"But not till after it happened?"

"Not till after the murder."

"He told you what she made him do?"

"He was very upset about it. He apologized."

Raynes looked thoughtfully at the young man.

"But he was more than a friend. He had been – perhaps still was – your lover?"

Philip Royle said nothing.

"You went to the College in Hastings?"

Philip nodded.

"But you dropped out?"

"It wasn't for me."

"But whilst you were there, you attracted Mr Middleton's attention? He took a close interest in you? I believe you sent him some photographs of a personal nature?"

Philip said nothing.

"It's no use denying it," said Raynes. "I've got the letters and the photographs. They were found in Lady Angela's safe. That's what she was using to blackmail your friend. If he wanted to keep his job . . . if he wanted to hold on to his wife and family . . . he had to do her bidding."

"I realize that." Philip spoke gently. "I don't hold it against him."

"But you hold it against her?"

"Of course. It was blackmail. It was cruel."

"Might it have provoked you to murder her?"

"I didn't touch her."

"You told me you were in Rye on the afternoon of the

murder."

Philip was silent.

"You were seen with Max in the main street 'laughing and joking'." Raynes watched the barman's face for any signs of guilt.

"You told me you went to the dentist."

"I did."

"Laughing and joking?"

Philip remained silent. He hated this man. He had you tied up in knots even before he put his questions.

"Why was Max with you that afternoon?"

"Well, it's not what you think. He was just giving me moral support. He hated Angela. He was very upset about what she did to me. In fact, if you want to know the truth, he paid for all my dental treatment."

"Did he?" said Raynes. "How very generous of him!"

"Well, he thought he ought to do something."

"After getting her the poison . . .?"

"He didn't get the poison."

"His wife's a chemist."

"But he didn't get it from her. He didn't want her to know anything about it. He told me he had got some technician to get it for him."

"Really?" said Raynes, thinking immediately of Liz Baxter.

To Philip, he said: "So if anyone did the switch – substituted the cyanide for something else – it would have been the technician?"

"Could've been." Philip looked thoughtful. "Of course, it might have been switched years ago. Not a very safe thing to have lying around. Perhaps Max told the technician to put something else in the bottle. But if he did, he didn't tell me."

"Nor Angela," said Raynes.

Another thought struck him.

"I suppose," he said, "Max could have changed the contents of the bottle but still given you the real stuff. If you had had the cyanide crystals, you could have diluted them, put them it in a bottle of brandy – and taken it to the studio. That could've been why you were 'laughing and joking'. You had got your revenge. Both of you."

Philip Royle did not smile.

"You're entitled to your opinion. But I'm not a man of violence."

"Oh, come on!" said Raynes. "Not a man of violence! What about Boxing Day? What about Easter Monday?"

"There was no violence on Easter Monday."

"Nothing at the meet. But who sprayed the stable walls with graffiti and slogans? Come on! You've got to admit that!"

"I'm not admitting anything."

At last, Philip showed some anger.

"The trouble with you," said Raynes, "is that you are a coward. You attack people – and when they hit back, you don't like it. You provoked Lady Angela on Boxing Day. Quite rightly, she hit back and kicked you in the teeth. You wrote her nasty, slimy letters. Anonymous. Poison pen. But she knew they came from you. She had your name on the envelope. You threatened her . . . frightened her. She wanted to kill you. She blackmailed Max into getting the cyanide. If he'd played her straight, she'd have killed you. But with Max's help, you got the cyanide. You had the last word. You attack animals and stables. Why not people? You had the motive and the means. The finger of suspicion points directly at you."

Philip Royle was silent.

Once again he picked up the cloth and wiped the bar.

There was nothing he could say. This policeman had built up a convincing case – most of it was true. He could not prove his innocence. If he said any more, he might incriminate Max. He was determined not to let him down. But the Inspector was right. He was a coward. His natural reaction was to do things by stealth. The events on Boxing Day had been the exception and he had suffered heavily for it.

Raynes said quietly: "When I leave this pub, I am going directly to Rye police station to speak to Inspector Appleton, who is in charge of this case. Is there anything you want to say? Any defence you wish to make?"

Philip shook his head.

Raynes looked at him long and hard – then turned on his heel. As he turned away, he thought there were tears in Philip's eyes. There would be many more to come.

35. *The Charnel House*

Raynes and Carlisle joined members of the Metropolitan police in Theydon Bois early on Wednesday morning. It was a crisp, chilly day – more February than April. Four police vans were parked in Morgan Drive; they contained sniffer dogs, sledge-hammers, shovels, body-bags – everything that was needed for the exhumation.

"Which house are we going for?"

"No. 87. According to our information, the house was owned by a friend of the suspect."

Raynes hoped that Carlisle had got his facts correct. It would be terrible to make a boob in front of so many witnesses.

The officer-in-charge looked at his watch.

"7.30am. Let's go!"

The team assembled in the garden of No. 87. The owner had been watching the scene from her bedroom window. When the door bell rang, she was quickly down at her front door. She was wearing a lace nightie and a blue dressing gown.

"What is it?" she said. "What's happening?"

"Are you Mrs Whitworth?"

She nodded.

"Are you the owner of the house?"

She nodded again.

"We have a warrant to search your garage."

"My garage?"

"Yes. May we come in?"

Three officers – including Raynes – went through to the kitchen where they explained the object of their visit.

"Bodies?" she squeaked.

The police asked her for the keys to her car and the garage and explained that that their operation might last several days. Would she like to move elsewhere?

"Oh, no!" Mrs Whitworth wanted to watch all that was going on. Nothing so exciting had happened since her husband's funeral eight years before. Bodies in the garage? Who would have thought it? The neighbours would be incredibly jealous! It was terribly exciting. Was there anything she could do to help?

"Tea?" suggested Raynes. "Lots of mugs of tea?"

Whilst Mrs Whitworth went upstairs to get dressed, her car was moved and the police team trooped into the garage and looked at the concrete floor. It was obvious where the inspection pit had been – but were there really bodies down there? Or was the whole thing just a hoax?

The area of the pit was chiselled out and the surface concrete broken up. Underneath, they were faced with a layer of rubble, bricks, stones, gravel into which someone had poured cement. The police removed the rubble in marked bags.

Sniffer dogs were invited to give their opinion – but showed little interest. Relays of police broke up the ground and worked down deeper into the pit. Having so much manpower, the job was swiftly done.

Raynes stood silently, looking into the long, dark hole.

If he was wrong – if Angela was wrong, he was going to look a bloody fool. Carlisle also stood anxiously at his side, wondering if he had chosen the right house.

Two feet down, the officers suddenly stopped. They called for lights. Powerful floodlights were set up and wires run back to the nearest van.

"What is it?" asked Raynes.

"Something blue. A shirt cuff, I think."

The lights revealed that there was indeed a blue shirt and an arm inside. It was slowly uncovered – and then the police photographer set to work.

Raynes relaxed.

At least there was one body in there. He could see the

hand. Or rather, what had once been a hand.

He looked at Carlisle.

The younger man was deeply relieved.

Bit by bit, the surrounding rubble was chipped away and the full body could be seen. It was a man with a beard. After exhaustive photographs had been taken, the body was moved on to a metal tray, strapped in position, lifted out of the pit and taken to the police forensic surgeon, who had established a temporary mortuary in a white tent on the front lawn. Raynes and Carlisle went with the body to see what had been found.

The moment the bearded man was lifted out, two more bodies were seen underneath. The same slow process of clearing the debris, releasing the bodies and photographing the remains continued. It was eleven o'clock by the time the third body had been removed. The police were becoming quite excited by their find.

"How many bodies d'you think there are?"

"Seven or eight, at least," said Raynes. "It should help you clear up your missing persons list!"

"What period did you say they were?"

"'64 to '70, I should think. Mrs Whitworth's been here for fifteen years. It was before that."

As each layer of rubble was removed, more bodies came to light. It was a grim business. By 3.00pm, they had reached someone whom Raynes felt might be the Italian waiter. The remains of a black suit suggested some such occupation, but the body was badly decomposed and the skull had been shattered.

As the search neared the bottom of the pit, Raynes and Carlisle watched more closely. The sixth body was that of a woman. She was to one side of the waiter. Raynes hoped it would be Helen Dimitriades. The torso was wrapped in a grey blanket tied up with rope. The remains were unearthed and brought to the surface. Raynes followed the corpse to the makeshift mortuary and watched the tests on the rope and blanket before the torso was uncovered.

It was a hideous sight – and Carlisle was sick. Raynes was also upset but turned away. It was terrible to think that this was a beautiful young woman whose life had just been casually snuffed out to protect a thief. On the assumption that it was Helen's body, Raynes told the surgeon the suspected cause of death – not that there was much likelihood of any surviving proof.

Eleven corpses were removed from the inspection pit; eleven bodies taken away for a full forensic examination elsewhere. During the day, more and more police came to visit the site. Mrs Whitworth ran out of tea bags at an early stage. By lunchtime, the press had begun to gather and were demanding information. They scented blood. Raynes could imagine the headlines: "House of Horror!" . . . "Gangland Graveyard." He hoped that the police would not say too much and give Tom Travers time to escape. With a bit of luck, an arrest could be effected that night before the story broke in the press. "A man is helping police with their enquiries" was all that was needed.

Mr Travers had a lot to answer for. Raynes wished the courts still had the power to pass the death sentence. He deserved every inch of the rope.

36. *The Turkish Bath*

Raynes enjoyed organizing the final gathering at Blake House. Even though his colleagues had always teased him about being old-fashioned and "storybookish", he felt that a fascinating murder – like a good wine – deserved a fine setting in which the search for truth could be revealed and the triumph of detection applauded. He felt that although the Sussex police and the Met both knew part of the story, only he had the full picture The background needed to be explained so that everyone could see their own part in the drama. Once that was done, he could put his finger on the villain – and expose him. True, it was theatrical; but modern life was so dull that it needed a roll of the drums and a blast on the trumpet.

Even George seemed to have captured the excitement of

the moment. He was rushing round organizing the seating, offering people drinks, exuding bonhomie. It was perhaps hard for him to realize that he was one of the prime suspects and that his liberty would soon be drastically curtailed.

The others had been rounded up at the last minute. Some had come willingly – like Simon and Brackles, Lesley and Janet.

Katie had come to support her dad, but Max was frightened that his private life might be exposed. He came with great reluctance.

Philip Royle had been ordered to attend; so had Charles Eastwood. The new Sir George Mallowan felt that he would have been better employed looking after the horses and Liz had said that she could not leave Cherry on her own. Mr Travers appeared in handcuffs, escorted by two officers from the Met. He was blazing with anger and his dark eyes flashed with hatred.

Even Mrs May had been persuaded to come down to see justice done. Raynes had been rather surprised to see her stepping out of a brand-new Jaguar XJ6. He had not realized that she owned anything quite so expensive. Lesley Travers had also been surprised – and jealous. She felt that the Inspector's whore had upstaged her. What was a BMW beside a silver-grey Jaguar?

Anyway, they were all there – including Bernard, stroking his beard thoughtfully in the back row.

Lady Angela was also there. Raynes had insisted that her picture be brought over to Blake House from Brackles' studio and given pride of place on the wall above the Chippendale cabinet. To Raynes' eyes, it looked magnificent; but George Proctor was embarrassed. Charles Eastwood and Tom Travers were visibly taken aback. Judging by the looks on their faces, it was deeply resented by Philip Royle and also by Lesley and Janet. Even though George was no longer the matrimonial prospect he had once been, both women felt in some strange way that the house was theirs. Brackles, of course, was over the moon. He was clasping a glass of George's finest brandy and expounding the finer points of the painting to anyone who would listen.

Six members of the Sussex police stood together in a group, looking somewhat confused. Why were they there? They hadn't caught anyone. Inspector Appleton was startled to see so many strangers – people he had never seen before – assembled as suspects. He recognized that he was out of his depth but Raynes had promised him that he could chair the gathering and arrest the murderer – and anyone else who had committed a crime – after the Inspector had completed his exposition. The presence of officers from the Metropolitan police and four other armed officers outside, gave him confidence that Inspector Raynes would be as good as his word.

As everyone settled into their comfortable seats, Raynes nodded to Inspector Appleton. His moment had come. He stood up and cleared his throat.

"I am very glad to see you all here today – including colleagues from Grasshallows and London. This has been a major investigation involving police from many counties. All of us have been working on the case but I have asked Detective-Inspector Raynes from the Grasshallows force to present the background details and explain how the murder was solved. Inspector Raynes . . ."

Raynes took his place in front of the Chippendale cabinet and the portrait of Lady Angela. He smiled disarmingly.

"The origins of this case go back more than twenty years. In those days – the 'swinging sixties' – there was in central London a night club called *The Blue Diamond*. It was owned by a man called Bernard and managed by a rather ruthless young fellow called Tom Travers. Twenty years on – how little things change! Bernard is still running a gaming club – the *Nightflyers* – and Tom is still his manager. One would have thought that by now both men would have earned enough to enjoy a comfortable retirement!

"Anyway, in those far distant days, a young woman from Hammersmith – Angela White – found herself attracted by the bright lights. She ended up working in *The Blue Diamond* and had a brief affair with Bernard. Like many people, she took an immediate dislike to Tom Travers who – even then – had a reputation for doing unpleasant things to women who got in his way.

"A young Greek girl also worked at the club – Helen Dimitriades. She had an affair with Tom – and then a stormy row about a bracelet. She vanished. So also did a waiter called Riccardo, who might have been able to tell the police what had happened to Helen – but was never seen again. Angela feared that she might be Tom's third victim, so she left. She moved to Peterborough and covered her tracks by marrying a man called Derek Anderson. But just in case anything should happen to her, she left a signed statement for the police – to be opened in the event of her death." Raynes paused. "I have found that statement most useful."

Tom Travers was examining his nails. He looked thoroughly bored by the proceedings. Raynes smiled. His time would come.

"Her marriage to Mr Anderson did not last long. She met an engaging rogue called George Proctor and was eventually the cause of his second divorce. Money was the chief object of Angela's life. And where better to find it than amongst the elderly and infirm who might be needing a housekeeper to care for them in old age? A few thousands could be siphoned out of their accounts before she moved on.

"Angela's exploitation of the elderly and infirm brought her to Sir Ian's door. There was no doubt that he was rich – a sober analysis of his business files and bank statements removed all doubt. But Sir Ian still possessed all his faculties. No wool could be pulled over his eyes. Any advantage to be drawn from this source required subtlety and skill. Angela had both. She discovered – presumably from reading his will – that Sir Ian had left the bulk of his estate to his grand-nephew. Who was this grand-nephew? Where did he live? Angela would have discovered that even Sir Ian was a little vague on this score. He had not heard from the young man for several years. Rumours may have reached him that he had gone abroad. There would have been cards with postmarks suggesting Australia – or New Zealand.

"Angela decided to capitalize on this uncertainty. The grand-nephew would be rediscovered. South Africa seemed a lively country for an enterprising young man. She decided that George Mallowan would reappear there. Before finalizing her plans, she made sure she gleaned every last detail about the grand-nephew. Any surviving letter, card, certificate or photograph was examined most carefully till she had the full picture. And then her lover and fellow-conspirator, George Proctor, was sent off to South Africa to prepare the way to the nine millions."

George seemed to be enjoying all this. He was sitting back in a large armchair, smoking a cigar and drinking his whisky. Now and again, he smiled and nodded.

"I imagine Sir Ian was delighted when George surfaced in South Africa. He had a slightly guilty feeling about his grand-nephew. He felt he had been a bit harsh – a bit mean – over the years. He was willing to make amends.

He was pleasantly surprised to find that George was now a salesman for lorries and earth-moving equipment. He had given up his earlier love of animals. He seemed to be doing well. He sent him a few letters and George responded from time to time."

Raynes sought confirmation from George.

"I imagine Angela wrote all the letters, typed them and sent them out to you?"

George coughed modestly.

"It was all her idea. She read Sir Ian's letters before she posted them – and then she sent me the replies. All I had to do was stick on a stamp and post them back."

Raynes smiled.

It was just as he had thought.

"Having established herself in Sir Ian's household as a trusted employee and an indefatigable doer of good deeds, she was able to persuade him that he should move to Bournemouth – which would be better for his health. Following his stroke, Sir Ian had had to move around in a wheelchair. A bungalow would suit him much better. So an attractive bungalow was found in Bournemouth and they moved there in March 1976. Here, Sir Ian became acquainted with Mr Charles Eastwood, an employee . . ."

" . . . a partner . . ." said Mr Eastwood.

" . . . a partner, no less, in the firm of Miller & Duckworth. Mr Eastwood handled all Sir Ian's legal affairs with great care and efficiency. He had no alternative because he was under the eagle eye of a great jurist. But what those eagle eyes did not see was Mr Eastwood's burgeoning love for the housekeeper, Mrs Anderson."

Raynes looked at the lawyer to see what impact this revelation might have on him. The reaction was just as he would have wished. Mr Eastwood looked thunderstruck. How had the Inspector discovered that?

The Inspector enlightened him.

"Lady Angela kept a number of letters in her safe. Eighteen of them were from her friend in Bournemouth. They revealed hazy, lazy, crazy days spent together on the Undercliff at Lyme Regis and other romantic places where kisses could be secretly exchanged and promises made. It seems that Angela agreed to become Mr Eastwood's wife. She would fill a vacant space in his heart; but not until Sir Ian died and all his affairs were settled. Mr Eastwood could scarcely wait till this treasure fell into his arms."

George laughed sarcastically.

"Poor sod! She conned him good and proper!"

Raynes could see tears in the lawyer's eyes. Even after all these years, he still smarted from Angela's rejection.

"Unfortunately, Mr Eastwood did not realize that this was part of the plan. He was being softened up to make sure the passage of the will was swift and smooth. If Angela was in love with him, there could be no likelihood of her showing the slightest interest in the new Sir George Mallowan.

"So the grand-nephew came back from South Africa, supplied with all the relevant documents and proof of identity – and inherited the estate. Angela and George then went off for a holiday in Mexico, where they got married in December 1977. Later, when they came home, they bought this house and lived here for the next twelve years.

"As we know, they lived in great style." Raynes looked round the beautifully proportioned drawing room with its high ceiling, its gilt mirrors and its fine furniture. "Sir George was Lord of the Manor and Angela was the life and soul of the county set. She loved riding and before long, she set up her stables and bought some fine horses. She shared this interest with her step-daughter, Katie. All went well – for many years. There was a lot of riding, a lot of sex and a lot of fun. Angela got into the habit of being able to buy whatever she wanted – to make demands on other people, to dominate, seduce, pick up and put down . . . She was very selfish, very greedy and very immoral; but as one or two of her admirers have said . . ." Raynes looked at Simon. " . . . she was irresistible.

"All went well until she met Brackles. He had established a studio in Rye and painted portraits of many local worthies. Angela thought it would be rather nice if she could have her picture done as well. So she made contact. What she did not know was that Brackles had a very profitable sideline storing smuggled brandy for an old friend in London. That friend was Bernard. In the course of conversation, Lady Angela told Brackles that she had once worked in *The Blue Diamond*, and Brackles – quite innocently – passed this information back to Bernard who, of course, told Tom.

"Mr Travers now knew who Angela was – and where she lived. He knew that she held the key to secrets in his past, which could still lead to his arrest. So Lesley was sent down to Rye to spy out the land. Not surprisingly, she caught George's eye and had soon wheedled her way into his heart. There was talk of divorce and remarriage.

"The appearance of Lesley – and her connection with Tom – unnerved Lady Angela. The suggestion has been made that George himself wanted to get rid of Angela; that he asked his son-in-law, Max, about the possibility of getting some poison . . . to kill off the pigeons which were defacing his stately home."

Everyone laughed – except George.

"But Max reckoned that what he really wanted was to get

rid of Angela."

"That's a lie!" said Max angrily.

"Of course it is," said George. "I never wanted to hurt Angela."

"But you were thinking of marrying Lesley?" said Raynes.

"She was thinking of marrying me. There's a difference!"

"Well, the thought was there. Lesley's friend, Janet, had the means. She worked in the jewellery trade where she had access to the poison. She and Tom could have provided the cyanide and cleared the way for Lesley to become the next Lady Mallowan."

Max was unhappy at being misrepresented by the Inspector.

"I told you it was *Angela* who wanted the poison! Not George!"

Raynes chuckled.

"So that she could murder Lesley? A much better idea!"

Lesley did not smile.

Raynes continued: "Since November, Angela had been having a very enjoyable affair with Brackles. George knew perfectly well what was going on. As he said: when he came back at five to collect her, all that Brackles had to show for the afternoon's work was a bit of fresh paint on the horse's tail! The portrait has now been completed and today it hangs in pride of place in this drawing room – as it was intended to."

Raynes gave the painting a casual glance before moving on.

"At this point, another suspect appeared on the scene. Mr Philip Royle is an active member of the anti-blood-sports brigade and he and his friends decided to stage a major protest at the Boxing Day meet. Much violence was done to dogs and horses – including an attack on Natal, Lady Angela's favourite horse. Lady Angela retaliated forcefully. She hit Philip across the face with her whip and kicked him in the teeth. This naturally caused the young man a lot of pain. He lost several teeth and it probably destroyed his long-cherished ambition of becoming a model. He also took legal action against her.

"Unfortunately, the wheels of justice did not move as quickly as he would have wished. Rather foolishly, he sent Angela a number of threatening letters which were also found in her safe. Angela became extremely frightened as to what Philip might do to her – and her horses – so it seems that she decided to get rid of him . . ."

Raynes was amused to see that he had now engaged the full attention of the Sussex police. One of them was busily taking notes.

" . . . Max has already mentioned the fact that Lady Angela asked him to get her some poison from the college where he worked. Max would have liked to have said: 'No', but Angela had a hold over him – as she did over many people – and she threatened him: 'If you do not give me what I want, you're for the high jump!'"

(Raynes thought he had described the situation as discreetly as Max could have wished.)

"So he did what she asked. Being himself a mathematics lecturer, he had no access to any laboratory; but his wife did – and he also had a friend at the college, Liz Baxter, who was a technician. He had helped her to get a job at the College when she first came to Rye. Perhaps he could ask her to help him? But it was a rather frightening request: 'Could you get me some cyanide?' and Liz may have seen the anxiety in Max's eyes. She realized that this request could cause trouble; someone might be killed. So she decided that she would substitute some less dangerous substance so that no harm would be done."

Raynes looked at Liz to see if there was any reaction. Liz was sitting with her arms folded tightly across her chest. Her face was completely expressionless.

"Mrs Baxter told me that she had no access to the poisons cupboard; the head of department held the keys. But we all know what happens. The cupboard is left open; the keys are lying about. It is the work of a moment to go through the jars and bottles and take what you want. It is equally amazing how often quite dangerous poisons are left lying about. So Liz passed over what purported to be potassium cyanide to Max, who passed it on to Angela."

Raynes was aware that he had moved from the realm of fact to speculation. He quickly moved back to safer ground.

"Lady Angela attempted to kill Philip Royle at the end of January. The young man was quite ill for a couple of days – but he recovered. Angela was annoyed; but there was little she could do. Max, not knowing about the substitution, felt extremely guilty. He had been a party to attempted murder. Philip Royle had been one of his students at the College and he had a . . . soft spot for the young man."

Raynes looked at Katie.

This was a bad moment for her. Her face was contorted with anger.

"Him? You were friendly with him! How could you – after all he's done?"

Max said nothing. He was terrified that worse secrets might emerge. He did not trust the Inspector.

Raynes continued: "Max told Philip what Angela had planned . . ."

" . . . Not till after the murder," said Philip.

"That's your story," said Raynes. "It remains to be proved. There is always the possibility that Liz gave Max the genuine stuff – and that *he* did the substitution. Then, when Angela's plan failed, he gave you the cyanide so that you could kill Angela!"

"That's not true!"

Raynes ignored Philip's feeble protest.

"You may like to know that Philip and Max were seen together in Rye on the afternoon of the murder. They were supposed to be going to the dentist's where Philip was receiving treatment; but the person who saw them said they were 'laughing and joking'. I leave you to draw your own conclusions."

Katie burst into tears.

Raynes looked at her.

"Of course," he said maliciously, "we could look at this from another angle. It could be that Mrs Middleton discovered the pressures her husband was under . . . the blackmail and the guilt which were driving him to drink . . . and *she* decided to take the cyanide from her own laboratory – as the local police believe she did . . ." Raynes looked to Inspector Appleton, seeking confirmation. Inspector Appleton nodded.

" . . . Then, of course,she would have had to cover her tracks. This could have been done well before the murder. Max may have got the cyanide from Liz – and given it to his wife! She would have had access to many substitutes which could have made Philip ill. But she would have had to replenish her stock, so that when the police came to examine the poisons book, there would be no discrepancy. These things can work both ways."

Katie's face was a picture. But not a pretty picture. Her eyelids were red and there were pink blotches on both cheeks. Raynes felt sorry for provoking her.

"Into this already crowded scenario, there came another person with a legitimate grievance against Lady Angela. The real Sir George Mallowan, Sir Ian's grand-nephew, who had been farming in New Zealand for many years. I was not aware of his presence amongst us until I saw his birth certificate – carefully retained at Blake House by Lady Angela."

Raynes noted the blank looks on most people's faces. They had no idea to whom he was referring. He would soon enlighten them.

"His date of birth was April 28th. That date rang a bell. Was it not the same day as that of Pat Baxter, Lady Angela's groom, whose daughter was also having her picture painted at Brackles' studio? And was this not a special birthday? His fiftieth? Sure enough, the birth certificate told me that George Mallowan was born in 1939. It was too much of a coincidence. I went to see Mr and Mrs Baxter and noticed that several of their daughter's pictures featured Mount Cook! So I discovered that the real Sir George had been living incognito in Rye for over a year and working for the bogus Sir George. How curious!"

A ripple of excitement ran through the audience. Pat

Baxter looked nervously to left and right. Inspector Appleton sighed deeply and put his head in his hands. Raynes reckoned it must be very galling not to have known these things.

For the benefit of the Metropolitan police who knew nothing about the background, Raynes explained:

"Now there was a reason for this. Mr Baxter . . . I shall continue to call him that . . . Mr Baxter had severed his connections with his grand-uncle and, for many years, had put him completely out of his mind. But when he married Liz – and, more particularly, after Cherry was born – he decided to get in touch with the old man. Perhaps he might have died? Perhaps he might have left him a few thousands in his will? 'Hope springs eternal in the human breast'. But letters proved unavailing, so he came over to this country to find out for himself what had been happening.

"He discovered that Sir Ian had died in Bournemouth so he went to see his lawyer. Mr Eastwood was not very forthcoming because he did not know who this man was; nor did he understand his connection with the Mallowan family. This was because Mr Baxter used a false name: Paul Cook. So Mr Eastwood was right to be suspicious. But Mr Baxter also had his doubts about the lawyer. Had he been a party to the fraud? Had he got his cut from those who had cheated him out of his inheritance, which he now discovered was a very large sum? Nearly nine millions."

Mr Eastwood rose to his feet.

"Sit down!" said Raynes. "I haven't finished. Mr Baxter went home to New Zealand and set various legal wheels in motion to establish his identity and press his claim to be the true heir to Sir Ian's estate.

"He employed a private eye to track down those who had cheated him out of his millions. And once he knew where Lady Angela was living, he and his family came over to Britain and, by immense good fortune, he obtained a job as groom at the stables at Blake House."

Katie was staring at Pat with complete amazement. To think he was the real Sir George! She had had no idea. All she knew was that he had been very kind to her – and she to him. Would

235

he remember all this when he recovered the estate? At least he would look after the horses. They would be in safe hands.

Yes. They were all thinking.

Sir George had finished both his whisky and his cigar. He was staring at the ceiling. There was now no hope of his escaping judgement. He would go to jail. It was all over.

Raynes tied the whole thing together.

"You may perhaps imagine the horror – and the repulsion – Pat Baxter felt when Lady Angela proposed that they should have sex together. Brutal – and perverted sex. This might have attracted some men . . ." (Raynes looked at Debbie) " . . . but not Pat. This was the woman who had cheated him out of his inheritance – and was flaunting her wealth day by day. Now she was inviting him to deceive his wife – to undermine the life of a happy little family." (Raynes allowed himself to wax sentimental.) "Naturally, he refused. But this did not do him much good. Lady Angela spread the story of their supposed 'affair' far and wide. She succeeded in her intention; she broke up his family. Liz left home. And but for Katie's kind help, their marriage would have been destroyed.

"Now," said Raynes, "I feel that this makes Mr Baxter – the real Sir George Mallowan – a leading suspect in this murder enquiry. He stood to benefit enormously from Lady Angela's death. He bore her a very deep grudge. He had been cheated and humiliated; his family life almost shattered. What better grounds for murder? On the afternoon that Lady Angela died, Mr Baxter had no alibi; and neither did his wife. He was supposedly at the stables; she was in Rye buying him a Valentine card!"

Pat Baxter looked confused.

"So that's why . . .?"

"The other Valentine was from Lady Angela!" said Liz.

"I thought you bought me both?"

Liz shook her head.

Raynes watched with interest.

"So then," he said, "we have nine main suspects, any one of whom might have wanted to kill Lady Angela – for a variety of different reasons. Her husband, because he wanted to marry Lesley; Philip Royle, because of what she did to him on Boxing Day – and because she later tried to kill him; Tom Travers, to silence a witness from the past; Lesley Travers, because she wanted to marry Sir George and become Lady Mallowan; Mr Charles Eastwood, in revenge for her rejection all those years ago; Pat Baxter, because she had cheated him out of his inheritance; Liz, because she had tried to break up their family; Max Middleton, because of her blackmail and cruelty towards Philip Royle; Katie, because of her anger at what Angela had done to her father and her husband. Beyond that inner circle, we should also consider Bernard, who received the smuggled goods; Janet, who may have supplied the cyanide; and two jealous lovers, Simon and Brackles, who were very close to the murder scene."

Raynes smiled.

"Take your pick!"

But, clearly, everyone was leaving the decision to him.

37. *The Mad Assassin*

"Alibis count for very little in this case," said Raynes. "All the suspects could have done it. I have already mentioned Liz Baxter going into Rye to buy a Valentine; and also that Max and Philip were seen in town on their way to the dentist. I am told that Brackles had gone shopping; George Proctor was driving home for a pleasant afternoon with Lesley Travers. Tom could have been dropped off on their way to Blake House. The real Sir George was at the stables, looking after the horses. Katie Middleton was suffering from a migraine; Simon was in his studio. I have not asked Bernard or Charles Eastwood where they were at 2.00pm on Monday 14th, but I am sure they will have some superb alibi – just like the young lady who was supposed to be in Paris but was seen on the doorstep of Blake House by Mrs Beaton!"

Lesley looked sharply at Janet.

Raynes smiled happily.

"I have indicated that three people had access to the

poison: Katie, Liz and Janet. Through their connections, either Katie or Liz could have supplied Max, George, Philip Royle, the real Sir George, Simon or Brackles. Janet could have supplied Bernard, Tom or Lesley. There is no evidence that Mr Eastwood had access to the poison; but had he wanted it, I'm sure he could have obtained it. Of course," said Raynes airily, "it is quite possible that there may have been other sources of supply we know nothing about."

The Inspector tried not to look in Lesley's direction.

"Neither does the brandy help us. It is a well-known brand – available in most wine stores and supermarkets. I saw a bottle of it behind the bar at the *Windmill*. Anyone who had access to Brackles' studio could have picked up a bottle. Mr Travers and Bernard handled vast quantities of the stuff. So – no help there!

"I have already outlined the possible motives for the murder, but perhaps I might now consider some of the inhibiting factors, things which might have prevented certain suspects from killing Lady Angela.

"First of all, I cannot for the life of me see what Brackles had to gain by murdering Angela whilst he was still painting her picture. They were having a most enjoyable affair; there was £5000 to be collected. Unless he himself had been threatened with murder, I cannot see Brackles poisoning her. Nor Simon, Brackles' neighbour. He spoke about her most tenderly. There was no jealousy or bitterness that I could see.

"Mr Travers, we know, was frightened of what Angela might say. But, over a period of twenty years, she had said nothing. Mrs Travers did not start hunting for the safe until after she died – for obvious reasons. Would not Mr Travers have been wiser to let sleeping dogs lie?

"The real Sir George and his wife, Liz, have been in this country for eighteen months. They have instituted legal action to claim their inheritance. The process is slow but it will get there in the end. There was no need to act precipitately; but if they had chosen to do so, why kill only Angela? Why not kill George as well? My personal observations have led me to believe that Sir George is not a man of violence. When he captured a man breaking into his stables and put a gun to his head, that gun was not loaded!"

Sir George smiled grimly.

Perhaps it would have been better if it had been!

"Equally, I find it difficult to see why Mr Eastwood should have waited all these years before seeking revenge. It is now twelve years since Lady Angela deserted him and two years since 'Paul Cook' alerted him to the possibility of a mistake. If he was going to kill anyone, surely it would have been better to kill the real Sir George rather than the impostors?"

Raynes turned to Katie Middleton.

"Now I know that Katie disliked her stepmother. She had always disliked her – even though they shared a love of horses. But, once again, I do not see Katie as a figure of violence. She is sensible and practical. And even though the local police have questioned her several times, they have not found any evidence to prove that she murdered Angela.

"Which brings me to Max and his friend, Philip. In their case, I do not see any inhibiting factors. Max actually took steps to get poison for his mother-in-law, even though he knew it was to be used to kill his friend." Raynes emphasized the point. "He was willing to be a party to murder. Now if Max had killed her before she tried to poison Philip Royle, I could have understood it. But he tamely handed over the 'poison'. If he didn't kill Angela then, why should he suddenly do so a fortnight later?

"Was he influenced by Philip? Did the young man persuade him that Lady Angela had become too dangerous? She had tried to murder him once; might she not try it again? Did he propose that together they should poison her – and hope that others would take the blame? Philip's attacks on Angela were mostly of a sneaky character. Anonymous letters. Nasty phone calls. That ties in with the detached nature of the murder. The means were provided for Angela to kill herself. But would Philip do this on his own? Would he not look to the older man for support?

"This was the conclusion I had reached after my visit to Max. I felt that he knew who had committed the murder – but was too terrified to admit it. If Philip was the murderer, then Max would have had to be involved. He would have been the one to provide the cyanide – the right stuff this time. Both men are by nature cowards; only with the other's fullest support could they have carried it off."

Raynes looked at Max.

The strain was beginning to tell. He was sweating – badly – and his eyes had a haunted look. His hands were gripping the arms of his chair. At any moment, he might stand up and scream. By contrast, Philip Royle seemed calm and controlled.

Raynes continued:

"But there were two things which challenged this conclusion. The first was that neither Philip nor Max had any connection with Brackles or his studio – at least as far as I knew. They would not have known the layout of the place; they would not have known of Brackles' habit of going out shopping on Monday afternoons. They would not have had access to the distinctive yellow writing paper on which Brackles pens his little notes.

"By contrast, Mr Travers is well acquainted with the studio. He was a regular visitor – mostly by night – collecting the booze and taking it back to London. He was an old friend of Brackles; he knew all his little ways. Many a time he had helped him when he was down on his uppers – getting him commissions for his paintings.

"He knew that Angela would be there that afternoon. Why else would Lesley be going to spend an afternoon with George? Tom knew exactly what time she would arrive at the studio. He knew her tastes in drink – her greedy, selfish habits. And Tom is no coward. He has proved many a time that if a person gets in his way, they will be 'removed'.

"The second thing was Lady Angela's statement to the police. It was a very detailed document. As I have said, it gave a very full report of the circumstances surrounding Helen's disappearance. She also did a little detective work to try and find where Helen's body might have been buried. She was able to pinpoint four houses in North London which had inspection pits in their garages . . ."

Tom looked up. For the first time, he seemed anxious.

"With the help of the Metropolitan police, we discovered the exact house where Helen was reported to be buried and we dug up the inspection pit last Wednesday. We found eleven bodies in the pit – one of them was Helen's, another the Italian waiter. This was conclusive proof of the truth of Angela's statement.

"All the bodies found on the site belonged to people who went missing in the period 1964 - 1970. Fortunately, the bodies were in quite good condition. The inspection pit was dry and so was the rubble which had been used to cover the bodies. A concrete surface acted as a seal. No air or water entered the cavity so the bodies were well preserved and identification quite straightforward. It is perhaps interesting to note that the person who owned the house was a friend of Mr Travers – who himself went missing a few years later. His body was not found in the pit."

Raynes paused before he dropped his next little bomb.

"Mr Travers was arrested early on Thursday morning. His office was searched and an envelope containing crystals of potassium cyanide were found in his safe."

That made Tom sit up. He looked startled – as well he might. He looked accusingly at Lesley; but her eyes were on the Inspector.

"It seems that cyanide was one of Mr Travers' favourite weapons. The police surgeon tells me that four of the victims probably died from cyanide poisoning. But that was not his only method. In her statement, Angela tells us that he took one young woman to Bulgaria for a holiday and drowned her in the hotel swimming pool. Mr Travers boasted that if any woman got in his way, he would soon deal with her. Angela would not have been the first."

Tom began to feel quite rattled. His past sins were raining down on him thick and fast. He stared at the Inspector with amazement. The episode in Bulgaria was something he had long since forgotten.

Raynes was pleased to see that everyone was giving him the fullest attention. Max seemed to have relaxed. But members of the Sussex police were still busy taking notes.

"I am reliably informed that after Angela's murder, Mr Travers was planning to get rid of Brackles. Another inconvenient witness! He had offered him a passport to help him get out of the country – but he would never have reached his destination."

Now it was the painter's turn to be astonished.

Raynes looked at him.

"He offered you a passport?"

Brackles nodded.

"Well, count yourself lucky you never received it. It could have been your death warrant."

Raynes was now approaching his conclusion.

"Most of Mr Travers' murders were . . . 'non-attributable'. They came to light later. And Lady Angela's was no exception. It was swift and silent. Very professional. No clues to help the police. If Lesley had been able to find the safe and had handed over Lady Angela's statement to her husband, Mr Travers would have walked free. No bodies would have been discovered. There would have been no case against him. We should not be here this afternoon. Lesley found the combination number in Lady Angela's address book; but she just could not find the safe itself. If she or her husband had been more 'horsey' people, they would have known where to look.

"From the grave, Angela and Helen – and countless others – will have their revenge. Justice will at last be done."

Raynes turned to Inspector Appleton.

"You have your man! You have also the former Sir George Mallowan – guilty of a serious act of fraud; Mr Charles Eastwood – guilty of professional misconduct, aiding and abetting a fraud; Mr Philip Royle – guilty of sending threatening material through the post; Bernard – guilty of smuggling thousands of bottles of brandy and other liquor into this country illegally. I hope that with all the bodies discovered in Theydon Bois, both you and the Met will have enough work to keep you busy for many months to come!"

Inspector Raynes sat down.

Inspector Appleton was somewhat lost for words. He thanked Raynes for his excellent work and then announced that no one would be able to leave the room until they had been given his permission. All five men named by the Inspector would be taken to Rye police station for further questioning. Detailed statements would be taken from each of them. Officers from the Met would continue to be responsible for Mr Travers.

Raynes watched Appleton gradually taking control of events. It was going to be a busy night in the police cells. He was glad that he would not be there. His hope was that he and Debbie could have another glorious night in the four-poster bed at the hotel. He felt that it would be only right to charge his expenses to the Sussex police. He had saved them a lot of money – and time.

* * * *

The Inspector was about to make his way over to Debbie when he was accosted by a very angry Charles Eastwood.

"Mr Raynes, I must tell you that I deeply resent the way you have handled this case. You have done both myself and my firm irreparable damage. If I am charged, I shall be forced to resign."

"I hope so," said Raynes.

"You hope so? Have you no feelings?"

The Inspector eyed him coldly.

"You failed to live up to the highest standards of your profession. You were party to a massive fraud. You've been lucky to escape these last twelve years but you would have been rumbled – if not by me. The real Sir George would have reported you to the Law Society. You wouldn't have escaped. It is only right that your career should end in shame. The sooner you admit your faults, the better."

Raynes turned away and headed towards Debbie who was now laughing and joking with Brackles. But once again he was waylaid. One of the officers from London came up to him.

"Mr Travers wishes to speak to you."

"Does he? Well, I'm not surprised."

He worked his way across the room to where Tom was drinking a final toast to freedom. Before approaching him, Raynes made sure that he was drinking from a plastic glass.

Tom eyed the Inspector with the utmost hostility.

"I should have got rid of you when I had the chance."

"Indeed you should. It's a great mistake to put things off. One often gets overtaken by events."

"I didn't realize you knew so much."

"I didn't. It was all thanks to Angela. She told me all I needed to know."

Tom's mouth twisted with rage.

"I didn't kill her!"

"You killed all the others!"

"But I didn't kill her. I should have done – but I didn't."

"Pity!" said Raynes. "Everyone thought you were the ideal suspect."

"You framed me, you bastard! Putting that cyanide in my safe! It wasn't there on Sunday night. You cooked it up with that bitch so that I would get sent down."

Raynes was feeling nothing if not charitable.

"I presume you are referring to your dear wife?" he said. "I think you probably underestimated how much she wanted to get rid of you!"

"And what will happen to the club?"

Raynes smiled.

"I don't think your departure will make much difference. She lacks your charm – but she's equally ruthless. Nothing will stop her."

Tom was still writhing with fury – even though he was handcuffed to the arms of his chair.

"It was a plant!" he said.

"It was," Raynes agreed – making sure that the two officers from the Met could not hear him. They were standing about six feet away.

"You admit it?"

"I do."

"Why?"

244

"Because it will give you greater kudos among the criminal fraternity. You will be able to live up to your reputation: 'No woman ever got in my way – and survived'. That's your boast. Surely it's better to go down with the reputation of having poisoned Lady Angela, rather than having to admit that, in the end, she brought you down? Better to let everyone think you were a winner right to the end. Even twenty-two years on, you still caught up with her – and silenced her! It makes you one of Britain's greatest serial killers. Don't spoil it!"

A glimmer of understanding dawned in Tom Travers' eyes.

"You mean . . .?"

"Go along with it. Blame me for your arrest. Most people do! But don't admit to anyone that it was a woman who brought you down. Say that whilst you were playing the field, you won every trick."

"Including Angela?"

"Including Angela. It won't cost you anything. You're going to get life for all the other murders. One more won't make any difference. So you might as well make it a round dozen!"

Tom sneered.

"There were more than that!"

"Far more," Raynes agreed. "I remember a case in Bermondsey when I was a young policeman on the beat. You managed to get off that one, but we all knew you were guilty . . . I haven't forgotten."

Tom clearly remembered the incident.

"Luke . . .? Luke something?"

"Luke Brown. A barman. He was drowned in his bath."

Tom nodded.

"That was years ago. There've been many more since then."

"Well," said Raynes encouragingly. "Take Angela on board and make it a grand slam!"

Tom looked surprised at the way Raynes had talked him round. He no longer felt so angry or bitter. A glow of triumph and achievement was slowly burning inside him.

"You're a clever bastard!"

"Just luck," said Raynes modestly. "Just luck. Would you like another whisky?"

38. *La Vie*

Simon said to Liz:

"I think I've found you a nice frame for Cherry's picture. Would you like to see it?"

"Of course."

Liz looked across the room towards her husband. He seemed deep in conversation with Inspector Appleton.

"I think he's going to be busy for quite some time."

"It won't take long."

So, with Inspector Appleton's permission, they slipped away from Blake House and returned to the studio. Simon had fitted the canvas into the frame and hung it on the studio wall. He put on the spotlights.

The lights immediately brought the picture to life. It was another of Brackles' superbly detailed paintings. The eyes were full of mischief and one could almost feel the texture of her straw hat and her pink dress.

As Simon had said, the frame fitted perfectly.

He put his arm round Liz's shoulders.

"They say that behind every painting, there's a story."

"And this one more than most."

As she spoke, they heard, behind them, the sound of footsteps coming up the uncarpeted stairs. They moved apart.

It was the Inspector.

"Admiring the picture?"

"Yes. I've found a suitable frame."

"Is it finished?"

Liz nodded.

Raynes said: "You must feel very proud."

"Of having such a beautiful daughter?"

The Inspector smiled.

"Of having such a faithful friend."

246

"Oh, Simon, you mean."

"I hope you will give him a little of your nine million. He deserves it."

Liz smiled lovingly at the artist.

Raynes listed his finer points.

"A man who will fetch and carry. Buy frames. Paint pictures. Take in refugees. Care for homeless women and their children. Wipe fingerprints off bottles . . ."

A slight chill filled the room.

Simon said: "What are you implying?"

"Nothing," said Raynes. "But I think it might be advisable if Liz and her family went back to New Zealand as quickly as possible."

"Why?"

Liz did not look pleased.

"In case your luck runs out."

"Why should it?"

"Because it may be only a matter of time before the police discover that Tom Travers did not kill Lady Angela. Then they will start looking elsewhere. It could be dangerous."

Simon looked surprised.

"But you were so convincing. You were able to prove every detail. Access to the brandy. Cyanide in his office safe. The plan to kill Brackles. All the other people he killed. The fact that he was in Rye on the day of the murder. Are you saying all that was a lie?"

"No," said Raynes. "All the evidence was correct. Tom had killed many times before – and planned to kill again. Much though he would have liked to kill Lady Angela, he was still frightened of the evidence against him emerging after her death. Because of that, he stayed his hand."

"But you said it was Tom. You completely convinced Inspector Appleton."

"And I even convinced you?"

"Of course."

"Both of you?"

Liz nodded.

"Even though you both knew differently?"

"Dick! Stop talking in riddles!"

Raynes shook his head sadly.

"You know that Tom Travers did not kill Lady Angela. You know that because you know who did kill her."

Simon tried to look blank.

"I'm afraid you've lost me."

"Me too," said Liz.

Raynes began to get irritated.

"You cleaned the fingerprints off the bottle," he said, looking at Simon. "Otherwise, how could you possibly know that there was only one set of fingerprints on the bottle? The police would never have told you that. It was the most stupid thing to say. I've spent weeks trying to figure out an alternative explanation. There isn't one.

"You cleaned the bottle to make sure that the murderer could not be identified. You removed every scrap of evidence before the police got there. So that bottle, glass, table were clean. Quite unnatural, don't you think? But why do it? Either because you are the person who killed Lady Angela – or because you are shielding someone else."

"I think you're building a lot on nothing," said Simon.

"No," said Raynes. "It's all true. All the evidence points one way. I'm sorry you got involved. You're probably sorry you got involved – because you were fond of Angela. Remember – you cried when you talked about her. You couldn't forget the fun, the excitement, the naughtiness . . . You knew all her faults but you still loved her – at least a little."

Simon said nothing.

Liz looked at him with anxious eyes.

Raynes smiled sadly.

"But even though you got involved, I don't blame you. It's not worth destroying other people's lives to get posthumous justice for a creature like her. She was a crook, a bitch, a blackmailer, a serial adulterer. She intended to kill Philip Royle." Raynes looked at Liz. "If you hadn't done a swap – and changed the crystals – Philip would now be dead and you would have found yourself in the dock as an accessory to murder."

"You said it was Janet who provided the cyanide."

"Well, it wasn't. It was Liz."

Raynes looked at the newly-discovered Lady Mallowan who was white-faced and shaking. She held on tightly to Simon's arm.

"Liz provided Max with the bogus cyanide. But whatever it was, it wasn't completely harmless. It upset Philip's stomach for several days. But what happened to the real stuff?"

"I put it in another bottle," said Liz.

She did not sound all that convincing.

"And could you take me to that bottle and show me where the cyanide is?"

Liz's eyes brightened.

"Yes, I could."

"But would it all be there? Would there not perhaps be a spoonful or two missing?"

"It would be difficult to tell. It wasn't a full bottle."

She sounded more confident.

Raynes smiled indulgently.

"I think that if the truth be known, there would be some missing."

"You couldn't prove it."

"Of course not," said Raynes. "But it's not where the cyanide came from that matters; it's how it was administered."

He took a deep breath.

"This murder has all the hallmarks of an inside job – which is why Brackles was arrested and held in custody for so long. Whoever did the murder knew that Brackles was a creature of habit. He usually did his shopping on a Monday afternoon. The murderer knew that Brackles would be out. He knew that the studio door would be open. That no one else would be dropping in till four o'clock. It would be easy to set up the brandy and the glass so that Angela, arriving at two o'clock and finding no one there, would help herself to a drink.

"The paper on which the note was written and sent to Angela was paper to be found in the studio. Pale yellow paper. Very distinctive. The writing on the note was done by someone used to receiving notes from Brackles; someone who knew his style and handwriting. It was delivered – without the slightest whiff of suspicion – to Blake House. Again no fingerprints. It probably travelled in a polythene bag and was posted through the letter box by someone wearing rubber gloves. It was all carefully prepared.

"And it was all arranged for St Valentine's Day! A nice touch that! A natural day for lovers to meet. To send each other cards – except . . ." Raynes paused. " . . . except that Lady Angela sent her Valentine to the groom rather than to Brackles!"

"He got one too," said Simon.

"Did he?" said the Inspector thoughtfully. "Then perhaps Lady Angela did not send one to her groom? Perhaps, as your husband thought, both Valentines came from you?"

Raynes looked sharply at Liz.

"A card from Angela would have given you an excellent excuse for being out shopping in Rye on Monday afternoon. A card which purported to come from the cruel lady . . . but which Pat thought came from you . . . and a genuine one which did come from you. A strange way to go about things," Raynes mused. "But an excellent alibi. If one was buying a Valentine, one could not possibly be doing a murder!"

Raynes laughed – but no one else did.

He turned to Simon.

"Now Liz lived here for a fortnight. I didn't know this. You didn't tell me – but Liz did. When Lady Angela accused Pat of dirty deeds in the stables, she came running to you. She would have acquired a clear picture of life in both households. She chose to get Cherry's picture painted by Brackles – not because she was frightened of tongues wagging – but because she wanted to get acquainted with the lay-out of Brackles' studio."

"That's rubbish!"

"Is it?" The Inspector's voice had a sharper edge. "You had decided to get your revenge on Lady Angela for the way she had deceived your husband, for the loss of his inheritance and for the allegations she had spread about their 'affair'. That was in November. When did Brackles start on Lady Angela's picture?"

"December."

"And Cherry's picture?"

"January."

"I make my point."

"It's only a hunch."

"No, I'm afraid it's more than that. The very absence of comment speaks volumes. You never mentioned Liz. Normally, you boast about all your conquests. You always have. But Liz was never mentioned."

Liz came to Simon's defence.

"I told you there was nothing intimate between us."

Simon looked at Liz.

He seemed surprised.

"I'm afraid I didn't believe you," said Raynes. "I don't see how you could have escaped – living under the same roof – for a fortnight! He even had designs on my friend, Mrs May, though he only met her for one afternoon!"

Simon laughed.

"Do you blame me?"

"No," said Raynes. "I know what you're like – that's why I didn't believe Liz. I think you were very close. I think you still are. That's why I followed you back to the studio."

"We weren't doing anything wrong."

"You can tell," said Raynes. "Anyway, once I knew that Liz was the mother of the little girl who was having her picture painted, my suspicions were instantly aroused. I had considered that this unknown woman might have been responsible for the murder. But I didn't see any connection. Had I known that she was the wife of Lady Angela's groom, I might have had one or two bright ideas. Had I known that she was the heavily-disguised Lady Mallowan, I might have started getting excited. To know that she was also your mistress – that she had lived for a fortnight in this house – I would have been quite convinced that she was the guilty party. The fact that you said nothing about her was most revealing."

"So what are you going to do?" asked Simon nervously.

Raynes smiled.

"I have arranged with my colleague, Detective-Constable Carlisle, to go to Liz's home and collect both Valentine cards. I saw them on the dresser the other day. They're probably still there. I'm quite sure that if one of them had come from Lady Angela, it would have been binned – long ago! We shall test both cards for fingerprints. If we find Lady Angela's prints on either card, I shall be wrong."

He paused.

"But I'm not wrong. Liz provided the cyanide! She 'borrowed' one of Brackles' bottles of brandy. She pinched the paper, wrote the note and delivered it to Blake House. Then she doctored the brandy. She's a technician. She knows what she's doing. She worked the morning shift at the College; she returned to Rye; she watched Brackles go out shopping. Then she dashed into the studio; set up the scene. It didn't take more than a few minutes. Lady Angela arrived; killed herself. Time passes. Cherry and her mother arrive for their appointment. A little early – before Brackles is due back. They find the corpse. They rush into your studio." Raynes looked thoughtfully at Simon. "You dash into Brackles' studio to see if what Liz is saying is true. You remove any trace of fingerprints; you wipe all surfaces clean. You return – and phone the police. Inspector Appleton turns up to find a weeping child and a distraught mother. And 200 crates of brandy! Enough to distract anyone! But the point is: Lady Angela is dead – and you were involved! You knew who had done it. And you protected her."

Simon was caution itself.

"Are you charging us?"

"No," said Raynes. "I'm just telling you I know who did it – and why. I can't really blame either of you. Lady Angela cheated you and the real Sir George for twelve years. She spent money like water. Your money! She tried to destroy your marriage. Sir Ian's wish was that his grand-nephew should receive the bulk of his estate. He would have been delighted to know that you were happily married and had a

252

daughter. He would have been pleased with your plans to buy a farm in New Zealand. He would have been proud of you for punishing a wicked woman. And as an accomplished lawyer, he would have made it his duty to defend you against the police. He might even have won!"

Raynes looked at Liz one last time.

"And so my advice to you is this – go back to New Zealand; buy your farm; bring up your family; have Cherry's lovely picture hung above the mantelpiece in your sitting room. Keep well away from Rye for another five years. And say nothing!" He smiled. "And if you would like to make a thank-offering for the fact that I am not charging you – make over the stables and the horses to Katie. She loves them. It'll give her some happiness whilst her dad's in jail."

"George was going to do that."

"A nice gesture."

Raynes turned to Simon.

"And as for you – you old scallywag! You've knocked off both Lady Mallowans. The genuine one and the fake. My advice to you is – keep your hands off Liz! Let her go. If you want to remember her – paint her picture."

"A nude?"

"It's up to you. But do it from memory. You've done it once; you can do it again! One for the bedroom this time. To be toasted in champagne drunk out of pink mugs!"

He grimaced. "And I hope it chokes you!"

* * * *

Raynes left the studio and walked over to the silver-grey Jaguar XJ6, where Mrs May was sitting impatiently at the wheel, wearing black gloves.

He sank back into the light-blue leather seat, enjoying the sheer luxury of an expensive car and overwhelmed by the subtle but all-pervading perfume of his chauffeuse.

He had told Detective-Constable Carlisle to hand over all the paperwork to Inspector Appleton and then take his car back to Grasshallows. He and Debbie would spend another memorable night at the *Mermaid* hotel.

"All done?

"Yes."

"Was he angry?"

"No. Just upset."

"He'll find someone else."

"He always has."

Debbie smiled provocatively at Richard.

"I might even come down myself!"

Raynes sighed.

"If you can afford to own and run a Jaguar, you can surely afford to give Simon a freebie!"

A mischievous smile appeared on Debbie's face.

"It's not mine, you know."

"I thought you said it was?"

"No. That was just to annoy Lesley." She smiled triumphantly. "And it worked."

"Most effectively," said Raynes. "You fooled me."

"I borrowed it from a friend. An old friend."

"He must be worth a bob or two."

"Not really. He works in a garage on the outskirts of Grasshallows. Does a bit of buying and selling on the side. I asked him to get me something swish. Of course he'll have to clock it when I get back!" She smiled sweetly at the Inspector. "He'd do anything I ask. He finds me quite irresistible!"

Raynes shook his head.

"That's what's been so difficult about this case. Nothing is what you think it is. Everything has been a fake!"

Mrs May dared to voice her darkest thoughts.

"Just like all that crap you were spouting at Sir George's house!" She mimicked the words of Raynes' peroration: 'From beyond the grave, Lady Angela – and countless others – will have their revenge. Justice will at last be done. You have your man!' Your entire presentation was a complete fake!"

Raynes was amazed at her perspicacity.

"You noticed?"

254

Debbie took both hands off the wheel.
"It takes one to know one!"
Raynes laughed. "I suppose it does."

———————————

If you have enjoyed this book, you may like to read other books which feature Detective-Inspector Raynes. They are part of our series – *Meadowside Crime*.

Copies of books already printed and news about forthcoming titles can be obtained by writing to:

MEADOWSIDE PUBLICATIONS
14 ALBANY TERRACE
DUNDEE DD3 6HR

Or by telephone:
01382 223510